Books by Mark Schorr

Gunpower
Overkill

Published by POCKET BOOKS

KENJI NAKAMURA: The youthful Japanese terrorist was experienced far beyond his years. He traveled the globe under assumed identities, leaving carnage in his wake . . .

WILLY ROSE: The wiry, skull-faced Australian arms dealer had been trained in Britain's elite commando unit, the SAS. He knew the game of death well, and had to remain the best. In his business there is no such thing as retirement . . .

GERARD DeVILLE: He'd amassed a fortune selling firepower to anyone who could pay. But no matter who you were, the price of crossing the suave Frenchman was destruction . . .

GENERAL TODD GRANT: As head of the U.S. Defense Intelligence Agency, the CIA's military rival, he called shots around the world. Now he was cashing in on moves he'd planned for years . . .

G U N
POWER

MARK SCHORR

POCKET BOOKS

New York   London   Toronto   Sydney   Tokyo   Singapore

An *Original* Publication of POCKET BOOKS

 POCKET BOOKS, a division of Simon & Schuster Inc.
1230 Avenue of the Americas, New York, NY 10020

ISBN: 978-1-451-67235-0

First Pocket Books printing May 1990

10 9 8 7 6 5 4 3 2 1

POCKET and colophon are registered trademarks of Simon & Schuster Inc.

Printed in the U.S.A.

PROLOGUE

The Cypriot immigration officer studied the picture in the red Hong Kong passport.

"How do you pronounce your name?" the officer asked.

"Wong Tai Lin," Kenji Nakamura said.

The passport control officer seemed to be taking hours staring at the photo. Nakamura, a lean Japanese in his early twenties, fought the urge to run. He toyed with the thin mustache he had grown for the mission and shifted from foot to foot. Behind him, fellow passengers from the flight from Amsterdam chattered, eager to see the sights of Cyprus.

Larnaca airport was hot and virtually indistinguishable from any other airport. Nakamura had stopped in three international airports since leaving Hong Kong nearly twenty-four hours earlier. His controller had given him specific instructions, which he followed dutifully. There was security in obeying orders.

"Welcome to Cyprus," the immigration officer said at last, handing back the passport.

Nakamura started to say, *"Domo arigato gozai mashita,"* Japanese for "Thank you very much," but bit off his words so only "dom" escaped his lips.

"Dom chai fun gai," Nakamura said, having no idea if the sounds meant anything. "Thank you."

He hurried away, waiting until he was out of sight to wipe the sweat from his brow.

He picked up his bag from the creaky carousel and took it to the customs inspector. The inspector had him open the case and tentatively poked around inside. He didn't realize he was rooting around in enough explosive to blow the entire inspection area halfway to the other side of the airport.

Nakamura passed through customs. The wave of hot air outside felt soothing. The only cab available, a Fiat with sagging suspension, already had three passengers in it.

"In, in," the driver said, beckoning Nakamura. He threw Nakamura's bag in the trunk. The Japanese tried not to wince. His handler had assured him that the explosive was completely safe until wired, but Nakamura couldn't believe something so deadly could ever be harmless.

Sharing the back seat with Nakamura was a bearded man and his overweight wife. The woman smelled of too much perfume but it dampened the odors of sweaty bodies, garlic, and rotting fruit in the back of the cab.

The bearded man—an American, Nakamura guessed from his loud English and equally loud shirt—launched into a tourist guide's description of the sights, a speech he continued nonstop as the cab made its way to Nicosia.

"This town was the major port for all of Cyprus until it fell to the Egyptians in the fourth century before Christ," he said. "Cyprus has been like that. Just about everyone has conquered it. Mamelukes, Venetians, Alexander the Great, Romans, Richard the Lionhearted, Turks, Greeks, Brits, everyone but the good old US of A has grabbed it at some point," the man said. "Aren't you glad I read up on things before we came? Doesn't it add to the trip?"

"Yes, dear."

The self-ordained tour guide launched into a frenzy of information as they passed through hilly land dotted with whitewashed, sun-baked houses and sparse clumps of green. A sign welcomed them to Nicosia.

"The capital of Cyprus, its only major landlocked town ... the Turks took over the north part of the island in 1974, and divided the city in half. The 'Green Line' is like the Berlin Wall." Facts spewed forth like antifreeze from an overheated radiator.

"Yes, dear," his wife said periodically.

The couple was dropped off at the Hilton Hotel. Nakamura studied the area carefully. It was where he was to do his work.

"Scat a mana fas," the cabbie muttered, in a tone that made it clear what he thought of the talkative American, who hadn't tipped. He continued with a long string of obscenities as he drove aggressively through city traffic. He dropped Nakamura at the Alexander the Great Hotel, just outside the walls to the old city.

Nakamura checked into the hotel. He laid his suitcase down on the saggy bed. The luggage had picked up a few nicks and a black smear during its travels. He donned a knit shirt and gray slacks he had picked up in Hong Kong. His "pocket litter"—business cards, coins, even a package of tissues—seemed to indicate that he was from Hong Kong.

With a camera around his neck, he ventured out, a typical tourist. He passed several hours in Archbishop Kyprianos Square, visiting the Folk Art Museum housed in a former Gothic monastery from the fifteenth century and the Museum of National Struggle. He doubled back several times and was satisfied he was not followed.

While continuing his apparent ambling, Nakamura scouted the "Green Line," the fortified border between Greek and Turkish Cyprus. He passed the police booth on Markos Drakos Avenue, and mentally reviewed the instructions his handler had given him for escaping to the Turkish side. He eyeballed the positions of U.N. peacekeeping troops, as well as Greek Cypriot and Turkish fortifications. There were fifty-five gallon drums filled with concrete, steel tank traps, machine gun emplacements, and rows of barbed wire.

"No pictures," a Cypriot policeman warned amiably, pointing to the camera around Nakamura's neck and shaking his head.

Nakamura nodded and moved on.

Back in his hotel, he read the English language newspaper, working up righteous indignation over U.S. imperialist aggression in Central America, skirmishes in Africa that were no doubt sparked by the CIA, and Israeli brutality against the Palestinians. When he crawled into bed, he was fortified. He was ready, and only regretted that he couldn't perform his mission that night.

CHAPTER 1

Robert Stark stood by the Boeing 747's bulkhead and gazed out the window at the sun setting on the glistening Pacific. As dusk turned to darkness, the sky was a muted rainbow.

"Is everything okay?" a petite, navy blue-uniformed Nippon Air Lines stewardess asked.

"Beautiful, *desu ne?*" he said, pointing out the window.

She nodded.

He bantered with her in Japanese for a few minutes. He made her giggle and she reflexively covered her mouth.

Stark was one of four non-Japanese in the first-class compartment. He was flying under a false name, with a cover story that he was a lumber company owner trying to get the Japanese to buy his Oregon grown fir and alder.

Actually his company, Halliwell-Stark Associates, was on retainer to a dozen major corporations as an antiterrorism agency. They had received word that there would be an attempt by the Japanese Red Army to hijack the plane.

Authorities had been notified and investigated the tip. They found no evidence. The NAL chief of security had asked Stark to fly undercover to be sure that the flight was as safe as both American and Japanese officials insisted it would be. In the event of an incident, he could aid negotiations, relay information to the outside, and if all else failed, neutralize the attackers.

Three times Stark had prowled the airplane, gazing out windows, walking to a rear rest room, stretching, feigning smoking a cigarette. He had chatted amiably with fellow passengers, while sizing up possible terrorists.

On the fourth trip, he recognized a man in his late thirties with close-cropped hair and an intense look. The man had been hidden behind his newspaper during Stark's previous reconnoiters. Stark, who had worked for the CIA in Japan and done plenty of business there since, tried to recall where he had seen the face.

Fukoda. Stark couldn't recall his first name. He was a Japanese Red Army associate. How had he gotten on board if authorities were supposedly giving the flight extra attention?

Stark ambled slowly down the aisle toward Fukoda. A woman near Fukoda held a crying boy, no more than four years old.

"Can't you shut that kid up?" an American man sitting near her demanded.

Japanese around the rude American gazed at him stone-faced. The woman didn't respond. She rocked the young child, who only bawled louder.

"Onegai shimasu," Stark said as he knelt down in front of the woman. The mother bobbed her head in response to Stark's "pardon me." The child paused to stare at Stark, eyes going wide. Then it returned to yowling.

Stark pretended to study the child, while eyeing Fukoda. He confirmed that it was the JRA sympathizer. Stark turned his attention to the crying boy.

"What's your name?" Stark asked in Japanese.

The child covered its face with tiny hands.

"He's normally not like this," the mother said in Japanese. "He has a cold."

"So desu," Stark said. "His sinuses are clogged. It must be very painful." Stark smiled at the boy.

"Can you do this?" Stark asked, pinching his own nostrils shut.

The boy looked to his mother, who nodded. The boy pinched his nose.

"Now, take a breath in through your mouth, and try and blow out through your nose.

Stark did it. His ears popped.

The boy did it. He smiled broadly.

The mother grinned too, thanking Stark profusely. The people around the formerly crying child were smiling as well.

Stark got into a discussion with a middle-aged man about the pressure equalizing trick called the Valsalva maneuver by scuba divers. Stark slid into an empty seat and they continued their chat. They swapped business cards and discussed scuba diving in Hawaii, favorite beaches.

Stark lingered, watching Fukoda while pretending to be absorbed in the scuba conversation. The JRA sympathizer feigned reading a newspaper, but Stark saw that he was alert, watching the plane, waiting.

Stark, his attention on Fukoda and fitfully on the man he was talking to, missed the first moves.

A chubby Japanese in his late teens got down a flight bag from the overhead carrier. He removed a gray windbreaker which bore the words "I Feel Sport." He donned the jacket. Concealed in the windbreaker was a Glock-17 9-mm automatic pistol, which he had in his hands before anyone knew what was happening. The lightweight gun had a steel firing mechanism built into a plastic frame.

A second terrorist about five rows away produced a similar weapon. He was even younger, with acne so bad it looked like his face had been peppered with a shotgun blast. Before he produced the weapon, he had been assaulting his eardrums with a Sony Walkman. The headset hung around his neck and poured out tinny heavy metal music.

"Nobody move," Jowls ordered.

"What's happening?" a bespectacled businessman asked, rising slightly from his seat.

Jowls cracked him across the face, the gunsight on the Glock 9-mm drawing blood as it raked his jaw and knocked his glasses askew. He fell back dazed.

Fukoda sat, seemingly as surprised as the other passengers.

"You passengers have just joined the struggle against worldwide imperialism," Pimple Face said in a squeaky voice. "Obey our instructions or you will be treated as enemies of the people."

There were curtains at both ends of the section. No one else in the plane would know about the hijacking until the gunmen moved on.

Gray Jacket moved back and forth, waving his gun and looking nasty with an expression he probably practiced in the mirror.

"You, foreigner," Gray Jacket said, pointing to Stark. "Come here."

Stark put a surprised expression on his face. "Me?"

"Come here, *gaijin.*" Gray Jacket yanked Stark's thick brown hair.

Stark had entered another world. All was calm. He wasn't thinking. *Munen muso.* Mind of no mind. It was as close to ecstasy as he ever got, the feeling when an athlete is in perfect form or an artist actually captures the image he sees in his mind's eye.

Gray Jacket pulled with his left, simultaneously bringing the gun toward Stark with his right.

A stewardess came through the curtain and saw what was happening. She gasped and turned to run toward the cockpit.

Gray Jacket diverted his gun from Stark. The weapon was inches from Stark's face. Only he could see the finger tightening on the trigger. Stark's hands moved with a speed developed through years of jujitsu training. His right hand seized the barrel of the gun and pulled down. His left hand locked on Gray Jacket's wrist and pushed leftward.

The move snapped Gray Jacket's index finger in the trigger guard before he even knew what was happening. As the first messages of pain were reaching Gray Jacket's brain, Stark's right hand was yanking the gun free and his left slicing into Gray Jacket's Adam's apple. A few ounces more

8

pressure, and it would be a deadly blow. But Stark held back. Gray Jacket would never talk the same way again, however.

Stark's arms and legs moved with practiced coordination. He was pivoting toward Pimple Face at the same time his fingers were rotating the Glock-17.

His index finger glided onto the trigger.

"Drop your gun," Stark ordered.

He sensed rather than saw Pimple Face's muscles tense as he deliberated what to do. There was the hint of a lift to Pimple Face's weapon.

Stark fired twice, aiming at Pimple Face's chest. The first bullet ripped into his sternum, the second his solar plexus. Pimple Face looked more surprised than hurt as he fell dead to the floor.

Stark spun again, back toward Fukoda.

The known JRA sympathizer was reaching under his coat. Stark sighted down on him.

"I'm with the Security Police," Fukoda said.

"Just keep your hands where I can see them," Stark said.

"Don't move," another passenger said, aiming his Walther PPK at Stark. He held a badge aloft in his other hand as he stood. The badge holder moved slowly, with dignity and caution. His lips, pressed tight, were his only sign of tension. "He's with us."

"Us?" Stark asked, his gun still trained on Fukoda.

Two other men stood, with badges and guns in their hands.

"He was supposed to identify any JRA members," the apparent leader said.

"They must be new," Fukoda said.

During the conversation, held over the heads of the passengers, no bystanders had moved or said anything.

Stark lowered his gun a few inches, but kept it ready.

The dignified cop moved down the aisle to where Gray Jacket lay gagging on the floor. He produced a pair of plastic handcuffs and snapped them on Gray Jacket's wrists.

One of his associates checked for Pimple Face's pulse and

found none. He barked a few words at a stewardess, who hurriedly brought him a couple of blankets. The second cop draped them over Pimple Face.

"I'll take that," the lead cop said, turning to Stark and indicating the Glock Stark had used.

"Let's see your ID," Stark said, keeping the weapon. The cop extended his shield case. The ID card inside identified him as Okada of the central police, captain in the security bureau. Okada matched his photo, which showed a distinguished looking man in his fifties, with streaks of gray in his black hair.

Stark handed over the weapon. The ID looked like Japanese police ID Stark had seen previously. Besides, he was outgunned three to one.

The cop took his weapon carefully and slid it into a plastic bag that one of his associates provided.

"I'm sorry for the inconvenience, but you will have to remain on board when we land," Okada said to the passengers. "We will make the questioning go as quickly as is possible."

"What the hell questioning do you need?" asked the American who had first snapped at the crying child. "You all saw it as plain as we did. You oughta give that guy a medal," he said, indicating Stark.

"Perhaps the incident might have been resolved more peacefully without such resistance," Okada said.

"Or maybe we would've been blown to kingdom come by those creeps," the angry American responded.

"Passengers, please return to your seats," the pilot announced. "We will be landing shortly."

Stark sat and buckled in. He wanted to be alone with his thoughts.

He had no remorse over killing Pimple Face. The terrorists had entered into a special dance with Stark, a sacred relationship. Like a primitive hunter thanking his prey, Stark felt only gratitude toward the terrorists. They had allowed him to transcend once again.

"You're under arrest," Okada said, interrupting Stark's

thoughts and producing another pair of handcuffs. The two other cops, guns at the ready, stood off to one side.

"I shot him because he was about to fire," Stark said.

"I'm sure we'll determine the truth," Okada said.

"Truth is relative," Stark said. "With any luck, you'll get the facts."

Okada frowned and sat next to Stark. One aide sat behind Stark, the other in front of him. Fukoda had stayed in his seat.

The plane's engines changed their pitch. The seat belt sign flashed on and then the No Smoking warning.

Stark leaned back and felt the plane descend.

CHAPTER 2

Willy Rose knew his approach had been spotted from miles away. His Land Rover trailed a giant cloud of dust that muted the unrelenting sun. The parched African earth hung suspended in the windless air. The bleak scene, dry and nearly lifeless, reminded him of parts of the Outback. The heat shimmered off the ground.

The vehicle bumped and bounced. Rose was glad he had taken the extra time to tie down his cargo. The weight of the guns and ammo made the four-wheel drive vehicle handle poorly. Even the reinforced shocks were straining.

He gulped boiled water from his thermos to clear the dust from his throat. His protruding Adam's apple bobbed up and down. Rose, a thin forty-year-old with muscle-corded arms and a skull-like face, wet his lips and blinked his eyes. He splashed a little cologne on his neck and under his nose. He had used the rose-scented cologne since he was a young man and taken all kinds of abuse for it when he was in the military. But a few drops refreshed him.

Out of the corner of his eye, he saw a crouched figure watching from behind a scrawny scrub brush. Rose continued down the primitive road, spotting other sentries and guards, watching. He knew what they had in mind. Every robber, pirate, or terrorist he dealt with had at one point had the same idea. Why not just take the guns without paying for them?

Rose loosened the flap on the .45 he kept on his hip. He patted the Ingram machine pistol on his lap.

Willy Rose had been born in Sydney, but his mother was widowed, remarried, and moved with him to London. Never that interested in raising a child, his mother had neglected Rose. As an outsider, he'd been picked on. He had responded by becoming the toughest child in the school, a feared bully and petty thief. Which made him more of an outsider, and more unloved by his mother and stepfather. It wasn't until he got into the army that he found peace.

Rose checked his map and compass again. He was on the right road. Only a few kilometers to go. King would be waiting. King's tribal name sounded like a burp to Rose, but he was happy to answer to his regal nickname.

King was the leader of seventy Toposa rustlers who terrorized settlers in the northwest corner of Kenya. Displaced from their tribal lands in the Sudan, they supported themselves by stealing cattle, sheep, and whatever belongings they found in the villages. Blood feuds and tribal rivalries dating back hundreds of years made them ferocious raiders.

The landscape began to change. More gnarled trees, bushes along low ridge lines. A few patches of grass. In the distance, Rose thought he saw a pond, but it could have been a mirage.

He rounded a curve, went over a rise and he was in the Toposas' camp. The houses were temporary structures, little more than lean-tos designed to keep out the sun. King waited by the biggest hut, with two of his wives, his favorite son, and a half dozen of his warriors. The tall, lean bandit leader, with tribal marks on his face, looked like a wire that had been stretched taut. He wore cutoff dungarees and a stained T-shirt that said "Spuds MacKenzie." Most of the men wore fragments of western clothing, while the women were wrapped in simple, more traditional fabrics.

"G'day, King. I brought the goodies," Rose said.

"Show me," King said. He and his entourage hurried to the car. They dropped their old Enfields in the dirt. Rose tried to imagine what his CO would've done to troops who treated their weapons as sloppily. Rose had been trained in the British SAS, the super elite commando unit that had given tips to the Green Berets and Delta Force.

Like kids opening Christmas presents, the Toposas tore apart the wooden crates and passed out the Stoner carbines. Rose sensed the change in mood as the bandits loaded the clips into the weapons.

"I was only able to bring a small amount of ammunition this trip," Rose said. "I'll bring back a truckload full as soon as these are paid for."

King studied him and a broad smile spread across his face. "When?" he asked in English. He had been trained in a British school, before the English colony gained independence in 1963.

"Will you be paying today?"

"Maybe. Times bad. And you not take cattle?"

"Hard to fit in my lorry," Rose said.

The Toposas thought that the height of hilarity. One of the warriors actually fell on the ground laughing. The women, who wore loose fitting tops, jiggled furiously as they laughed. The chief saw Rose watching.

"You want a girl, I give you. I have few we took on last raid. None older than twelve. Make old steer feel like bull."

One of the wives gave King a dirty look. She was about twenty, but the hard life made her look much older. She had probably lived at least half the time she'd have on earth. Her unsupported breasts sagged down to navel level.

"Maybe later. I know a way you can make the money pronto," Rose said casually. "If you're interested."

The chief barked out commands and everyone but his favorite eight-year-old son and one of the warriors hurried away. The advisor who stayed had a cunning, brutal look and battle scars across his powerful torso.

"What do you say?" King asked.

"I hear that the Lion Lady has lots of gold," Rose said, emphasizing "lots" with his Australian drawl.

The advisor shook his head and said something in the Toposa dialect. Rose could almost get by in Swahili, but had no idea about the various tribal dialects. Swahili was Bantu, with an Arabic influence. This dialect had a Bantu flavor, but Rose could only guess at meanings. The chief and his advisor exchanged quick bursts of sound. The chief's son watched and learned.

"Lion Lady bring much trouble," the chief said to Rose in English.

"I heard she's got more than six thousand dollars' worth of gold," Rose said. "If we find it, I take half as payment for the guns. You keep the rest."

King and the advisor argued in the Toposa dialect. The chief's son sat on his haunches off to the side, listening.

More conversation.

"Of course, if you don't think you can handle it . . ." Rose said, letting his words trail off. "I think I know someone who might be able to."

There were two other rival bands operating in the area. Rose knew that King planned to use his new guns to reduce the competition. The thought of Rose arming his enemies should be enough of a nudge.

It was. The chief overruled his advisor. "She's white. That means attention from government," King said.

"I know a way around that," Rose said.

"How?"

"I'll show you. I'll lead the raid."

As he crept forward, Rose wasn't worried about succeeding. He'd stormed much more fortified targets. He was concerned about his troops. That they didn't shoot him in the back. Accidentally, or intentionally. Rose had worked as a mercenary, training native soldiers in southern Africa. He saw himself as a freedom fighter, a rabid anti-Communist. He felt that it was his job to keep the natives from giving in to an evil they were too simple to recognize.

Rose stayed near King, his gun drawn, ready to take the bandit leader hostage if he sensed treachery.

Thirty of the Toposas made their way through the trees.

The zoologist known as the Lion Lady was camped in a dense clump on the edge of a forest. It was a moonless, cloudy night and the bush-wise Toposas had to move slowly. Twice bandits nearly stumbled across the venomous green mambas that slithered after prey in the night.

The Toposas signaled each other with various whoops and trills. They had an elaborate language that allowed them to coordinate as well as modern troops with walkie-talkies.

The lone sentry on guard was more to discourage night-time predators than to keep out raiders. The sentry had an old M-1 slung across his shoulder. It did him no good as Rose soundlessly came up behind him, clamped a hand over his mouth and slit his throat.

King was impressed. There had been no wasted move-ment, no hesitation.

Rose counted four tents. "Have your men spread out," he whispered to the chief. "Five to each tent. The rest provide perimeter security."

"Perimeter security?"

"To watch our backs."

King nodded. He began a series of whoops, trills, and chirps. Rose heard the men dispersing. In a few minutes, the rustling stopped and there was more signaling with mim-icked animal sounds.

King gave a cough like a lion and the men moved forward, an eerie sight as their dark figures skulked across the landscape.

A man strolled out of a tent to relieve his bladder. An attacker fired. Then they all let loose and charged. Rose stayed low and waited.

The natives were brave but unused to Western style weapons and warfare. Only with months and months of training could he get them to not empty a clip at the slightest noise.

When the firing died down he got up and advanced. The Toposas were already tearing the place up.

The Lion Lady turned out to be a somewhat chunky, late middle-aged blonde. Her mane of hair, as well as the beasts

16

she studied, had sparked her nickname. She wore a flannel night robe which she pulled tight against her. The Toposa bandits tugged at her hair and the robe like a pack of cats playing with a mouse. She was remarkably composed, considering she had been awakened in the middle of the night by an invading force.

"Where's the money?" King demanded.

There were screams of pain in the night.

"The little I have is in the trunk over there," she said.

The advisor smashed the lock off the trunk with his rifle butt.

Inside they found two hundred dollars, a few hundred dollars' worth of simple gold jewelry, and a pearl necklace.

"Where's the rest?" King demanded.

"That's all there is," she said in a schoolmarmish voice.

King smacked her across the face. She retained her composure, which enraged him more.

He ripped her robe off and his men pulled her down. First he took her, then the advisor, then another then another. They knew their place in the pecking order, and though they acted in a frenzy of rage and lust, no one moved out of turn.

The bandit chief's son silently watched. His expression betrayed neither revulsion nor interest.

Rose stood off to the side, arms folded across his chest. The woman didn't cry out. She locked her eyes on his. Rose could feel them boring into him, feel the pain and the anger.

After about the tenth man, her eyes changed. Rose could sense her spirit leaving.

King stomped in front of Rose. "No gold!"

"There'll be some goods worth scavenging. And the two hundred."

"No gold!"

Rose held his gun loosely. "Guess not. Better luck next time."

"Big trouble now," King said. "Government send troops."

"I'll fix that," Rose said. Keeping a wary eye on King and the advisor—he doubted the others would have the initiative to attack him without their permission—he took out a spray can and wrote "Death to White Colonialists" and "KFA." The KFA was an outlawed Communist guerrilla group.

"They'll get the blame," Rose said.

King was slightly appeased. He went out to keep face with his men and see if they found any valuables.

The bandits were still taking turns on the woman. They no longer needed to hold her down.

"Get away," Rose said, shooing the remaining natives out with a wave of his gun.

The Lion Lady lay motionless on the dirt floor. Her eyes regained their focus and met Rose's.

"Sorry, luv," he said. The shot from his .45 took off most of her head.

As day broke at the Toposas' camp, the returning raiders were in a foul mood. The total haul hadn't been even half of what Rose had promised. About five hundred dollars' worth of cash and jewelry and a few dozen head of cattle and sheep. Three Toposas had been injured. Two had been slain by friendly fire. One had shot himself in the foot. The Toposas had used up three quarters of the bullets in an attack that could've been done with machetes.

"Time to settle our debts. I'll return tomorrow with the ammo," Rose said.

"I don't think you will," King said, the threat clear in his voice.

Rose saw the circle forming around him.

"I give you my word. All I need is my money and I'll be on my way."

"Maybe we just keep the money and guns, and let you go. Or maybe we don't let you go."

"You'll let me go. And you'll pay me."

The chief scowled.

"You are an honorable man," Rose said.

"You lied. You knew there was no big money at Lion Lady," the chief said.

Perceptive beggar, Rose thought. "I understood there was money."

Rose heard the click of a weapon being cocked. He jumped forward, coming up right next to the chief. He grabbed the chief's eight-year-old and put the .45 in his ear. The weapon looked even larger next to the small boy's head. The Ingram was pointed in King's direction.

"I leave now with the money. And the pearls."

Silence. A slight breeze stirred the dust.

The chief nodded.

The first wife brought Rose's payment out of the chief's hut. She stared at her boy, a silent prayer for safety in her eyes.

Rose walked carefully to his Land Rover, the money and string of pearls in his bush jacket pocket. He had tied a rope around the boy's neck and tied the short leash around his waist. Both hands held guns. One was kept unwavering on the chief, the other tracked slowly back and forth over the other men.

He put the Land Rover in gear. The boy had the same emotionless expression he had shown in the Lion Lady's tent.

Rose drove off. As he did, the Toposas broke ranks and, led by the advisor, charged after him, waving their guns above their heads in a futile gesture of frustration. The chief didn't move from his spot. Rose wondered if the advisor would give him an "I told you so" or simply try to usurp leadership.

A few shots pinged down the road, kicking up dust trails.

Rose drove five miles. "All right, time to take a hike," he said to the boy.

The boy stood with supreme dignity and got out of the Land Rover.

"You got the stuff, lad," Rose said. He fetched a Kenyan fifty-shilling coin from his pocket and tossed it to the boy. The boy let it drop into the dirt. He spat on it.

"Suit yourself," Rose kicked the car into gear and drove off, spraying the youngster with dust.

Rose took the strand of pearls out of his pocket and studied them. A good bluish luster. He rolled his teeth across one. A nice gritty feel.

He twirled it around his finger and began humming "Tie Me Kangaroo Down."

It was a long drive to the airfield where the two-seat Piper was waiting. Then a short flight to Nairobi. He couldn't wait for a hot shower and a cold beer. The joys of civilization. He wouldn't have long to savor them. After a few hours in Kenya's capital, he had to catch a plane for Istanbul.

CHAPTER 3

Kenji Nakamura strolled down the sunny street in Cyprus's capital. His blue American Tourister suitcase was light in his hands, half emptied of his clothing. Yet it had a certain awesome weightiness, a magic, because Nakamura knew the power within.

No customs official had detected any contraband or hidden compartments in the case. That's because the entire case was itself the bomb, Semtex explosive which had been compressed and covered with a laminate veneer of ordinary plastic. That made it undetectable even to bomb-sniffing dogs.

To prepare it for use, Nakamura that morning had scraped away a tiny patch of the laminate on the inside. He'd taken two small bits of wire and soldered them into place using a spoon heated over the hotplate in his room. He'd taken the heavy Seiko watch from his wrist, and attached the other end of the wires to the small contact points that were all but indistinguishable from the textured pattern on the crown. Then he'd tucked the watch into the customized cosmetics pocket, designed to hold the timer in place.

He'd been so excited, he'd nearly forgotten to set the timer. Fortunately he had not yet snapped shut the locks. That was a secondary trigger, which would detonate the bomb if it were tampered with. Nakamura's hands were slick with sweat.

Everything had been supplied by his handler. The watch had an extra strong mercury battery which would deliver the charge. Neither battering nor sparks would detonate the plastique, but a charge of nine volts would turn it into the equivalent of ten sticks of dynamite.

The handler had explained that it was equally important where he placed the bomb. Ideally, it should go off inside a confined space. Expanding gases are what make explosives powerful. Confined inside a space, the device would become like a bomb within a bomb.

If a confined space weren't available, the bomb should be tamped, that is, directed. Instead of blowing up and out in all directions, the blast would focus out one side, multiplying the destructive force.

Nakamura strolled by the Aphrodite cafe on Archbishop Makarios III Avenue. The cafe was busy. He saw three servicemen in American uniforms sitting under umbrellas at the small round tables outside. Many others in suits looked to be Americans. The American embassy was nearby, at Dositheos and Therissos streets, and several luxury hotels were within walking distance. If not Americans, at least capitalist imperialists from other countries would feel the force of his outrage.

He requested and got a table against the wall of the restaurant. He slipped the suitcase down behind him, out of sight. The waiter brought a menu.

Nakamura wiped his sweaty hands on the white tablecloth. He wanted to shout, to boast, and to warn them simultaneously. He was glad he saw no children in the lunchtime crowd.

"Your order?"

It was the waiter. Nakamura had no idea how long he'd been staring.

"Uh, here." Nakamura picked out the special.

"Very good. Thank you."

The meal came quickly, steam still escaping from the pita bread. Nakamura had thought it would be hard to eat but the smell reminded him he hadn't had a meal in twenty-four hours. He devoured the bread wrapped around lamb, tomatoes, onions, and peppers. He was so hungry, he ordered a second. Then he realized that the timer was still ticking. He checked his watch—a much cheaper Citizen on a worn leather strap—and saw that he had less than a half hour until detonation.

He paid the bill and hurried out, wondering if he had acted so strangely that he'd be remembered. Then he realized that it was doubtful anyone who had seen him would survive.

Nakamura walked several blocks before hailing a cab. It was three quarters of a mile to the Green Line, the fortified border between Greek and Turkish Cyprus.

The cab dropped him by the Ledra Palace Hotel, which was occupied by U.N. forces, and the only way to cross the border to the Turkish side. The front of the building was pockmarked with bullet holes. There were sandbagged fortifications and rolls of barbed wire.

Nakamura checked his watch while the Cypriot Border Police checked his Chinese passport and recorded his passport number.

"You must be back by sundown," the khaki-uniformed border policeman said, clearly disapproving of Nakamura leaving the Greek side. "Do not buy anything or it will be confiscated."

Nakamura nodded. He could almost hear the bomb ticking.

He began the long two-hundred-meter walk to the Turkish border. Any moment he expected to hear shouts and shots. He checked his watch.

Then he was at the Turkish side. More barbed wire and sandbags. The border marked the furthest point of the Turkish advance during the invasion in 1974. The Greek junta at the time had sparked an uprising in Cyprus to oust the Turks. But the move had backfired, the Turkish government had sent forces to defend the Turkish Cypriots, and seized the northern third of the island.

"What is your business?" the Turkish guard asked.

"Sightseeing."

"You may not go outside Lefkosia without permission," the guard said.

"How do I get permission?"

"Permission is never given." The guard handed him back his passport and waved him through.

Nakamura was admitted to Northern Cyprus, a country recognized only by Turkey. The streets were more crowded, the shops more cluttered, the buildings appeared older. There was less of a Mediterranean flavor, more of a hint of an Arab bazaar.

He glanced at his watch. He tried to appear casual, a sauntering tourist, while putting as much distance as possible between himself and the border.

Any second now. Or was it overdue? Would the bomb work? It seemed like people were watching him. He dismissed it as paranoia.

He heard the distant blast. People on the street perked up their ears. Most had lived through at least one invasion, some had been through wars, revolution, and invasion. Sirens howled in the distance.

He took a cab to the Museum of Barbarism, the Turkish answer to the Greek Museum of National Struggle. The museum, just outside the walls northeast of the city, was once the home of a Turkish regiment doctor. He and his family were killed by Greek terrorists in 1963.

Nakamura wandered in, checking his watch again. He was a few minutes early. The stocky man with a bushy mustache sat at a small desk just inside the door. A jar invited donations but there was no admission charge.

Nakamura didn't have any Turkish currency, and a Greek Cypriot coin wouldn't be well received. The guard glared at him as he wandered past. There were less than a dozen people in the museum.

Mounted on the walls were photos and newspaper clippings reporting Greek atrocities. Nakamura made his way through the spacious house to the second floor bathroom. A rope blocked access. Inside, he could see bloodstains on white tile. A plaque explained that this was where the doctor's wife and children were gunned down.

"It's a bad day to be indoors," the stranger said, sidling up to him. There was no one else around.

"I am usually at the beach, but I was badly burned last time," Nakamura responded.

The stranger, a short man with thick glasses and a squint, whispered, "Give me the Chinese passport. Quickly."

Nakamura handed it over. The man handed him a Korean passport and hurried away.

Inside the passport were a few hundred dollars in Turkish lira, an airplane ticket to Istanbul, and a ticket for a 4 P.M. tour of the cathedral-turned-mosque-turned-museum called Hagia Sophia.

Nakamura hailed a cab outside to take him to the airport. On the ride over, he memorized the Korean name in the passport and the particulars of the Korean's life. He noticed that the passport had a forged entry stamp showing that he had arrived in Turkish Cyprus four days earlier.

CHAPTER 4

Gerard DeVille waited in the antechamber of the Kenyan defense minister's mansion. DeVille lit his fifth Gauloise of the day. It was a little past nine o'clock. The harsh cigarette gave the Frenchman's voice a husky warmth that had charmed many a woman. He was a corpulent fifty-five-year-old, with a net worth of over fifty million dollars.

DeVille puffed on his cigarette and admired a colorful landscape painting on one of the walls.

"That's an original Gauguin," a voice said, and the minister strode into the room. He was dapper in a thousand dollar Saville Row suit, his voice as imperious as a member of the British Parliament. "I'd prefer you didn't smoke so close to it."

DeVille stepped back. The minister's arrogance would cost him an extra $100,000, DeVille vowed to himself.

"In fact, let us walk in the garden," the minister suggested. He was a Kikuyu, the elite tribe which led the Mau Mau uprising. The minister claimed relation to Jomo Kenyatta, the late revered leader who had guided Kenya to independence, and kept her on track in the years following the revolution.

The minister pointedly sniffed the fresh air as they

stepped onto the broad porch. The day was beginning to heat up. Three gardeners tended clumps of bougainvillea and the ten-foot-high hedges which gave the minister privacy on his fifty-acre estate. All the creature comforts, on a salary that was no more than twelve thousand dollars a year. Of course that didn't count bribes. Which were considerable. And why DeVille had chosen to visit the minister at home, rather than in his office near Uhuru Park in downtown Nairobi.

"You said it was urgent I meet with you," the minister said. "Now what do I need from one of the largest mercenary brokers in Africa?"

"I supply very few mercenaries nowadays."

"How refreshing. Especially since mercenaries tend to work for the white supremacists. What will you do when South Africa falls?"

"I'm not here to debate politics with you. I have an excellent deal on hardware."

"We have all we need."

"Hah."

"Perhaps you know something I don't?"

DeVille rattled off a detailed account of the tanks, planes, rifles, and automatic weapons in the Kenyan army.

Grudgingly impressed, the minister asked, "How do you know all of that?"

DeVille tapped his ear. "I also know you are having trouble in the northwest area. Communists."

"More likely bandits."

DeVille gave a Gallic shrug. "The respected Lion Lady brutally murdered. *Tres mal.*"

"We are working on it."

"You must present a strong front to show foreign investors. You cannot be seen as being soft on communism. An announcement about re-arming would be reassuring and good for the morale of the troops. Send them off with M-16s, and you can't go wrong. If you would like, I have just got my hands on a few Mowag Piranhas. They're the Swiss internal security vehicle. They can swim, climb a seventy percent grade, travel seven hundred and fifty kilometers. They can transport up to eleven men and take up to a 25-mm automatic cannon." DeVille leaned forward confidentially. "But if you desire real firepower, I have a few reconditioned M-1 tanks available. Never been used in combat. Perfectly maintained."

"Are you trying to bankrupt my country?"

"What is a few million dollars more or less?"

"Perhaps we can get the armaments in aid from the Americans."

"*Oui,* but if you get it from me, the true price is between you and me."

They had walked around the house grounds and were standing near the front drive. "I quote you a price of six and a half million. I'm sure the treasury would accept a quote of seven. A half million private commission to you."

The minister hesitated barely a moment. "Do you still have my Swiss account number?"

Nakamura landed at Ataturk Airport, about a half mile southwest of Istanbul. He half expected police waiting for him on the tarmac. His moods went up and down, from elation over the success of his mission, to terror over being caught.

A cab dropped him at the Grand Bazaar on the European side of Istanbul. The city, divided by the Bosporus strait, sits astride both the European and Asian continents.

He wandered the bazaar, periodically checking for surveillants, assailed by the pungent smells of spices, the shouts of vendors trying to convince him of the quality of their wares, the bump and shove of thousands of sweaty shoppers moving through narrow, poorly paved streets. Rugs, jewelry, antique guns, knitwear, leather gear, and every kind of bric-a-brac imaginable were offered by merchants who shouted their products' merits and their low prices.

The only item Nakamura bought was a copy of the English language Istanbul newspaper. There was nothing about his bombing in Nicosia. He supposed it was too early.

Nakamura presumed his handler had arranged for the suitable notification of the news media. It was important that the proper credit be given.

He didn't notice the wiry, skull-faced man who had him in the cross hairs of a 400-mm telephoto lens mounted on a motor-driven Nikon. The skull-faced man snapped away.

Willy Rose was as accurate with a camera as he was with a rifle.

Nakamura was eager to see his handler. He mentally reviewed the operation for the hundredth time, to convince himself that he had done everything as directed. He was more scared of his handler's anger than of prison. Only once had Nakamura dared to question his handler.

"Why do I have to go to all these tourist sites? Why can't I just go and do the job?"

His handler's pale blue eyes had gone flat. They were in a noisy *yakitori* restaurant in Tokyo's Roppongi district. The handler had picked up a used skewer, an eight-inch-long piece of wood that looked like an oversize toothpick.

"Do you know how easy it is to kill a man?" the handler asked.

Nakamura shook his head. Despite the fact that he was elbow to elbow with dozens of other customers in the smoky restaurant, he felt cold and alone.

"If you can't use your hands, a simple tool like this," the handler held up the skewer, "shoved into the eye, can instantly take care of a problem."

His handler picked up a skewer with broiled chicken on it and slid the pieces into his mouth. He ate slowly, savoring the salty taste, then said, "Don't ever question my orders. Understand?"

Nakamura nodded.

"Good. Now I'll tell you why. You're going to be a stranger in a new city. The safest place for you to be is surrounded by other strangers, tourists. Unless you think you can pass for a Turk. And an Istanbul native at that."

Nakamura shook his head.

The counterman set down another half-dozen skewers.

The handler picked up one, but Nakamura had lost his appetite. It was one of the few times since he had first joined the cause that he regretted it.

Nakamura's involvment had started at age sixteen, after his older brother died while protesting the construction of Narita Airport. The two surviving brothers had become activists after the oldest's death. Numerous times, Nakamura professed that he was willing to die for the right cause. He would be in the front lines in demonstrations against Narita Airport or American bases on Japanese soil.

Somehow word was passed. At a rally, a grim-faced woman had grilled him. Later, he learned she was one of the survivors of the Japanese Red Army. He wished he had known so he could have sworn his fealty to her.

He'd gotten a phone call a few nights later and gone to meet a man on a busy street corner in Shinjuku. The man was to become his handler. Nakamura never questioned just who the white man represented, but from little dribs and drabs, he came to realize the man was KGB.

Nakamura hung back toward the end of the gaggle of tourists. He was disappointed. His handler was not in the group. The guide led them forward, her voice echoing off the stone walls. Other guides nearby lectured their charges and the speeches sometimes blended into a confusing blur.

Nakamura barely heard the spiel about the various administrations and how they had altered Hagia Sophia. It had survived earthquakes, plundering by thieves, and Muslim leaders who ordered murals plastered over because they violated Islamic edicts against re-creating human imagery.

The group walked up the wide, winding ramps, designed for the sultans to ride up to the gallery on horseback. The tourists admired mosaics of Christ, the Virgin Mary, and tenth century portraits of the Emperor Alexander and Empress Zoe. Nakamura grew fidgety, waiting for contact.

The group was down in the main sanctuary, passing by the famous weeping column of Saint Gregory, when Nakamura's tension was relieved. The guide was pointing to the spot where centuries of pilgrims have poked their fingers, resulting in a three-inch hole in the marble.

"Some people believe the water, which springs from a mysterious source, causes clear eyesight and aids fertility," the guide was saying.

"I wonder if there's any relationship between the two," a man quipped. A few others laughed.

Nakamura looked past the pillar. A familiar figure. His handler. Nakamura nearly waved.

But his handler had seen him, been watching him. With a slight nod of his head, the handler signaled for Nakamura to come over. The Japanese drifted away from the group.

The handler sauntered to the narthex, the entry hall with mosaics of Justinian and Constantine.

"Congratulations, Kenji," the handler said, his voice a whisper that was inaudible more than a few feet away.

Both men stared at the mosaics, apparently wrapped up in their colorful artistry. They were practically shoulder to shoulder.

"Did everything work out?"

"Very nicely." The handler took out a tour book on Istanbul and pretended to read.

"How do I get delivery of the SA-7?" Nakamura asked.

"We have one more little chore for you," the handler said.

"I thought all I had to do was the bombing."

"It's for the good of the cause, Kenji. You have to trust our judgment. The time isn't just right."

Nakamura had been promised an SA-7, a Soviet shoulder launched surface-to-air missile. His handler knew Nakamura's intention—to blow a jet out of the sky at Narita Airport. It was to be the ultimate revenge for Nakamura's brother.

Nakamura frowned.

"Don't let us down, Kenji. Central was pleased with your performance. Your actions were discussed at the highest levels of government."

"In the Kremlin?"

The handler just smiled. "You did well. This next little jobbie is easy. There is a woman in Thailand. The daughter of an imperialist. Her brother is a big capitalist in the United States. She's working in a refugee camp. We want her kidnapped."

"A woman?"

"All men and women are equal. Isn't that true?"

"Yes, but I find it difficult."

"Then this challenge will help you grow."

"But what kind of imperialist can she be if she's working in a refugee camp?"

"It's part of the way they keep the masses down. A bandage here and there, when the entire body is diseased," the handler said. He set the tour book on a small shelf near him. "There are a couple of local blokes who will help out. Their ideology is questionable, but we will give you an operating fund to encourage them."

"I don't know if I can do it."

"There is no backing out. If you abandon us, we abandon you. It will be too easy for the authorities to learn who was behind that bombing. You could wind up back in Cyprus before you know it. They have capital punishment there. And the prisons are even worse. Neither guards nor inmates would be sympathetic to the cause."

"But I did what I promised."

"Yes. And after you finish this assignment, you'll be doubly rewarded. Pick up the tour book as soon as I leave."

What a crock of Commie crap, the handler thought as he strode away. He had only contempt for amateurs, fanatics, and Communists. Nakamura was all three.

The man Nakamura believed was a KGB case officer was in reality Willy Rose.

CHAPTER 5

Diana Hancock grew up in San Marino, a small city in the suburban sprawl of Los Angeles, where having an unmanicured lawn is a major offense. To San Marino residents, anyone who makes less than two hundred fifty thousand a year is a pauper, and any family that hasn't had money for several generations is *nouveau riche.*

Hancock's great-grandfather had been one of the first to settle in the Golden State. His family owned a major dry goods store in New York and he was able to take a shipload of necessities to California just as the Gold Rush boomed. He sold shovels, picks, pans, and bedrolls at exorbitant prices, and bought land with the proceeds.

By the time Diana was born, the Hancock family was one of the ten wealthiest in California. She seemed destined for a life of decadence. Her first car, given to her for her sixteenth birthday, was a pink Porsche Targa. Two weeks later, she got drunk at a party and wrapped it around a phone pole. Daddy's little girl had a new one by the next morning.

She moved out of San Marino, which was too stodgy for her taste, to a hillside home in Bel Air. Her stereo system alone cost twenty-five thousand, and she blasted it so loud that neighbors a mile away, across a canyon, called the police.

Her older brother, Edward, took over the family publishing and real estate business. Edward Senior had spoiled his daughter while demanding perfection from his heir. Edward Junior became a super achiever. He graduated summa cum laude from Stanford, got his MBA at Harvard, and excelled at polo. He married the daughter of a wealthy banker, had two children, and owned a house that was featured on the cover of *Better Homes and Gardens.*

By the time she was thirty-five, Diana had enough sex, drugs, and parties to cripple an older person. Then her best friend died of a drug overdose. Her latest boyfriend, who claimed to be part of the Saudi royal family, turned out to be a Brooklyn con man who was charged with stock fraud. Her pet terrier, who was the living thing she was closest to, ran out of the house during one of her parties and was killed by a car.

She went into a depression and attempted suicide. Psychiatrists, gurus, and drug dealers didn't help her.

She was sitting in a Thai restaurant, picking at a plate of ginger chicken, when she saw a small, elderly man walk in. He was treated with reverence by the owner and numerous patrons. She tried to eavesdrop but couldn't understand the language.

"Who is he?" she asked in her best bored and cool tones.

The restaurant owner explained that he had run a refugee camp in Thailand. He had saved the lives of several members of the owner's family when they fled the Khmer Rouge in Cambodia. She had never seen such respect not brought on by fear or greed.

She packed her bags and was on the next flight to Thailand.

That had been three years earlier.

None of Hancock's friends would recognize her now. Her once elegantly coiffed hair was cut short. The druggy glaze was long gone. She exuded a lean, healthy vitality. She had four changes of outfit. The rest of her clothing she'd given away to people who had fled Cambodia, Laos, or Vietnam, with nothing. The first time she gave one of her silk shirts to a refugee, and saw the woman's face when she understood it was a gift, Hancock was hooked. Virtually all of her ten thousand dollar a month allowance went to the camp.

Despite occasional bouts with dysentery, body lice, poisonous snakes in the brush, a crude hammock to sleep on, often unpalatable food in small quantities, and little privacy, Hancock was happier than she had ever been.

She had learned enough Thai, Vietnamese, Cambodian, Laotian, and Chinese to reassure orphans, calm widows, help the injured. She functioned as teacher-nurse-mother.

Hancock's camp was in northeast Thailand, about a hundred miles from where Burma, Laos, and Thailand met in the infamous Golden Triangle. Karen, Lisu, and Meo hill tribes made up a large part of the population. Their colorful outfits, frequently adorned with silver bangles, looked expensive. In reality, they were all the villagers had.

The camp was a mix of corrugated tin shanties, thatched lean-tos, and several Quonset huts. Children, dogs, and an occasional chicken played in the dirt streets. The adults worked at crafts which they sold in the city of Chiang Rai.

Her schoolhouse was a roof on four poles. There was a dirt floor, with long hard wood benches, and a blackboard at the front. On it was written the numbers from one to ten in English and Thai.

Most of the students in her morning class were hill people from the Meo tribe. The group customarily lived in an area for ten to fifteen years, using slash and burn agriculture, and then moved on. But the ravages of guerrilla war and urbanization had forced many of them into the dirty and depressing camps.

Hancock was teaching her students to count when the soldiers burst in—a sergeant, a stocky one, and a tall one.

"Come with us," the one wearing sergeant's stripes said.

"Who are you?" Hancock demanded.

"Come with us."

The children, who had lived through revolution, bandit raids, and drug lord skirmishes, had scattered. The stocky soldier grabbed her arm.

A tattooed Lisu man, returning from chopping bamboo, stepped in and demanded, "What's going on?" He held a machete loosely in his hand.

The tall soldier lifted his gun and shot him. The sergeant snapped a few angry words at him in what sounded to her like Japanese.

Hancock tried to pull away to tend the man who'd been shot but the soldier held her firmly.

"Let me go!" she demanded.

More men came over. The soldiers fired. There were screams from a woman who had seen what was happening. Hancock struggled. The stocky soldier swung the muzzle of his gun, hitting her in the jaw and knocking her unconscious. He easily lifted her over his shoulder and, firing into the crowd, the three men carried her to a jeep parked at the edge of the compound.

"Where am I?" Diana Hancock's voice cracked, her throat parched. She was blindfolded, sitting in a chair.

"You are a prisoner of the Asian People's Independence Party," Kenji Nakamura said. He had played the role of the sergeant. The other two were Yokohama hoodlums that had been referred by Rose. Both were in their late teens, but had already been arrested several times for minor crimes.

Nakamura had had angry words with them while Hancock slept. He was enraged that they had gunned down refugees, whom he saw as the oppressed people he was fighting for.

The stocky punk laughed, the tall one grunted.

"We did what had to be done," the stocky one said.

Nakamura had been careful to fire over the heads of the crowd as they fled. But he had seen his two accomplices shoot low, and at least one child went down.

"Who are you?" Hancock said, moving her jaw. It ached, but didn't feel broken.

"That's not important," Nakamura said.

She strained against the rope that bound her wrists behind her. Her ankles were tied to the chair.

"How long was I unconscious?" she asked.

"No more questions," the stocky one said, slapping her.

"I'm in charge," Nakamura said in Japanese.

The stocky man worked the action on his gun and smirked. He tweaked Diana's breast and sauntered away. He whispered something to the tall one and both laughed rudely.

For the first time in her life, Hancock felt completely helpless. She prayed that the kidnapper who had protected her would keep her safe.

CHAPTER 6

Nakamura's bomb had killed eight people and injured another nineteen. Among the dead were two American servicemen, three low-level British embassy officials, a Dutch tourist, and two waiters. The injured were largely Greek tourists and Cypriots.

In the hours after the blast, a half dozen groups took responsibility for the bombing. Shiite and Sunni Muslim groups, a Lebanese Christian organization, two rival Palestinian factions, and the IRA contacted newspapers or authorities to demand credit and publicity.

It was the Associated Press office in Athens that ultimately got the most believable message. A caller told the news desk to pick up a note from the phone booth across the street. A fledgling reporter was dispatched and brought back the message that the Japanese Red Army was behind the "blow for freedom of the oppressed peoples of the world." The Greek Cypriots were being oppressed and sheltering "Fascist Imperialist Deathmongers" by allowing two British bases to remain on the island and allowing ships from the American Seventh Fleet in the port.

Not released to the public was the fact that the note writer, alone among all those who had taken responsibility, knew specifics, that a Czechoslovak Semtex high explosive had been used.

The Cyprus police bomb squad was quite adept. During the turmoil in the 1970s, numerous bombs were planted by Greek and Turkish loyalists. But those went off in the middle of the night, or at deserted facilities, or in empty cars.

The bomb squad did a first-rate job of preserving the scene, pinpointing the source of the blast and the type of explosive used.

The bomber was presumed to be Oriental—because of the JRA call—and there were only a couple dozen on the island at the time of the blast. Investigators quickly targeted Wong Tai Lin, the name on the forged passport Nakamura had used to cross the Green Line.

When it was discovered that he had passed over to the Turkish side of the island, all hell broke loose in Athens.

"It is a matter of national honor," a conservative politician bellowed on the floor of Parliament. "Once again the Turks have proved their barbaric inhumanity."

Greek tabloids screamed for vengeance.

In the Turkish capital of Ankara, they denounced the incident as a Greek provocation, an attempt to stir up trouble. They noted the Communist tone to the letter, and how strong the Communists were in Greece.

They said there was no record of Wong Tai Lin ever leaving Turkish Cyprus and promised to check into the movements of all Orientals on the island.

Greek officials blasted them for foot dragging, pointing out that the entire area controlled by the Turks held less than 150,000 people, and most of it was small villages where any stranger would be immediately noticed.

Once a month General Todd Grant, head of the Defense Intelligence Agency, found himself whacking a golf ball on the links of a Virginia country club. It was defense industry execs' favorite way to meet with him. For Grant, the only thing worse was appearing before some candyass liberal congressional committee.

The American Dynamics president was a dedicated golfer, and as he stepped up to the tee, a vision in a green checked golf outfit, he was completely focused on the ball. He connected solidly and the ball landed within a few feet of the green.

He drove the golf cart with the stocky, stiff-spined general as a passenger. Grant's ball was in a sand trap. The other two players, also defense industry execs, rode in a second golf cart.

"Todd, we're disappointed with the way things are going," the American Dynamics president said. "Several of the companies have been forced to lay people off. Three plants have closed down, and probably won't be reopened. Your intelligence forecasts don't paint a pretty picture."

"The Israeli-Arab situation provides a steady market."

"Yes. That's accounted for. The market's already divided up among fifteen countries and twice that many companies."

"Greece and Turkey are beefing up their defenses. As I predicted."

"Yes. Your advance notice allowed us to get a leg up on the others. We do appreciate that. But the market is limited."

"Turkey's got the second largest standing NATO army after the U.S.," Grant continued. "They should provide quite a few customers."

"It's an existing market. We need new ones. Besides, from what I understand the superpowers won't tolerate an escalation in that region. It's too sensitive a spot."

"Who told you that?" Grant asked angrily.

"You're not our only friend in high places," the exec said.

"Who else?"

"C'mon now, Todd. Surely you believe in compartmentalization." He smiled. "Now what about Thailand? You mentioned an arms cache there?"

"Right. It's in the works."

"Any other southeast Asian countries?"

"Most of the ones in that region don't have a pot to piss in. Cambodia, Laos, Burma. They're a couple of notches above the Stone Age."

"Vietnam?"

"Piss poor," Grant said. He had been a colonel in Vietnam, leading troops in combat. He had earned several medals in the war, but some said his most ferocious fighting came when taking credit for other people's work. Grant was quick to tell everyone he met that he was a direct descendant of General Ulysses S. Grant, though his claim had never been verified. "The Vietnamese have got tons of leftover arms from the war, though most have become dysfunctional. More than a million and a half rifles were left behind by our troops. Close to a hundred thousand .45s. Vietnam's made some of its scant hard currency by selling them on the black market."

"What do you have in mind?"

"Japan."

"It's been tried."

"I've got a new plan of attack. In fact, I've already set things in motion."

The meeting room looked like a corporate boardroom. Hidden behind the off-white walls was several million dollars' worth of electronic gear, controllable through panels recessed into the table. The hardware provided an antibugging, white noise generator, access to computers at the CIA, National Security Agency, and Defense Intelligence Agency headquarters, as well as a direct link to three U.S. surveillance satellites. Other telecommunications gear allowed direct, secure contact with the White House.

The weekly meeting was called to order by Dan Creange, the DCI, Director of Central Intelligence. An Ivy Leaguer with a strong business background, he had concentrated on intelligence gathering and cut back on covert operations. When the agency did get involved with a covert op, it was with the complete approval of the President.

"Our first order of business is Cyprus," Creange said, after all the members had settled around the big boat-shaped table. In a second concentric ring, set farther back, were staff members for each agency, ready to reach into their attaché cases and produce statistics to back up their boss's claims.

Around the table were members of a select Restricted Interagency Group. RIGs had gotten a bad name during the Contragate fiasco when it was revealed that a National Security Council RIG had endeavored to run their own covert operation. But RIGs, like ad hoc committees or task forces, were often the most efficient and effective way to get things done in a bureaucracy grown too cumbersome.

This RIG included General Grant; the director of the National Security Agency; the chief of the National Reconnaisance Office, and the deputy secretary of state. The NSA had primary responsibility for electronic eavesdropping, while the NRO handled satellite intercepts. Both are supposed to do little more than supply raw data to the CIA and DIA. The RIG focused on terrorism and Low Intensity Conflicts, small wars.

"We have a guest from State's Bureau of Intelligence and Research. Please," Creange gestured for the visitor to make his presentation.

The lights were dimmed and a screen rolled down from its place in the ceiling. A map of the Mediterranean flashed on.

"Cyprus is located in the eastern Mediterranean," said the BIR speaker. "It is forty miles from Turkey, a hundred miles from Israel and Lebanon, and more than three hundred miles from the nearest Greek island."

"How far is it from Broadway?" the NSA chief quipped. There were a few chuckles.

"I think everyone here is up on their geography," Creange said gently to the speaker. "Please continue, and get to the meat."

"May I provide a quick historical perspective?"

"I hope we're not going to hear about Alexander the Great," whispered the NSA chief, loud enough for everyone to hear.

They couldn't see the young man from the State Department blush red. He had planned to include it all. He had worked hard on his presentation, his most important to date. The only audience more significant would be the president himself.

"Make it very quick. I'm sure my learned colleagues know

about its long history of conquest, going up to British occupation, then the Turkish invasion of the north. Let's start with the events of last week."

The BIR expert clicked through a half dozen slides and rustled papers. "Very well, sir. A bomb exploded in the Aphrodite cafe. Eleven people were killed, sixteen injured." Slides on the screen showed the restaurant blackened, and bodies and parts of bodies lying amid chaotic rubble. Someone gulped.

"I thought only eight were killed," Grant said.

"Several injured subsequently died, sir," the speaker said, stressing the "sir." The BIR expert was glad to be able to put one of the inquisitors in his place.

"The numbers aren't really important," Creange said. "Even though we know how the military loves its body counts."

There were a couple of chuckles. DIA chief Todd Grant harrumphed.

"Are there indications that any of the victims were specifically targeted?" the NRO chief asked.

"None. As far as our investigation has shown, the cafe was chosen because of its use by foreigners. Targets of opportunity. It was pure bad luck for those people that they were there."

"Damned bad luck," the NSA head muttered.

The BIR expert clicked to a slide with an organizational chart of the Japanese Red Army. "The Japanese Red Army is believed to be behind it, but according to our investigation, the perpetrator appears in none of the files on JRA. There're only a few hardcore members left, after their mass homicide-suicide in 1972."

"I'm not familiar with that," the NRO chief admitted.

"Thirty members were trapped in an empty hotel with a female hostage," the BIR expert explained. "Half sentenced the other half to death for absence of revolutionary sincerity and for bourgeois deformities. That's their language."

"I guessed as much," the NSA head said.

"So who is it then?" the NRO chief asked.

"I'll field that one," Creange said. "From everything

we've been able to piece together, it was a clean-cut Japanese man, in his early twenties. Now, the plot thickens. Someone delivered a photo of an individual fitting this description to Greek counterintelligence. The suspect is walking on a street in Istanbul."

"Who is he?" the NSA chief asked.

"We're trying to get that out of the computer. Matching his facial type is rather time consuming. The photos are reasonably good quality, but not close-ups."

"Who supplied the pictures?" the NRO chief asked.

"The Greeks are as vague about their sources and methods as we'd be with them. But our man in the government there led me to believe it was received anonymously."

"Why is it credible then?" Grant asked.

"It isn't. But it's significant. It's an open secret in Athens."

"What's the connection between the Cyprus incident and the kidnapping in Thailand of the Hancock woman?" Grant asked. "That's Japanese terrorists too, isn't it?"

"We've looked for links," the State Department speaker said. "There does appear to be a JRA resurgence. We don't understand why."

"You never can with terrorists," Grant said. "Let's go back to the Mediterranean for a minute. The Greeks have put in a request for a large arms order. They want AWACS, fighter planes, several naval vessels, tanks, attack helicopters. It's a whopping shopping list, from .45 automatics to F-14s. If we provided everything they wanted, it would be more than a half billion bucks."

"Are they planning on hocking the Parthenon?" the NSA chief quipped.

"What they're planning is what worries us," Creange said. "I'm sure if our guest had been allowed to give a more detailed presentation, we would've heard about the long history of animosity between the Greeks and the Turks. The bombing at the Aphrodite cafe can only exacerbate a bad situation." He turned to the NRO chief. "What's the most recent input from the satellites?"

"The Greek army is involved in a training exercise. It's

not a major mobilization, but we do see a lot more traffic. Several divisions' worth."

"So what do we recommend to the President?" the NSA head asked.

"We should pass on the sale. Turkey has too much strategic value," Creange said. "Even if the Greeks do nothing but rattle sabers, our supplying the sabers will alienate Turkish officials."

"Why don't we sell the Greeks some of what they want, and let the Turks know we'll give Athens more if they don't let us expand our bases there," Grant said.

"I vote with Todd," the NSA chief said. "If we don't supply the Greeks, they'll go shopping elsewhere. There're already too many Greek politicos in bed with the Communists."

"I'm aware of that," Creange said. "I know you scoff at geography lessons, but are you aware who Turkey's neighbors are?" Creange asked. "The Soviet Union, Bulgaria, Iran, Iraq, Syria, and Greece. The potential for a flare-up there is enormous."

"Which is exactly why we have to keep the Turks off balance," Grant said.

"Turn up the lights," Creange said.

The lights went on, the projector went off, and the screen rolled up. "Thank you," he said to the guest expert. "I'd like to excuse the various staff members."

The staffers got up and left, leaving their bosses around the oak table.

"Todd, we're not in a position to play hardball with the Turks," Creange said. "There's a growing Islamic fundamentalist movement there."

"Screw 'em. Do you know how many arms suppliers there are? We're the biggest and the best, but the Greeks can turn to a half-dozen different countries, and even more independent operators, and get just about whatever they want."

Creange sighed.

"If we don't supply them, they go elsewhere. We lose an ally and get a war," the NSA chief argued. "This way we keep some control over them. And make money to boot."

The deputy secretary of state, who diplomatically tried to avoid taking sides, responded to Creange's questioning gaze by stroking his chin. "That large an order means more work for the defense industry. And more jobs."

"What do you say?" Creange asked the NRO chief.

"You can present your opinion to the President as a minority opinion. You know he respects you."

"Okay, a compromise," Creange said, thinking quickly. "We recommend delaying the deal for a month. Perhaps things will cool down. We can spread a little information in the right places stressing how much this will cost the Greek treasury."

"They'll never go for a month," Grant said. "They'll want something on paper within a week. The best we can do is delay delivery."

After several minutes of haggling, Creange got an agreement that they would advise the President to stall the matter for one week.

CHAPTER 7

Police Captain Okada had asked that Stark not leave Japan after he aborted the hijacking on the NAL jumbo jet. The two policemen who followed Stark every time he left his hotel made it clear that Okada's request was more than just a suggestion.

Stark's partner, Les Halliwell, had been impatient for his return. While Halliwell had the business sense and contacts, it was Stark's abilities that kept the agency going.

"The papers here wrote it up as if you were a kill-crazy cowboy," Halliwell said after more than two weeks had passed. "That the Japanese are talking about charging you with endangering the lives of the passengers."

"I've read the papers here. They're not much better. Unfortunately the hijacker I killed was only fifteen. And my traveling under a fake passport didn't earn me Brownie points. I was arrested, but not formally charged with anything. Yet."

"You think you'll be charged?"

"I find out more from the papers than I do from the government. I've got a lawyer over here working on it, but you can't rush them."

"Jesus Christ. This is costing us money. What are you doing?"

"I've touched base with a few old contacts. And I'm spending most days at the *dojo.*" Stark didn't mention how much time was devoted to meditation. Halliwell considered that a fancy form of napping. Stark sometimes found the meditating more rigorous than a jujitsu workout. Quieting the mind was harder than exhausting the body.

"Well, I'm glad you're having fun," Halliwell said bitterly. "Why do I get the feeling you're not trying very hard?"

In truth, Stark didn't mind his stay in Japan. He enjoyed working out at the Kamakura *hombu,* the jujitsu school headquarters that had been in his teacher's family for several hundred years.

The incident on the plane was an embarrassment to the government security agencies and NAL. Even though officials had been warned, they had been unable to stop the hijackers. Why hadn't they been able to detect the hijackers? Who had failed? Why was a private security company hired? How come Stark, and not the three police officers on board, had stopped the incident? Was a shooting on a crowded aircraft justified?

Three passengers—including the loud-mouthed American who had proclaimed Stark a hero—had filed multimillion-dollar lawsuits claiming they were too traumatized to fly ever again. Left-wing politicians criticized Stark for not resolving the incident peacefully. Right-wing politicians chided him for overstepping his authority and usurping the Japanese police function.

The incident seemed to have sparked a controversy over gun control. Several outspoken politicians were calling for a loosening of Japan's gun control laws. Although the idea of a gunfight on an airplane was universally denounced, these leaders felt that if Japanese were more familiar with firearms, they could've coped better with the situation. Others called for even more stringent weapons penalties.

After nearly a month in Japan, Stark received a phone call from Pedro Quesada. Stark's trusted aide was a fifty-year-old Mexican-born émigré with one arm. He was an ex-L.A. gang member, a crack shot, and a skilled investigator.

"We've got a good client," Quesada said after initial

pleasantries. "Diana Hancock was kidnapped. You know who she is?"

"I read a sketchy account in the paper."

"She's been working with Southeast Asian refugees in Thailand. Three armed men snatched her a few weeks ago."

"Why?"

"They want three million from her brother for her return."

"Why'd he come to us?"

"They think the terrorists might be JRA. He knows you know Japan like nobody's business."

"I'm flattered."

"Besides, they didn't come to us first. He tried another outfit. The kidnappers sent back a piece of Diana. Her ear."

"Any leads?"

"Thai police think she's being held near Chiang Mai. Any chance you can jump in on it?"

"I'll see what I can do."

That was the polite Japanese way of saying no. But the more Stark thought about it, the more he realized that he had delayed too long. The time for passivity had passed.

One cop trailed about twenty feet behind Stark. The second was about ten feet behind the first. They had had the assignment for several weeks and were used to Stark's routine.

Four days a week he went to the Kamakura *hombu* and worked out from 10 A.M. to 4 P.M. The rest of the time was spent wandering Tokyo streets, visiting other martial arts schools and old friends. But today Stark had someone to see who he didn't want the police to know about.

He led the two cops to the Ginza district, where the high-priced shops were clustered. He stood outside the huge Mitsukoshi department store, studying his Seiko scuba diving watch and glancing at the busy traffic on Harumi Dori Avenue.

Then he hurried inside the store, past the two white-gloved girls endlessly chanting their welcoming *"Irasshaimase."*

He was out of sight of the cops for a few seconds. He pulled off his jacket while briskly moving toward the exit at the far side of the store. Timing was everything.

As the cops entered, he stepped back out into the street. The light was just changing. He sprinted across the street. The second cop spotted him and tried to follow, but traffic had already resumed.

Stark hurried around the corner and down into the Ginza subway station. One of the cops had somehow figured out his destination. Stark was standing on the platform as the cop came running. The train pulled in and Stark boarded.

The cop did the same, a few doors down.

At the last possible second, Stark jumped off. The doors closed, and the cop was whisked away, glaring at Stark through the train window.

"I've been expecting your visit," Saito said, as he waved Stark into the apartment. The two-room apartment itself was unremarkable. Saito was a widower and kept it spare but clean. All his energy was devoted to his terrace, which housed a spectacular bonsai display.

"I didn't want to trouble you," Stark said.

"Horsefeathers," Saito said, and Stark smiled. The old man had an affinity for outdated American slang. "Sit and I will bring us tea."

Stark positioned himself looking out on the bonsai. With a little imagination, he could envision it as a vast garden. Saito had even arranged a small waterfall, two feet high, but in proportion to the trees, as grand as Niagara.

Saito took his time, allowing Stark to lapse into a relaxed, but alert state. There was a faint smell of incense in the apartment. Saito was a Zen master, a *roshi*. In his time, he had also been a skilled swordsman. Only his slow movements and crevices in his face betrayed his eighty years on earth. His spirit was as strong as a youth's, almost a palpable force.

Saito brought the tea and sat down near Stark.

"You haven't called because you haven't wanted my help to leave Japan," Saito said.

Stark bowed his head. The old man's sharp words were as jarring as the whack of a Zen master's stick.

"You are angry over the reaction to the incident on the plane. You feel you should have been given a hero's welcome, not arrested."

"I was just doing my job."

"I was just doing my job," Saito said, mimicking Stark. "If you were on a lake and an empty boat brushed yours, would you be mad at it?"

"I know."

"You know but you don't know."

"I came here."

"Even with my old eyes I can see that. What do you want?"

"To see your garden."

"The right answer. I'm sure your visit has nothing to do with my government connections." Saito had taught *kendo* to the Japanese prime minister and several members of the Diet. It was rumored they consulted the irascible old man when faced with particularly troubling problems.

Stark stared at the bonsai. "You don't let up, do you?"

"When you are doing a jujitsu technique, do you let up if you sense your opponent wobbling?"

"Am I your opponent?"

"You are your own opponent. You have gotten too far from your true nature. A warrior doesn't care if the fight he fights is unpopular. You must overcome yourself, then you can think of overcoming others."

"So I shouldn't let anything affect me?" Stark asked. He regretted his words. They sounded like a whiny complaint. Saito always managed to bring out the worst in him. But it was like a whetstone sharpening a blade. The grinding was necessary for the proper edge.

"The moon's reflection on the surface of the water moves incessantly. Yet the moon shines and goes nowhere; it stays but it moves."

"I think I understand."

"You don't understand anything. Go back to your room and think about it."

"Thank you, Saito-*san.*"

"Next time you come, bring groceries. I hate shopping."

The next day, Stark received an invitation from Captain Okada to lunch at a sushi restaurant.

Stark and Okada were escorted to a rear table. A deferential waitress brought them specialties that Okada ordered.

After a few minutes of eating and obligatory polite phrases, Okada said, "Where did you go yesterday?"

"I just wanted to be alone. I sat in Ueno Park."

"I see," Okada said, his words thick with skepticism. "I have read your file. I'm impressed. However, I still don't understand why you left your Agency of Central Intelligence."

"I had an agent I was running who my superiors believed was working for the Russians. They wanted me to set up his execution. I didn't, but they went ahead and killed him anyway. I subsequently learned he was innocent."

"Such mistakes are made. It's difficult to judge the loyalty of informants," Okada said sincerely.

"That's why I got out of the business."

"But you stayed in a related field."

"Yes, but now I don't have to take orders from anyone. If such a mistake is made, I accept the blame." Stark swallowed a chewy bit of sea urchin flavored with eye-watering *wasabi* horseradish and said, "Okada-*san,* I have a question. How did the hijackers get the guns on board?"

Before Okada could answer, the restaurant was flooded by martial music and a male Japanese voice haranguing the patrons. It was one of the loudspeaker-equipped buses that cruise Tokyo streets, blasting ultranationalist slogans. Stark, sensing Okada's annoyance, didn't comment, but eventually Okada muttered, "Sasaki."

"Sumi masen?"

"Sasaki. The industrialist. He's a *kuromaku* who is coming out from hiding. You are familiar with the term?"

"From the kabuki. They're the curtain pullers who work hidden in darkness and control the action."

"Hai, so desu. He is calling for my country to expand the

military. Reclaim the Northern Territories, what you call the Kuril islands, from the Russians. Throw U.S. military bases out of the Pacific."

"The usual ultranationalist line," Stark said.

"That, plus loosening gun control laws."

"I've read about that. In the U.S., police are pretty divided on the issue. A lot are gun buffs, yet too many have seen what handguns in the wrong hands can do. What do you think?"

"We are a much more homogeneous society. We would never reach the level of violence that your country has. But I think guns will do no good. Once you have allowed them in, they are difficult to get rid of. Although Japan did, once before."

"In the sixteenth century," Stark said. "So a samurai with his swords wouldn't be challenged by peasants with guns."

The sound truck drove on and the noise from outside subsided.

"The guns on the plane?" Stark prodded.

"They were the plastic Glock-17 weapons."

"I know. But even with the plastic polymer frame, the steel in the barrel and firing mechanism is detectable. Your airport security is as good as the Israelis'. And officials had been alerted."

"Yes?"

"I read in the newspaper that the surviving hijacker refuses to say anything."

"That's true."

"If you could find out how the guns got on the plane, it could prove fruitful. All passengers were diligently searched?"

"*Hai,*" Okada said, slipping into his native tongue as he waited for Stark's next words.

"Then I would guess the crew, or perhaps, and I mean no offense, one of the police officers."

"I take no offense. Fukoda smuggled them aboard."

"What's his story?"

"He was a radical, then changed to our side early on. A previous administrator used him as an *agent provacateur*. It wouldn't surprise you to learn that, as the British say, Fukoda is assisting us with our investigation."

"Not at all."

"Let me make this clear. There will be no coverup," Okada said. "Have you expressed your suspicions to anyone? In your government? In the media?"

"I wouldn't do anything to jeopardize your investigation."

Okada toyed with his chopsticks. "I have argued that you did the right thing from the start. You showed restraint in not shooting Fukoda. A *budoka* like yourself wouldn't needlessly jeopardize himself or others. I presume you felt it necessary to scuffle with the gunman."

"He was about to shoot the stewardess."

"Fifty witnesses, fifty different stories," Okada said. He swallowed a *norimake,* and used a toothpick to clean the seaweed from his teeth. "I am sure it has nothing to do with your slipping away from my men yesterday, but somehow officials at the highest level of government have decided that you should be free to go. I gather you want to go to Thailand."

"And I gather you listened to my phone call."

"I am sure you expected it," Okada said. "The incident in Thailand allegedly involves Japanese nationals. We are, of course, interested."

"You understand that I have a client on this. My first loyalty is to her."

"Yes." Okada reached into his suit jacket pocket. "Here is a ticket to Bangkok and an Interpol report on the incident. I hope you will be able to resolve this quietly."

CHAPTER 8

General Todd Grant kicked his chestnut mare's side and she galloped forward. Arms dealer Gerard DeVille tried to spur his bay gelding on, but the horse could barely keep pace.

DeVille had landed by private jet at Washington D.C.'s National Airport early that morning. He had business in Greece that evening. But a meeting with the head of the Defense Intelligence Agency was a priority matter. They were on a bridle path on Grant's two-hundred-acre estate in Virginia. More than six miles of oak and willow-lined trails snaked through the property.

Even though DeVille knew he would be sore for a week, he had agreed to the trip. Grant, a superb horseman, was in his best mood after time in the saddle.

Grant was waiting up ahead.

"Did I tell you I'm a descendant of General Ulysses S. Grant?" Grant asked.

DeVille was breathing hard and craving a cigarette. But he dared not light one. He needed both hands clutching the pommel of the hand-tooled leather saddle. "You had mentioned it."

"He was an interesting fellow. Sam got a rough deal from historians. But the great ones sometimes do."

DeVille dismounted clumsily and quickly lit up. "Yes," he said between heaves. A few puffs, and he felt much better. "You said there was an urgent business matter to discuss?"

Grant dismounted gracefully and stroked his horse's nose. The mare tossed her head, then rubbed up against him. He took a sugar cube from his pocket and she gobbled it down.

"Horses are the best friends there are," Grant said. "Better than dogs, cats, children. And especially women."

"I suppose."

"They're smart, loyal, and you can ride them whenever you want," Grant said. He grinned, waiting for a reaction to his homespun wisdom. Grant took out another sugar cube and the mare rubbed her head against him. "Try to get that kind of affection out of a woman for just a sugar cube," Grant said.

DeVille preferred a medium rare, horse meat steak to a ride on the beasts, but he didn't think Grant would enjoy his tastes.

"Okay, let's get down to brass tacks," Grant said. "We'd like it if an arms shipment would turn up in Thailand, and look like it came from Cambodia."

DeVille didn't know exactly who "we" was, but he assumed it was some heady mixture of what Eisenhower christened the "Military Industrial Complex." He had been involved in numerous secret deals with Grant. The transactions always took place in Africa, the Middle East, or Asia. DeVille avoided Europe and Central America. Too many Catholics. He was a devout Christian. The idea of Buddhists, Muslims, or assorted heathens slaughtering each other did not bother him. But he had personal reasons for wanting peace in Thailand.

"I would hate to cause trouble in Thailand," DeVille said. "What about the condition in Cyprus? It seems to be a promising market."

"Maybe. Maybe not. The President is pussyfooting around. He doesn't want to piss the Reds off."

"Japan?"

"Don't jump the gun. No pun intended. It's Thailand

where I want the action right now. I know about your plans there. This is just a little diversion. It shouldn't affect anything. In fact, your plans in Thailand and mine for Japan might just mesh."

"Perhaps I could plant the load in Laos?"

"They don't have enough money to buy a slingshot. It's Thailand. Or maybe you want us to find someone else?" Grant paused to let his threat settle in. "If you want to keep the pipeline open, you'd better remember who controls it."

The only sound was the husky heaving of the horses. Grant cleared his throat and spat on the ground.

"I've got a load of Skorpions," DeVille said reluctantly, referring to the Czech-manufactured Skorpion 7.65-mm machine pistol. "And some AK-47s," he added, referring to the famous Kalashnikov 7.62-mm assault rifle. The weapons DeVille was thinking of had been water damaged. They'd require extensive stripping and cleaning to be usable. "You just want a load of weapons that will be discovered?" DeVille asked.

"Yes. And a Japanese tie-in again."

"I will try my best."

"This is a rush order."

"Hmm. It will cost more."

"How much?" Grant asked.

They haggled and finally set a price, which included DeVille getting a half dozen TOW missiles that would be listed as defective. The TOW—Tube launched, Optically sighted, Wire guided—missile was a shoulder fired antitank weapon, much in demand by Third World guerrillas. "How soon can I count on it?" Grant asked.

"A couple of days at the most."

"Great. Let's ride back."

"If you don't mind, I think I'll walk," DeVille said, holding the horse's reins.

"Suit yourself," Grant said. He took off at a gallop, his horse kicking up dust on the trail. DeVille coughed, dropping his cigarette.

"*Merde,*" he muttered, then a string of curses in French. He fingered the heavy gold cross he wore around his neck.

He lit a new cigarette, yanked on the horse's reins and began the walk back.

"Mr. Robert Stark?" the Thai assistant police chief asked as Stark deplaned.

Other passengers stared. Stark hated calling attention to himself but the sight of a ranking uniformed officer waiting at the foot of the jetway had drawn a small crowd of curiosity seekers. Stark wondered if the Thai policeman were deliberately blowing his cover.

"I'm afraid your trip here is unnecessary," the policeman said after guiding Stark to a quiet spot. "We have located the kidnappers. The Border Patrol Police Bureau has already surrounded their hideout. Our Border Patrol Police are experts at subversion, insurgency, and terrorism. They will raid the premises as soon as night falls."

Stark looked at his watch. Sundown was about four hours away.

"How many kidnappers are there?"

"We know of at least three."

"How heavily are they armed?"

"We are not sure."

"Explosives?"

The official shrugged.

"How can you storm them, then?"

"Mr. Stark, we have received word that the victim's brother is willing to pay the ransom. We do not allow that here. We do not encourage terrorism in your country and trust you and your fellow Americans will not do the same here."

"I understand." There was no point in arguing with the stiff-necked bureaucrat. "Thank you for your consideration."

Stark went to a pay phone and called New York. The policeman watched him from across the terminal.

After a few minutes for the long-distance call to go through, Stark got Les Halliwell on the line. Halliwell was a former Secret Serviceman with extensive government contacts.

"The authorities seem intent on storming the place," Stark said. "From what I've heard, it's a dumb move. This girl's brother must have some clout. Have him use it."

"I know people on the Asian desk at State."

"Use them too. Tell Hancock if he doesn't stop them, his sister will come home quick. In a box."

CHAPTER 9

M y family farmed the same land for eight generations," Kenji Nakamura said softly. "Then they decided to build Narita Airport. Now the farm is under asphalt. My father has to work at the airport to support the family. Instead of tending his land, he cleans toilets."

Diana Hancock nodded. She was still blindfolded and tied to a chair. She had come to think of Nakamura as the gentle one. She looked forward to the sound of his voice. The other two would poke, pinch, slap her by surprise. She was allowed to get up to go to the toilet three times a day. That was her only exercise. She hadn't been allowed to shower.

But the worst horror had been when the visitor came. She guessed he wasn't Japanese, maybe British or possibly Australian. He was in the other room when he spoke, and his voice was too low for her to make out his words. But he had the sound of authority.

Then someone came in, grabbed her head, and cut off her ear. The pain made her pass out. She woke with her head bandaged. She could feel the blood caked on the side of her neck, in her hair. The ear stump throbbed.

The gentle one had tended her, keeping the wound clean, even slipping her a pill that numbed the pain. As she listened to him speak, she could sense his vulnerability. She wondered what he looked like.

"My brother was among the first to demonstrate against the airport. He was as brave as a samurai, going up against water cannons, police with clubs. He led an expedition into the airport offices. They broke in through a sewer tunnel. They set back the construction by several months."

She nodded along.

"He was killed during a demonstration. Officials said he was trampled by rioters. I know he was beaten to death by police. I vowed he would be avenged."

"It won't bring him back."

"It will restore honor to my family name and show the imperialist exploiters that they cannot oppress the proletariat."

"Are you a Communist?"

"Ideological labels are not important," Nakamura said sternly as he mouthed learned slogans. "Justice for all people, not just the rich, is what matters."

"But the hill tribe refugees who were shot down weren't rich?"

"They were ignorant tools," Nakamura said. He lowered his voice. "It was regrettable that they had to die."

"And me?"

"I am prepared to die for the class struggle. We all must be prepared to die."

"You sound like a good person. I don't understand how you can talk like that."

Talking to Hancock had softened Nakamura's attitude. He no longer felt so eager to die for the cause. She was a beautiful woman, and strong. Even when his handler came and cut off her ear, she had barely screamed. He had begun to regret the path his life had taken. He was mouthing the rhetoric as much to convince himself as her.

"Revolutionaries must be strong. Have foresight. It isn't easy to do what is right. Like the bombing last week. When I . . ."

"Kenji, there's movement out in the field," she heard the stocky one shout.

The gentle one, who she now knew was named Kenji, hurried away. She heard the sound of guns being cocked.

Bars and dark teak shutters covered the numerous windows. Nakamura opened a shutter a few inches.

The four-room rented house bordered a six-acre lot, used by Chiang Mai University agricultural students to practice agronomy. The field was overgrown, lying fallow, and provided an ideal escape route. The kidnappers had three Honda 750 cc motorcycles, with knobby off-road tires, hidden nearby. It was little more than fifty miles to the Burma border. A Burmese contact there held forged papers and plane tickets out of Rangoon.

"The birds have stopped singing," the tall one said from the other side of the house. "Something big was moving in the brush not that long ago." The palms and bushes were so dense that visibility was limited to a few yards.

"An animal?" Nakamura asked hopefully.

"I saw a camouflage uniform," the tall one said.

"Up there, on the roof," the stocky tall one said from the other side of the house. Nakamura hurried to the other side of the building, which faced out on Bumrungan Road Lane. Nakamura followed the stocky one's line of sight. He saw the movement. Someone had stuck his head up, and dropped back down. A police sniper?

"Are we surrounded?" Nakamura asked.

The stocky one grunted assent.

The tall one opened the knapsack he had been carrying. Inside was a detonator and a book size wad of C-4. The white explosive was three times stronger than dynamite. Nakamura noticed tiny wires trailing out the window.

"What are those?" he asked.

"While you spent so much time talking to the *gaijin*, we've been working. There are Claymore mines planted all around the house. If they attack, boom!" the stocky one said, his hands flaring wide to indicate an explosion.

"Maybe we should negotiate?" Nakamura suggested.

The tall one snapped open the folding stock on his Beretta Model 12 submachine gun. The nine-pound gun held forty rounds of ammo. He took out several full magazines.

The stocky one had an M-1 carbine. It had only a fifteen-shot magazine, but it had a greater muzzle velocity and was much more accurate up to three hundred and thirty meters. He checked that his three spare magazines were full.

"Negotiation is for cowards," the stocky one sneered.

On the plane ride from Bangkok to Chiang Mai, the Thai assistant police chief explained to Stark that the Japanese trio had pretended to be exchange students attending Chiang Mai University. They had rented a house that once belonged to a university administrator. The cop volunteered little else. Hancock and Halliwell had used their connections, and he was forced to oblige Stark. But he clearly was unhappy about it.

A police car picked them up at the airport and drove them to two blocks from the house.

"We cannot guarantee your safety," the assistant chief said. "Would you like a bulletproof vest? I might have one big enough for you."

"No, thanks. It wouldn't fit my cover story. *Mai pen rye.*"

"Whatever happens, happens," the assistant police chief echoed.

"There's a white man walking up the street," Nakamura said.

"I can see that," the stocky one snapped.

Police had closed off the road and hustled neighbors away. A few chickens and dogs wandering the street were the only signs of life. Stark walked slowly, like a gunfighter going to a shootout. Behind him, hidden in doorways, on rooftops, and behind windows, several dozen black-bereted Thai cops waited for a signal to fire. In front of him, the kidnappers waited.

"Should I kill him?" the tall one asked.

"No," Nakamura said.

The stocky one wiped a bead of sweat that stung his eye.

The tall one kept his gun trained on Stark and waited for the stocky one's decision. His finger cramped on the trigger.

"Let us see what he has to say," the stocky one said.

Stark had his hands up. He was jacketless. He neared the front gate. The house was ringed by a five-foot-high brick fence that was covered with concrete and topped with steel bars. He could see the glint of a gun in the window.

Stark concentrated on his breathing, focusing his attention on his *tanden*, the point two inches below the navel that Japanese and Chinese consider the center of the being.

"I'd like to come in," Stark said, stopping at the open gate.

"Enter," the stocky one said. As the crisis had developed, he had usurped Nakamura's authority.

Stark stepped forward. He could feel the police guns on his back, the kidnappers' guns on his front. He inhaled and exhaled slowly, drawing strength and composure.

CHAPTER 10

The stocky kidnapper grabbed Stark's shirt and jerked him in. He shoved the shotgun in Stark's face. The three kidnappers had donned stocking masks.

"Who are you?" the stocky one demanded in choppy English.

"My name is Alex O'Dell. I'm with International Insurance." Stark reached into his wallet and produced fake ID which identified him as a vice president with the nonexistent company.

"What do you want?"

"To verify that the victim is okay before we can settle the claim."

"Are you crazy, marching in here like this?" the stocky one asked after roughly frisking Stark. "We could kill you."

"I don't think I'm worth three million dollars to you. If I verify she's okay, I'll recommend payment. If she's dead, or you injure me, I won't." Stark tried to sound as nonthreatening as possible, maintaining a fussbudget demeanor.

The trio conferred. They didn't realize Stark was fluent in Japanese and could understand what was said. He assessed that Nakamura and the stocky one were rivals for leadership, with the stocky one more hardnosed. Nakamura seemed ready to crack. He also gathered that they had laid traps in and around the house, and felt confident they could handle a police assault.

"What about the police?" Nakamura finally asked in English.

"I can arrange to keep them back," Stark said.

"I don't like it," the tall one said.

"We have no choice," Nakamura responded.

The stocky one led Stark, shotgun at his back, to the smaller room where Hancock sat bound and helpless.

"Miss Hancock?"

"Yes," the blindfolded woman answered.

"What's your brother's name?"

"Edward."

"What was the name of your childhood pet?"

The stocky one poked Stark with the shotgun. "You are wasting time with stupid questions."

"I am verifying that your hostage is indeed Miss Hancock. Now, please, the dog's name?"

"Boopsie," Diana said. "She was a Labrador retriever."

"Very good. How are you?" Stark asked, taking a step closer to the woman.

The stocky kidnapper with the shotgun tensed.

"Take it easy," Stark said. "I just want to inspect her injuries."

"Make it quick."

Stark leaned in close to Diana and studied her cut ear. "Don't worry. You'll get out of this fine," he said reassuringly.

"The leader's name is Kenji. He had a brother killed at Narita," she whispered.

"What did you say?" the stocky one demanded, cracking her across the face. She rocked back in the seat. Stark moved reflexively to protect her. The stocky one hit him with the shotgun.

Stark could've disarmed the man, but he didn't know what booby traps there were around, and where the other two kidnappers were. He let the stocky one get in a couple of blows, rolling with them to minimize their impact.

"You think you're a hero?" the stocky one scoffed.

"No, no, just let me out of here," Stark said. "I see she's okay."

The tall one kicked Stark in the backside as the counterterrorist walked out the door.

Stark reached police lines. The assistant chief of police had seen the kick.

"They seem to have the upper hand," the cop said. "Or the upper foot at least. Now are you ready for us to act?"

"I need access to a secure line and about six hours. With any luck, I can resolve this without anyone getting killed."

The cop frowned, but shouted for an assistant.

Stark called Captain Okada in Tokyo.

"How many people have been killed at Narita Airport?"

"I would guess about a half dozen."

"Can you see if any of them have a brother named Kenji? He's about five ten, maybe a hundred fifty pounds. I'd guess he's somewhere between twenty and thirty."

"This relates to the kidnapping?"

Stark told him what had happened.

"I'll do what I can. Call me back in a half hour."

When Stark called back, the police computer had already spit out a printout. Okada read from it. "Kenji Nakamura, twenty-four, two arrests at Narita for disorderly conduct. He's a self-professed Communist, has been identified at numerous rallies. Considered a fringe member of radical groups."

"He just moved in from the fringes. Does he have any family?" Stark asked.

"Another brother. Two years younger. Minor arrests. Father works at the airport."

"Can you get me a copy of the brother's driver's license that looks like the original."

"It can be done. What do you have in mind?"

When Stark explained, Okada laughed.

CIA director Dan Creange took the phone call himself. "Bob, how's it going?"

Stark explained where he was and what he was involved in.

"You wouldn't be phoning now unless you were calling in a marker. What do you need?"

"I want a Thai coroner to do me a favor."

"What kind of favor?"

When Stark explained, Creange chuckled. "Let me know what happens."

"I'll give you a complete rundown as soon as I get back to the States."

Again Stark walked down the street, only this time he had a small aluminum Haliburton case in one hand. He reached the door of the house and was yanked in by the kidnappers.

"Is that the money?" the stocky one demanded.

"It's your payment," Stark said, setting it down on the table.

"What if there's a booby trap in there?" the tall one asked.

"Let him open it," the stocky one said, indicating Stark by jabbing him with the muzzle of the carbine.

"What if there's a gun in there?" Nakamura asked.

The stocky one scratched his head.

"I'll open it," Nakamura said. "He stands next to me."

Stark was shoved forward. Nakamura unsnapped the case. The others greedily hovered nearby.

He opened it and gasped. Then he looked at the Japanese driver's license inside and screamed.

The two other kidnappers surged forward, distracted.

Stark grabbed the carbine and shoved it back hard into the stocky kidnapper's abdomen. Keeping his momentum, he jerked the weapon toward himself. He pivoted, swinging the gun like the *bokken*, the wooden practice sword he practiced with in the *dojo.*

It caught the tall one right on the ear, stunning him and making him loosen his grip on his gun. Stark kicked him in the knee, and the tall one fell.

Nakamura hadn't moved, but the stocky one had recovered, and produced a foot-long *balisong* knife. He lunged. Stark was off balance, facing the taller kidnapper. Thought and action were as one. He spun to avoid the blade, using the stock of the carbine to block. He dropped the weapon, grabbed the stocky man's knife hand and stepped in, simultaneously pivoting. He locked the man's arm up.

The attacker resisted, and Stark yanked, dislocating the stocky man's shoulder. He fell to the floor, yowling in pain and dropping the knife.

Nakamura held onto the table, about to pass out.

The tall one got up and swung a wild roundhouse punch.

Stark stepped in, blocking and delivering a knife hand chop to the man's neck. The man stiffened, and Stark landed two more quick blows, then threw him with a straightforward *ogoshi*, a judo hip throw.

The stocky one scrambled to his feet and jumped out a window. He got about twenty feet before hitting a trip wire from a Claymore. The explosion sent seven hundred ball bearings—driven by a pound and a half of C4 plastic explosive—tearing through him.

It also knocked Stark to the floor, and gave the tall hood a chance to recover his gun. Stark couldn't make it across the room in time.

Stark scooped up the *balisong* and flung it as the tall one aimed. The knife caught the tall one in the throat. In his death throes he sprayed the entire clip of ammunition around the house. Stark pulled the knife from his throat, wiped it on the tall one's shirt, and kept it at the ready as he checked Nakamura.

Kenji lay unconscious on the floor. Stark found the heavy tape they had used to bind Hancock, and used it to tie Nakamura. His fainting had saved him from the deadly spray.

Stark hurried into the other room.

"Are you okay?" he asked Hancock, using the knife to sever her bonds.

"What happened?" she asked.

"You're safe. The kidnappers have been neutralized."

"Dead?"

"All but the one you know as Kenji," Stark said.

"Good."

"I'm going to take the blindfold off," Stark said. "Close your eyes. The light will be painful after so much time in darkness."

She did as she was told, gradually blinking and squinting until she could keep her eyes halfway open. He draped a blanket over her and pulled it around her as gently as a mother tucking in a child. She nearly toppled over, her legs were so weak from lack of use.

"I can't believe this," she repeated several times. "Who are you?"

"Stark. Robert Stark. Your brother sent me."

They stepped into the living room. Flies were buzzing around the Haliburton case. Stark shut it before she could see what was inside. She looked down at Kenji.

"He's alive?"

"He'll be around to stand trial."

"He was the nicest of the three."

"Everything's relative."

The assistant police chief gave Stark a *wai*, fingers steepled, head slightly bowed. It was a traditional Thai gesture of respect and thanks.

"My men didn't realize how well prepared the terrorists were," the assistant police chief said. "More lives would have been lost if we stormed them as planned."

"I appreciate the cooperation you extended me. Your men were extremely professional in the way they held their fire and kept the perimeter secure." Stark *wai*ed back. Thinking of Okada, he said, "I have a favor to ask. The Japanese government is concerned about their terrorists giving the country a bad name. Would it be possible to play down the nationality of the suspects?"

"In fact my men have discovered Japanese, Chinese, and Korean passports," the assistant police chief said. "The press will be told only that they were Orientals, and not Thais."

More thanks, and then Stark hurried Diana away before the first journalists could arrive at the scene. In Bangkok, a mob of reporters was waiting at the terminal. Stark and

Diana had successfully evaded the press at police headquarters thanks to a cordon of police.

Her brother had arranged for a private jet. The crowd of reporters watched from the terminal as she was led out onto the tarmac and to a Hancock Publishing jet.

She stared out the window of the plane as they sped across the Pacific. She dozed fitfully. The copilot came back with a light meal. Finally, she made eye contact with Stark.

"Feeling better?" he asked.

"I feel halfway back to human."

"It will take a while."

She was silent. "What will happen to Kenji?"

"He'll stand trial. He might get off with life imprisonment."

"He wasn't so bad," she said.

"He helped kidnap you, didn't he?"

"Yes, but . . ."

"He didn't stop them when they cut off your ear, did he?"

She patted the bandage. "You don't understand." She turned her back to him and curled up on the seat. He watched her back rise and fall, then closed his own eyes again.

She was a remarkably strong woman. He'd seen people take weeks to reach the stage of recovery where she was already. She was through the denial stage, into anger. Then would come bargaining, depression, and hopefully, acceptance.

When she awakened again, he gave her a smile.

"What did you do exactly?" she asked. "I heard Kenji scream." Her tone was cool, removed.

"I faked him out."

"How?"

"I got someone at the morgue to cut the genitals off of a traffic accident victim. Then I got a copy of Nakamura's brother's driver's license."

"That's horrible."

"It saved your life, his life, and probably the lives of a few cops," Stark said.

"He believed in something."

"Your venting your anger is normal. Although misdirected."

"What about the Kenji Nakamuras of the world? They're helpless, they need to call attention to themselves. Haven't you ever felt frustrated, tempted to lash out violently?" When she was done with her tantrum, she went back to sleep.

A spoiled child, Stark thought, an empty boat.

He thought of Saito's bonsai and tried to call up the beautiful scene.

CHAPTER 11

Isao Sasaki was barely five feet tall, but wielded the power of a giant. Sasaki Industries was one of the massive industrial combines, successful in electronics manufacturing, real estate speculation, and mining of various raw materials throughout South America and Southeast Asia.

He stood off to one side, watching as Kowa took the podium in the huge hall. There was absolute silence. Behind him, a twenty-foot-high picture of the emperor gazed down. Kowa was artfully lit, and the microphone picked up his rumbling voice and spread it to speakers throughout the hall. Kowa was a former actor, who made up what he lacked in intelligence with a surplus of charisma.

"We have been too long the little brother to the United States," Kowa said, repeating the words Sasaki had written as if they were his own. Kowa spoke softly, but the high-tech sound system made every word clear. "Now, we are like the little brother who is more successful than his older sibling. It is an uncomfortable situation. But our actions are inevitable.

"Our big brother has been our protector. Now we must stand on our own. Perhaps even help our big brother. We must be like the Swiss. Every man a soldier, armed and ready to fight to protect the homeland. A peaceful Japan is an armed Japan."

Shills in the audience of nearly a thousand shouted "Banzai!"

"It is more than just the right of the younger brother to help his older brother. It is *giri*, his duty. For the good of the family. For the good of Japan."

"Banzai!" the shills shouted, with the enthusiasm of teenage girls at a Bon Jovi concert.

The crowd picked up the chant. Applause. The shills stood, and others followed. Feet stomping. Someone who hadn't seen a Japanese rally would never believe "inscrutable Orientals" could be so noisy, so visibly emotional.

Sasaki had written two more pages of material. But he signaled Kowa to stop on an emotional high note.

TV crews from Nippon Broadcasting recorded his triumph. Sasaki's cameramen filmed Kowa from a low angle, so he appeared larger than life. The hall would be photographed with a wide-angle lens, making it look even more crowded.

Shouts of "banzai" washed over Kowa, and Sasaki smiled.

Stark hit the oil-slick road at sixty miles an hour and immediately skidded wildly. He fought the urge to stomp the brakes, went with the skid, and brought the Volvo under control after hitting only a few road cones.

"Not bad," the instructor said. "Turn into it more, keep the arms loose, and you'll do well."

The course was aimed at chauffeurs, bodyguards, and anyone who might encounter man-made road hazards. Eighty percent of all terrorist attacks have taken place in or near the victim's car. The school was set up on the runway of what had once been a small airfield in southern New Jersey.

Stark continued to drive down mock streets. He thought about Diana Hancock. He was used to ungrateful victims, it was part of the Stockholm syndrome. Named after hostages in a Swedish bank who fell in love with their captor, psychologists blamed it on transference of a parent-child relationship.

He was frustrated that her rescue had resulted in two deaths. And there had been the shooting on the NAL airliner. So many other deaths over the years. Too often terrorists were young, idealistic. But that didn't make them any the less deadly.

"Look out!" the instructor shouted. Stark saw the woman with the baby carriage at the last minute.

He slammed on the brakes, burning rubber, but pulling to a stop inches in front of the cardboard figure.

His forward momentum had barely stopped when a man with a gun jumped out and shoved it in his face.

"You're dead, running dog imperialist lackey dogfucker," the man said.

"Okay, you made your point," the instructor said.

The man with the gun smiled and strolled back to his hiding place.

"You know how many incidents there've been with a baby carriage used to stop the car?" the instructor asked. "The terrorists keep their weapons in the carriage."

"I know. I know," Stark said. If he hadn't been daydreaming, he might've reacted differently. When you stand, stand. When you sit, sit. Don't wobble. He'd been guilty of wobbling. And if it had been the real world, he'd be dead.

He met CIA director Dan Creange a few hours later. They were the only two whites in a noisy soul food joint in northeast Washington. Creange wore his Ivy League alumnus uniform——khaki chinos, blue blazer, topsider shoes.

"So what would you do in an incident like that?" Stark asked, describing the scene with the baby carriage. "Take a chance on killing a baby or risk your own life and the person's you're guarding?"

Creange reflectively gnawed a sparerib smothered in a spicy brown sauce. "I'd probably commission a study to analyze the feasibility of forming a committee to assess and evaluate the proper response." Creange set down the rib thoughtfully. "I suppose I would probably brake and not hit the pram. Though I would want a chauffeur who would be willing to run her down."

"Your honesty is very becoming."

"My honesty will get me back into the private sector."

"What's going on?"

A reggae tune blasted in the background. Patrons talked to each other by shouting, except for Creange and Stark, who leaned in close to each other. The background noise made bugging extremely difficult.

Creange moved so he was virtually whispering in Stark's ear. He recounted some of the RIG power plays. "Our President is surrounded by a group of men who like to think in football metaphors," Creange said, wiping his lips with a napkin. "The President wants to show that he's tough, can handle foreign policy. I think if he could arm wrestle Gorbachev to decide the next treaty, he would."

"Personally, I'd put my money on Gorbachev to win. He's got good wrists."

Creange tried to smile. "It's tiring. This Cyprus situation had the possibility for real problems. There were a few ugly demonstrations with the usual anti-American tone. But fortunately things have quieted down. Now I have a question for you. Did you notice any unusual undercurrents when you were in northern Thailand?"

"No. But I wasn't looking for anything. What's up?"

"I don't know. We lost one of our best people. Heart attack. Another one disappeared. I gather the KGB lost one of theirs as well. Satellites don't show anything."

"Shan Army?"

"DEA shows no increase in drug activity. The poppy crop was bad this year."

"Burmese rebels? Laotian troops?"

"I was hoping you'd have the answers."

"Not when I didn't even know there were questions."

"What about Japan?"

"Dan, I wasn't tasked before I went traveling."

"I know. But I also know you're the sort who keeps his eyes open. Once a spook, always a spook. And I did do you that favor with the coroner."

After slowly finishing a piece of chicken, Stark said,

"There were signs of increased militarism. It had the feeling of a well-funded, vocal minority."

"That's our assessment too. Would you be interested in going back there? We would like—"

Stark held up his hand, interupting Creange's words. "Don't tell me what you're looking for. I'm out of the business."

"The intelligence trade is like the Mafia, Bob. Like it or not, you're in it until you're carried to your grave."

CHAPTER 12

Bob, you've got to go," Halliwell said.

"I don't have to go," Stark said. He was seated behind his desk, a stack of papers before him. At the bottom were the Halliwell-Stark profit and loss statements. On top of that were various intelligence reports. Two weeks after his return to New York and the paperwork only seemed higher.

"Hancock paid us a hundred grand for rescuing his sister," Halliwell said. "And I think he's got more work for us."

"No, he probably wants to show me off to his country club friends," Stark said. "A genuine terrorist hunter-killer."

"He just wants to thank you personally. He's a classy guy, footing the bill for you to fly out there. Probably put you up at his mansion, provide hot and cold running starlets."

Stark just grunted and returned his attention to his paperwork.

"I'm asking you to go to California," Halliwell said. "It's not such a big deal. Hancock's worth more than two hundred million. If we could get a contract for some of his businesses . . ." Halliwell let the words trail off.

"We're okay the way we are. Terrorism is a growth industry," Stark said, holding up a few intelligence reports.

"What's with you anyway? You're not your usual effervescent self," Halliwell said with a mocking smile. "I think your semen's built to dangerous levels. You've got to get out more, go hand to hand with the most dangerous creature on earth—the single California woman. Do me a favor, go to L.A. Bake in the sun. Go surfing. Roll in the sand with beach bimbos. Just bring back the Hancock account."

"What about time to ponder the eternal questions of life?"

"Do that between the legs of some hot little beach bunny."

The limousine drove through the arched gate, along the curving driveway, by a row of palms. A couple of gardeners were trimming the boxwood hedges. Two romping Dobermans were watched by a burly handler with leashes dangling from his waist.

Edward Hancock lived in a mansion at the foot of the Santa Monica Mountains in Bel Air. The hill had been notched, and the six-bedroom home slipped in. The Spanish tile roofed house was three stories high, white, with archways over a long veranda.

There was a party going on as Stark arrived, and casual but elegant people sipped drinks, chatted, and mingled. A few splashed in the Olympic-size swimming pool, a few more boiled in the Jacuzzi, two couples played mixed doubles, while several others kibitzed from the sidelines.

"Mr. Hancock is waiting to see you in the study," the chauffeur said, dropping Stark at the front door. A white-jacketed manservant took over the escort role.

Stark felt like a private eye in a Raymond Chandler novel as he was led through the mansion. The house had old-world elegance, hardwood moldings and wainscotting, dark built-ins filled with books and art objects. The furniture was antiques from the Colonial era. Straight clean lines, solid wood frames.

The manservant pushed open the eight-foot-high fruit-wood doors. Edward Hancock sat behind a huge mahogany desk, speaking into the phone. He gestured for Stark to have a seat in one of the leather chairs facing the desk.

Stark had accessed the numerous data bases his agency

subscribed to and read up on Hancock. Good intelligence on a potential client could be as rewarding as good intelligence on an enemy.

Hancock was forty-eight, ten years older than his sister. He was married, with three children, two dogs, and a cat. He had inherited a small, twice a week newspaper chain, and land holdings worth about two million dollars in 1958. Through real estate and stock market speculation, getting in early on the transistor and then the computer boom, Hancock had built a fortune.

In part because his family had come to California around the time of the Gold Rush, Hancock was a respected member of the elite that runs Southern California. He had been considered as a political candidate, but withdrew his name, since it would require public scrutiny and actually a loss of power.

He hung up and stepped forward, his tanned and manicured hand grabbing Stark's for a warm shake. Hancock had prematurely gray hair and a regal bearing, more old-world dignity than California mellow. But he was perfectly tanned and had a robust freshness about him.

"Mr. Stark, it's a genuine pleasure to meet you," Hancock said. "My sister's told me about you."

"I'm not as bad as all that."

"She regrets her behavior," Hancock said.

"She was under a lot of stress," Stark said. "She had great grace under pressure."

"Hemingway's definition of courage," Hancock said, showing that the leather bound classics on the wall weren't just for decoration. "I have a business proposition to make. How would you like to do a series of articles for my newspapers? About the terrorism network, how they arm themselves, where they train, what they believe, trends for the future. The specifics could be worked out."

"My writing is pretty much limited to reports," Stark said. "I doubt if readers would find it as interesting as Dear Abby."

"I'll pair you with one of my best writers. You provide the

raw material, he'll whip it into shape. All expenses paid. Take as much time as you need."

"Why?"

"I don't like what happened to my sister, Mr. Stark. If I were as physically competent as you are I would probably go out and, excuse my French, kick some butt. As it is, I have a certain amount of influence. I'd like to use it, and my publications, to put pressure on our officials, other countries. This terrorism has gone on long enough."

"I doubt a series would change much. As long as you have disaffected people with nothing to lose and people who'll supply them guns and bombs, you're going to have violence."

"I understand that. But we in the media have become a partner to terrorists. Albeit an unwitting one. Terrorism is great theater. The perpetrators get an audience, newsstand sales increase, TV ratings climb. I believe it was Margaret Thatcher who called us the oxygen that fuels terrorism's fire." Hancock slammed his fist into his palm. "I want to do something. What good is money and power if you can't use it to help mankind?"

It sounded hackneyed to Stark, but Hancock was a charismatic and convincing speaker. Stark had occasionally considered doing something more about terrorism than just cleaning up messes and Hancock's offer definitely had a certain appeal.

Hancock sensed his wavering. "You'd reach hundreds of thousands of people through my papers. Perhaps influence politicians, educate the public." Hancock grinned. "Of course, I'd sell lots of papers in the process."

He was a good salesman, Stark thought, knowing just when to take the edge off the hard sell.

"Think about it, Bob." Hancock walked Stark to the French doors that opened onto the lawn. "For now, I know Diana wants to say hello."

The party had divided into a dozen clumps of people, oases of chitchat in a green landscape. There were giggles and laughs coming from some clusters, serious voices coming from others.

Stark drifted to the bar and got a glass of ginger ale. He sipped it and wandered, his mind inevitably turning to work, and mulling over the security of the Hancock estate. Strong steel gates stood at the foot of the driveway, but they hadn't been locked. Fences were high, topped with an insulated wire that could either be electrified or used as an alarm sensor. The many windows on the house had been wired. Then there were the two Dobermans, and the staffers with the broken nose, cauliflowered ear, wary eyes look.

Stark considered Hancock's offer. It would allow him to snoop around the world of terrorism from a different perspective, with the backing of a media empire. But how would he structure the story so a layman could appreciate the complexities?

Maybe he'd profile the three major kinds of terrorists: revolutionaries, usually left-wing, like the Tupamaros in Uruguay or the Italian Red Brigade; separatists, like the IRA or Basque's ETA; and right-wingers, like the Latin American death squads or neo-Nazi survivalists.

But where would he begin? In Persia in A.D. 1090, with Moslem fanatic Hassan ibn al-Sabbah, who terrorized the Crusaders with his Assassins? Or maybe on Skyjack Sunday, September 6, 1970, when the Popular Front for the Liberation of Palestine targeted TWA, Swissair, and El Al flights? He wanted to show the roots of frustration from which terrorism grew, and yet make readers see that terrorism was a genuine threat to civilized nations. Maybe he would——

"I suspect your thoughts would be worth much more than a penny," a woman said.

It was Diana Hancock. She wore a clingy, gauzy white outfit. She had regained some of the weight she had lost during her ordeal. She wore a floppy hat that shaded her face and covered her missing ear.

"You look good," Stark said.

"I'm feeling better. Why were you staring so intently at the house?"

"Admiring the architecture."

"Edward had it custom built, modeled on a villa in Valencia." She grabbed his arm. "Come with me. I'd like to introduce you to a few friends."

Stark let himself be led. There was something wrong with Diana. He couldn't place it until he saw her group. They had that artificially animated look. Cocaine.

There were about ten people, none older than fifty. Several of the older ones clearly did their best to hide their age with face lifts. All dressed in bright colors, designer beach clothes. They were on the rear patio of the house and looked like a layout from a trendy magazine.

"This is my knight in shining armor," Diana said. She rattled off the names of the people. The only one Stark made an effort to remember was Sam. He was almost six feet, four inches, but no more than one hundred and sixty pounds. He had deep set brown eyes that glared at Stark as if he knew him.

The group peppered him with questions he'd heard before.

"Who's the worst terrorist?"

"How many people have you killed?"

"Is it hard to kill someone?"

"Are you ever scared?"

Their attention wandered even before he answered. Cocaine uncoupled trains of thought. Stark felt like an outsider, but Diana kept her hand on his arm. He realized that it wasn't so much to welcome him in as to draw support for herself.

After about fifteen minutes, Sam sidled over. "Di, you want to do a toot?"

She hesitated.

"Whistle?" Stark asked, playing an innocent.

Sam snorted. "Coke, moron."

"What's a cokemoron?" Stark asked.

The dealer was getting annoyed. "Mind your own business. Diana? I've got some more nearly pure Colombian."

"I don't think the lady needs any coffee," Stark said. He sensed that Sam and Diana had once had more than a dealer-customer relationship.

"Fuck off."

"You're hostile. I've heard that that is an unwanted side effect of several illegal substances," Stark said prissily. "You might reconsider your lifestyle."

"You want trouble, I can give it to you."

Stark gently disengaged Diana's hand from his arm, but continued to talk in a level tone. "I don't want trouble. I just want Diana to have time to get her bearings back. Then if she wants to snort Drano from the can, it's her business. So why don't you go peddle your crap elsewhere."

The dealer reached toward his waistband. His fingertips had just gotten near his belt when Stark pinned that arm flat against his body. Stark's other hand went to the dealer's throat.

Both Stark's arms were extended in a basic aikido "unbendable arm" position. The elbows weren't locked, but the arms were solid. He stepped forward, pinning the dealer against the wall.

"I hope you were reaching into your pants to scratch an itch," Stark said.

Sam choked and gasped for air.

Stark reached under Sam's hand, and pulled out a Sterling .25 automatic. "This gun doesn't really have much stopping power," Stark commented, continuing to put pressure against Sam's throat. "You should get yourself a better one." Stark dropped the small gun in his pocket. He used his free hand to roughly frisk the dealer. He came up with a cigar-sized vial filled with white powder.

Stark snapped the cap off with his thumb. "Dust in the wind." He waved the arm holding the vial and the cocaine blew out in the night air.

The people who had been watching and murmuring gasped. Stark had just thrown out a week's pleasure.

Stark let the dealer go and Sam slumped to the ground.

"You bully," one woman said to Stark.

"Uncool, very uncool," a man muttered.

"I guess the entertainment's over," Stark said to Diana. "I'd better be going."

She burst into tears and ran into the house.

"It's her party and she'll cry if she wants to," one of the men quipped, and everyone laughed. Stark fixed them with a dirty look and headed inside.

He was directed by the manservant to where Diana had run. Stark found her inside the game room. It had a pool table in the middle and shelves packed with every game imaginable. She was sitting in a wingback chair, which faced another across a small table, and sobbing softly.

Stark pulled six darts from the board and began tossing. He threw five, getting one in the bull's-eye. Diana continued to cry.

"You want company?" he asked, when her sobs had lessened.

She sniffled a "yes."

He threw the last dart, just outside the center ring, and sat facing her. There was a half-completed game of chess on the small table.

"Interesting friends you have," Stark said.

"You don't know how badly I wanted that coke," she said. "I thought about getting down on all fours and sniffing the grass."

"It's easy enough to find another dealer. I've heard there're one or two others in Los Angeles."

She struggled to smile and failed. "What was that you did to Sam?"

"It's a variation on a basic aikido move called 'unbendable arm.'"

"Can you show me how?"

"You don't try and lock the joint, just let energy flow out like water through a hose." He demonstrated, then positioned her arm and guided her through it.

After a few minutes, she had a rough idea. They were standing very close, his hand on her arm. It felt firm and yet feminine. There was long eye contact, which he broke off.

"My life sucks," she said.

"Living in the ghetto like this is tough."

"You don't understand."

"Maybe not." He patted the side of her face. She leaned into his hand like a puppy craving affection. "You've been through a hard time. You might try a martial art. When I bottomed out, the discipline helped me."

"I don't see how kicking and punching will make me feel better."

"The goal of any real martial artist is inner calm, self-control, learning how to stay in motion without moving."

"What's that mean?"

"Think of a top. It appears motionless, except when it slows down."

She bit her lip and wrinkled her brow.

"If you can react calmly to a fist coming at your face, you can handle most of life's little problems."

"I guess that makes sense."

"A true martial artist doesn't want to hurt other people. He, or she, wants to develop himself. Anyone else is just a fighter."

"You came on pretty strong with Sam. And the Japanese terrorists." She turned her face down so she didn't have to meet Stark's eyes. "I keep thinking about Kenji."

"I'll give him your regards."

"You're going to see him?"

"Your brother has hired me to look into terrorism," Stark said. "I'm going to start by talking to Nakamura."

CHAPTER 13

Willy Rose watched from his third-floor room, nearly a half mile from Thailand's Nonburi prison. The ceiling fan overhead spun feebly. The guest house accommodations weren't even good enough to be called shabby. But they furnished the view he needed.

Near the window was a modified XM-21 sniper rifle resting on a bipod. The gun, similar to the U.S. military's M-14, fired a 7.62-mm NATO round. Rose's gun had been customized, for increased precision and portability. It could be broken down to fit into a small attaché case. The German gunsmith who had done the work was a master. Each time Rose screwed the Sionics noise suppressor onto the barrel or clicked the Adjustable Ranging Telescope (ART) sight on top, he felt a twinge of admiration for the German craftsman's micrometer-accurate tolerances.

Rose had paced off the distance from the prison wall, and estimated another fifty yards from the wall to where the target would be. A total of more than a thousand yards. He had adjusted the knobs for windage and elevation.

It would be a difficult shot, but Rose had made tougher. The key was knowing the schedule of the prey. When he'd led big game hunts in Africa, he'd been able to time it so his fish-belly pale tourists could wait at the water hole and have gazelle, antelope, and wildebeest all but fall into their lap.

Still, they'd often blown the shot. Buck fever. Or grazed the animals, so he had to track them down and kill them. He didn't miss those days, sitting around, drinking beer and trying to be sociable with a bunch of rich doctors, dentists, or businessmen—Yanks who would shoot themselves in the foot if he didn't watch them.

Now his prey was more challenging.

Kenji Nakamura was allowed a half hour each day in the yard. He'd walk in a large circle, never looking up or out, lost in his thoughts. The rest of the time was spent in a six-foot-by-six-foot cell, with a hole-in-the-floor toilet and a one-inch-thin straw mattress. The heat and humidity in the solitary confinement cell were crippling.

Nakamura looked forward to the walks. He hadn't been in prison very long but all his time was spent brooding. He kept imagining what it was like for the people in the Cyprus cafe. The suffering survivors more than the dead. What had they done to deserve their fate? He thought often of the Hancock woman. He wished he'd had more time with her.

The guard rattled the bar of his cell with a nightstick and gestured him forward. The guard didn't speak English or Japanese and clearly hated Nakamura. He grabbed Kenji's arm and shoved him down the hall.

The prosecutor and a policeman would be coming to see Nakamura soon. He debated whether he would make a full confession. Let the world judge his actions.

From the cells along the corridor, prisoners shouted and hooted at Nakamura. There were close to five thousand prisoners at Nonburi, a maximum security facility located a few hours from Bangkok.

The Japanese shuffled along. He couldn't understand much of what was shouted, but the derision was clear. They were common criminals, he decided, unable to understand the difference between themselves and a political prisoner.

He stood straighter as they approached the third set of steel doors. It was an old building, but all the gates and bars had been modernized and many gleamed.

He breathed in deeply as he stepped out into the sunshine.

* * *

General Todd Grant puffed his inch-thick Cuban cigar. He had joked to Pentagon buddies that Fidel's island was worth invading, just to be assured a supply of first-rate cigars.

As Grant leaned back in the high leather chair behind his desk, thumbing through briefing reports, he mentally counted down the days until he would retire. His Swiss account held several million dollars. And his job with the second largest arms manufacturer was guaranteed. He'd be a consultant-salesman-lobbyist, pulling in three times what he was currently making. That, plus his military pension and a few good investments assured that he wouldn't wind up on the breadline in his golden years. Visions of his father, a once wealthy man who'd been stripped bare by the 1929 crash, still haunted him. A descendant of Ulysses S. Grant reduced to farm laborer.

The ash on Grant's cigar was nearly two inches long. He tapped it off and puffed. He studied a report from northern Thailand. It had been properly adjusted so no one would know what was going on there. Not that DeVille wasn't discreet. But certain names, certain pieces of equipment, could give away the arms dealer's whole operation.

Grant made a mental note to let DeVille know, again, all he was doing for him. The arms dealer should cough up another hundred grand. At least.

Grant picked up his private line and called a New York number. He assumed that the line was tapped and planned to file a contact report. He knew the man he would be calling, the top Soviet Military Intelligence (GRU) official in New York, would file a similar report with his Kremlin bosses.

When the two men were connected and past initial pleasantries, Grant asked him, "What's going on with Cyprus?"

"I could ask you the same question, comrade," the GRU general said.

"C'mon, these disruptions have Moscow red all over them," Grant said.

"I see them as typical imperialist provocations," the GRU

general responded. "Turkey is one of your NATO allies. They suffer the same expansionist greed as you do."

"You mean those riots in Greece just happened? And the Greek Communist Party is making noise without express permission from the Kremlin?"

"There are those here who do wish to see an escalation. Notably a couple of Armenians who are well placed in the Defense ministry. You are aware of how they feel about Turks. They have not forgiven the genocide of 1916."

"Which may not really be a genocide."

"We will not debate history, comrade. They are being kept reined in. Our general secretary is a man of peace."

"Glad to hear it. You start giving us a hard time and I'm gonna cancel your subscription to *Aviation Week* and *Space Technology*. You wouldn't know what the hell is going on here without them."

"We have other ways," the GRU general responded defensively. "It is not in our interest to see an acceleration of turmoil between Athens and Ankara."

"Glad to hear it. We don't want trouble there either, comrade."

"*Dasvadanya*, the GRU general said.

"*Stolichnaya*," Grant responded.

As he hung up, he jotted down a few notes. The GRU general would only lie to him as much as he had to. The information about the Kremlin's position was good raw intelligence, which Grant could use to perk up the next RIG meeting.

Willy Rose checked his watch. It was time. He adjusted his breathing, slow and deep. He anointed himself with the scented rose water. He moved to the rifle and peered through the ART sight.

Nakamura would step into the cross hairs within seconds.

Nakamura stretched his shoulders, bent and touched his feet, went up on his tiptoes. He looked at the walls, the high guard towers on top of stone walls. Some primitive instinct caused him to turn and look through the cyclone fences, topped with ribbon wire, toward the rows of houses.

The muzzle of Rose's rifle was two feet back from the window and not visible from the street. Rose had a flash arrester on the weapon that reduced noise. A silencer would throw off the accuracy of the weapon. His fingers, clad in surgical gloves, embraced the weapon. He exhaled. Just as his lungs were empty, Nakamura stepped into view. Perfectly timed.

Willy Rose fired twice. The first slug tore into Nakamura's heart. The second went through his shoulder as he fell.

The guard standing only a foot from Nakamura thought the prisoner was faking a faint. He kicked Nakamura in the side. Then he saw the blood. He threw himself to the ground. His hand shook as he blew his whistle.

The sirens went off. Cell doors were slammed shut. Guards carrying shotguns raced across catwalks. Prisoners, shouting questions and obscenities, were shoved into their cells. Lock down.

Two full minutes had passed. Rose was already a couple of blocks away. His hair was dyed black, his skin tinted dark. He had a thin mustache glued to his upper lip. The surgical gloves were in his pocket. The attaché case carrying his custom XM-21 was gripped firmly in his hand.

An hour and a half later, at Don Muang airport, he flushed the mustache and gloves down the toilet. He checked in his precious gun, regretfully unable to carry it with him on the plane. His flight took off on time. He ordered a martini as a reward for a job well done.

Robert Stark passed within a few hundred yards of Willy Rose. Stark couldn't know that the man boarding a flight on the upper level had just killed the prisoner Stark had flown eighteen hours to see.

Stark got the bad news when he arrived at the prison. He viewed Nakamura's body and verified his identity. The kidnapper had never made any statements. Stark was allowed to go to the guest house where police deduced the shot had come from. He was shown the room where technicians were beginning to dust for prints.

"You won't find any," Stark said.

"How do you know?" the detective asked suspiciously.

"Too professional." Stark gazed out through the window toward the yard. He could barely see the pool of blood where Nakamura had fallen. "How many people do you think could make a shot like that?" Stark mused.

The cop didn't answer. "What do you know?" the cop asked.

"I know that this doesn't look like a terrorist hit. Too quiet and clean. They like noise and hoopla."

"Who did it then?"

"A professional."

"A professional what?"

"A professional killer."

CHAPTER 14

Stark called the Thai Foreign Ministry and was put through to Assistant Foreign Secretary Nawowarat Thanom. Just under the top rung of power, Thanom was adept at gleaning classified information, thanks to his large family. His nineteen siblings and cousins occupied posts in Defense, Justice, and Foreign ministries. The Thai official hadn't been one of Stark's CIA assets, but they had swapped information on an informal basis.

"Nakamura," Stark said after greetings.

"We'll meet tonight. You know where?"

"Yes."

Stark knew of Thanom's obsession, *muay thai*. Every chance he could get away from his wife and kids, he'd be at either Rajadamnern or Lumpini arena watching the Thai kick boxing. Most of their meets had been held at the huge, hot, and smoky arenas.

Half the crowd were chain smokers. Stark's clothing stuck to him as if it were pasted on. The audience was ninety percent male but the few women were among the loudest enthusiasts. The betting outside the ring was as ferocious as the fighting inside.

The boxers were stick figures of bone and gristle with a savage determination. Punches and kicks were used to soften up the opponent—the knockout blows came from elbows and knees. The canvas mat was stained with blood.

Stark and Thanom were seated on the tiered, padded wood benches, about ten feet back from the arena. Top price tickets. Of course Stark had paid. He also covered Thanom's bets. The assistant secretary was up about two hundred dollars. Thanom cheered as loud as anyone and whispered to Stark, out of the side of his mouth, during lulls.

"Did your government arrange Nakamura's death?" Stark asked.

"Not as far as I've heard," Thanom said, watching the fighters in red and blue trunks go through the prefight *ram muay* boxing dance. "Why do you ask?"

The *pi,* which sounded like an oboe, warbled in the background as the boxers each had five minutes to perform the warmup ritual honoring their guru and spirits. They wore sacred head and armbands containing an image of the Buddha.

"It's happened before. Remember how the whole Baader-Meinhof gang simultaneously committed suicide in prison? It saved the Germans time, money, and annoying publicity," Stark said.

Thanom frowned, his attention divided as the fight began. "It is my understanding that my government wanted to put him on trial, to show the world how well we handle this problem. Aiiiiieh! Did you see that roundhouse?"

Stark had missed the punch, which had knocked the fighter in blue trunks to the floor. He got up, wobbly. The referee checked him quickly. The fighter in red trunks bobbed up and down, waiting to be unleashed. The referee signaled for the fight to resume. The fighter in red closed in.

"This whole case is very unusual," Stark said. "The Japanese Red Army didn't particularly go for kidnappings. Bombings and shootouts with an occasional robbery were their style."

"That has been noted," Thanom said.

"Then the killing itself. More like a mob hit or an assassination."

"Like your President Kennedy," Thanom said. He

jumped up and shouted something in Thai. Stark could understand a little. It was some sort of combination. Jab, jab, hook. Left, left, right. Then kick. Kill him.

Thanom sat down, breathless.

"Is there anything you can tell me about Nakamura?"

"Why are you so interested?"

"I'm doing an article for a newspaper."

Thanom giggled, a funny noise coming from a man who had just been shouting violently for violence. "You have become a newsman?"

Stark told him about Hancock.

"It's not my department," Thanom said.

"C'mon, I know you too well. After I mentioned Nakamura's name to you earlier, I suspect you called around."

There was a flurry of punches in the ring, then knees.

"See! See!" Thanom shouted, taking credit for the red-trunked fighter's attack on his opponent. The blue-trunked fighter fell to the mat, flat, his chest heaving.

The referee held up red trunk's hands.

Thanom had bet heavily on the fight. Stark saw the glow in his contact's eyes.

"Thanom, you probably know more about Nakamura now than his own mother did."

"You think you can flatter it out of me." Thanom grinned. "But you brought me good luck, so I must repay you. Nakamura made many trips to Hong Kong. Never any sign of trouble while he was there. Singapore too. He was shopping," Thanom said coyly.

"For what?"

"A SAM-7 or a Stinger. He would have settled for any shoulder-launched rocket. He approached several arms dealers. Basically, he was laughed out of their offices."

"Any idea why he wanted it?"

"No."

"Or who he specifically approached?"

"No. We are receiving much of our information from the Japanese. They want to reassure us they had nothing to do with Nakamura's execution. At this point, we believe them."

"Did Nakamura ever go anyplace else in his arms hunt?"

"He went to the Mediterranean a couple of weeks ago, his only trip there."

"Lebanon?"

"We don't know exactly where. There is no sign he was able to buy what he wanted."

"Ever go to North Korea?" There was a well-known terrorist training camp favored by the JRA less than a half hour northwest of the capital, P'yŏngyang.

"No."

"What do you think?" Stark asked.

"I think I better go collect my winnings and head home or my wife will do to me what the red fighter did to the blue. She's become an independent lady. Too much American television, I think."

"Shitsurei shimasu," Stark called out, knocking at the door.

"Dozo," a woman's voice entered.

Stark stepped into the apartment. It was located in Chiba prefecture, not far from Narita Airport in Japan. The smell of jet fuel was strong and planes roared frequently overhead. The apartment house was gray concrete, with long halls and small windows, the cell block architecture common in Tokyo.

"My name is Robert Stark. I wonder if you might have a few minutes to speak with me?" Stark offered a business card that identified him as the president of Halliwell-Stark. Establishing rank was all important.

"I would be honored to have you as a guest in my home," the woman replied. She looked to be about seventy, but Stark decided it was more hard years than actual years. Probably in her late fifties.

She guided Stark to a room with tatami floors and offered fresh brewed, strong and bitter, hot green tea. He sipped it, commenting on how well it was prepared and the beauty of the cup. She in turn dismissed his praise. The expected rituals.

"I wish to express my condolences over the death of your son," Stark said.

She gave him a polite Mona Lisa smile, masking her emotions. "He set out on his own path."

"Yes."

"Your Japanese is very good," she said.

"I was fortunate enough to live in your country for a few years."

A long silence passed. Planes roared overhead.

"Would it be too painful for me to ask a few questions?" Stark asked.

"I knew so little about him, I'm ashamed to say. But please ask."

"He made many trips to Hong Kong. Would you know when? Or why?"

"I'm afraid I cannot help you. I don't know."

"He also made a trip not that long ago to the Middle East. Do you know exactly where? And when?"

"It was no more than a few weeks ago. I might remember the name of the country if I heard it."

"Turkey?"

"No."

"Israel?"

"No."

"Lebanon?"

"No."

"Cyprus?"

She hesitated, then nodded. *"Hai, so desu."*

"Would it be too much to ask for a picture of him?"

"Why?"

"There are some people who might have seen him. I would like to check into it. Perhaps he was forced into the situation that led to his demise."

Nakamura's mother shuffled away, returning with a couple of pictures of her son. Stark took the most recent, which showed Nakamura with a baseball cap, squinting unhappily at the camera.

"Perhaps you can tell me more about your son," Stark

said as he pocketed the shot. "Who his friends were, where he would go to socialize?"

A burly young man barged into the room. "Who are you?" he demanded.

"My name's Stark. I came here to offer my condolences."

"You! You killed my brother."

"Don't be rude," the mother cautioned her youngest son.

"I didn't," Stark said. "I arranged for him to be arrested."

"And then he was killed in prison."

The son, about twenty, was standing nose to nose with Stark, his fists clenched at his side.

"Please," his mother said plaintively.

Stark edged toward the door, keeping an eye on the son. He bowed to the mother, still wary. "Thank you for your hospitality. Perhaps it's best if I no longer intrude."

"Get out of here, murderer," the son said.

The mother looked on sadly as Stark backed out.

"You again?" Zen *roshi* Saito said when he opened the door for Stark.

Stark handed over a sack of groceries. He had spent more than a hundred dollars on the contents, buying Kobe beef, several Satsuma melons, papaya, and other expensive fruits that he knew the old man enjoyed.

Saito unpacked the bag, examining each item and grunting approval.

"No rice crackers?" he asked, when he was done.

"I thought you didn't like them."

"I don't. But sometimes it is good to eat what you don't like."

"You confuse me."

"Good. I thought you wanted to leave the country so badly."

"I did. I came back. I need your opinion." Stark recounted what had happened with Nakamura. "It might be in the interest of the Japanese government for Nakamura to die in prison. I would like to rule out that possibility before I go further."

"What makes you think they didn't do it?"

"It doesn't feel right. It's just not in the Japanese ethos. Assassinations are done face-to-face, with a sword or a knife. Or even a Molotov cocktail, like those Okinawans tried with then Prince Akihito."

"Balderdash," Saito said. "You're using your intuition, which is good, then slapping a Western-style explanation on it, which is bad."

"Do you think Nakamura was killed on orders from Japan?"

"What I think doesn't matter."

"Could you make inquiries with your friends?"

"A lot to ask for a bag of groceries. Hmmph. You bought too much food. Most of it will go bad before I have a chance to eat it. You'll join me for supper tonight."

Saito took the groceries into his tiny kitchen and began puttering around. Stark knew Saito wouldn't accept any assistance. Stark sat on his haunches, meditating before the bonsai garden.

When Saito laid the meal out, it was a feast for the eyes as well as the palate. Each fruit had been perfectly cut; the flavors of the beef, the purity of the rice, the tang of the miso soup harmonized like instruments at a symphony.

Saito was absorbed in the food. Stark secretly watched him. He had known the Zen master for two decades. They had been introduced by Stark's jujitsu teacher, who was also a *roshi*. Stark had been forced to be his teacher's second when the instructor committed hara kiri. The teacher had chosen suicide after his brother disgraced him.

"*Go chiso sama deshita,*" Stark said sincerely as they finished.

Saito dismissed the customary compliment. "I'll see what I can find out regarding the death of Nakamura. You must promise me you will study harder."

"What should I study?"

"Life. You must live each moment impeccably. Like the way you held your chopsticks. Very bad."

Stark had eaten the entire meal without the smallest morsel slipping off the slippery black lacquer chopsticks. He regarded the old man quizzically.

Saito indicated that Stark should hold his chopsticks the way he had been. The old man moved quickly, tapping them. Stark had been holding them perpendicular to his mouth, and the tips plunged inside, tapping the back of his throat and nearly making him gag.

The old man picked up his chopsticks and held them parallel to his face. "This is the way a samurai eats. An enemy could shove the chopsticks into your mouth and kill you. You must always be ready."

"I'll remember that."

"Now you can wash the dishes. Do it perfectly. Remember every action has meaning."

CHAPTER 15

Stark called the New York office through a pay phone at Narita Airport. "Can you check data bases for a first-class marksman?" he asked Pedro Quesada. "Used an XM-21. Possible ties to terrorist groups."

"The Nakamura hit?"

"You got it."

"Was it that good a shot?" Pedro asked.

"You would've been proud if you had made it."

Quesada gave a low whistle. "I'd like to meet the guy that did it."

"I'd like to meet him too. Face to face. Not at five hundred yards, through a crosshair."

Security was tight as Stark passed through customs at Cyprus's international airport at Larnaca. His bag was thoroughly inspected by an unsmiling man.

Stark bought a map of Nicosia and drew a series of concentric circles, with the center on the cafe which had been blown up. He showed the photo of Nakamura to passersby in the area of the cafe.

"Pretty sure I saw him the day of the bombing," said a fruit market owner a block from the cafe. "You don't see many Chinamen around here." But the man wasn't sure.

Stark tried cab drivers, shopkeepers, shoppers who looked like area residents. The Cypriots were obliging, friendly. He got a half-dozen tentative IDs but nothing that made him confident. From a cab driver he learned that someone fitting Nakamura's description had been dropped off at the north end of the city, near the Green Line, the border with Turkish Cyprus.

The bombing had occurred on a Wednesday at noon. Stark waited until Wednesday, then began showing the picture near the Green Line.

Stark showed the picture to pedestrians and soldiers. He identified himself as the brother of one of the victims, doing his own investigation. Everyone but policemen were generally tolerant, if not outright helpful. Stark got a lot of sympathy, but no solid evidence.

Until he met the soldier who had checked Nakamura across the line.

"That's him. No question about it. I remember how nervous he looked. I told the police. What's his name?"

"I'm not sure," Stark lied.

"Police didn't know it either. They had some grainy shots of him on a street in Istanbul. Shit-eating Turks. They're animals. Get a Chinaman to do their dirty work. I hope they catch him and string him up."

"Me, too," Stark said.

"Stringing up is too good for the bastard. They should boil him in oil."

Stark nodded. The soldier went on for a few minutes, suggesting more and more gruesome punishments for Nakamura. Stark remained listening, politely agreeing. Finally the soldier wound down.

"Good luck to you," the soldier said, giving a polite little salute and marching off.

Stark guessed that Nakamura had gone from Turkish Cyprus to Istanbul. He followed what he imagined Nakamura's path to be, crossing the border under the watchful eyes of Greek, United Nations, and then Turkish guards.

He began showing the picture of Nakamura in Turkish Nicosia. People were more suspicious. A few wanted a "tip" before they'd give him any information. It took a solid day of canvassing, but he was able to trace Nakamura to the Museum of Barbarism. The only reason Nakamura would go there, seemingly minutes after the bomb blast, was for a contact.

But the guard at the museum, the same one who was on duty when Nakamura visited, didn't remember any other patrons from that day.

"Him, yes, no one else," the guard said, after pocketing the money he had hustled out of Stark. "No can help."

Stark toured the museum briefly, looking for clues, but found nothing of value. Just signs of the festering hatred between the two countries.

With what he had, he could provide enough for an article for Hancock. It would be an exclusive, since the identity of the bomber had not been made public. Either authorities hadn't been able to ID Nakamura or they were keeping it a secret.

But the article would do nothing but exacerbate tensions between the two countries, confirmation that the bomber had fled across the border to the Turkish zone. Stark decided to hold off.

He crossed the Green Line, back into Greek Nicosia. As he walked from the border, a voice shouted, "Mr. Graham! Halt, Mr. Graham!" A motley mix of soldiers, guns at the ready, surrounded him.

It took Stark a second to realize they were talking to him. Graham was the name on the false passport he was traveling under.

The Graham passport belonged to a Canadian. The name had been taken off the gravestone of a child in Vancouver who died a few weeks after birth, around the year when Stark was born. Stark had requested a copy of the birth certificate. Since birth and death certificates were not cross-referenced, the clerk gave it to him after he paid a nominal fee. Using that as ID, he'd built a false identity. Stark had followed the same procedure in several U.S. cities, building up a library of six fake identities. The name Robert Stark was on too many terrorist hit lists.

The soldiers surrounding him were with the U.N. forces, Swedes, Finns, and Austrians, based at the Ledra Palace Hotel. Their job was to supervise both sides, and get caught in the crossfire if either side violated the truce.

"Let me see your passport," an Austrian with pale blond hair on his arms and upper lip ordered.

Stark handed it over. He showed a little fear. Being completely cool while held at gunpoint would be abnormal. "Anything the matter?" Stark asked.

"Earlier today you questioned people in the vicinity," the Austrian said, looking up from the passport. "What was your business?"

Stark figured they had spoken to the Greek soldier already. He gave them the same story.

"We did not see anyone with the name Graham on the list of victims," a soldier wearing a Finnish uniform pointed out.

A crowd of Cypriots was beginning to gather, watching from a distance.

"Go away!" the Austrian shouted, gesturing with his gun. The people stepped back a few feet, but continued to watch. The soldiers' attention was divided between Stark and the onlookers. The crowd was more curious than hostile.

"It's okay," Stark shouted in Greek. "No problem."

The crowd bobbed their heads. Stark's words took the tension down a notch. But the fact that he had spoken in Greek made him more of a home boy. About thirty-five people had gathered. Tourists on the fringe of the crowd peeked over heads and asked what was going on.

"What is your business here?" the Austrian soldier repeated, still holding Stark's passport.

"Perhaps we should just release him," a Swedish soldier suggested, eyeing the growing crowd.

"*Nein*. We should take him in for questioning. I don't believe his story."

Stark decided to gamble. He produced a business card with a British name and number on it. "Perhaps you might want to call this number. The phone will ring on Whitehall Street." It was an intercontinental tie line, direct to Halliwell-Stark's Los Angeles office. The line was kept for cover stories. Gina, the secretary-office manager and a talented mimic, would answer by repeating the digits and pretending to be the secretary of an MI5 official, or a corporate exec, or an insurance company president. Whatever cover they had previously agreed upon.

"MI5?" the Finn asked.

"I'm not at liberty to say," Stark responded.

The Austrian and the Finn huddled while the other soldiers kept wary eyes on Stark and the fifty-person crowd. Finally the soldiers agreed to let Stark go, providing he left the area immediately. He showed his plane ticket for that afternoon and the Austrian was mollified.

As Stark walked away, the Finn hummed the theme from the James Bond movies. Stark winked at him, and he gave a "thumbs up" gesture.

The museum guard had lied. He knew exactly who Nakamura had met. Nakamura's contact was a veteran smuggler, a petty career criminal who had no more interest in history than he did in attending church. The guard let the smuggler know that he had valuable information for sale.

After they struck a price in Turkish lira equal to about twenty dollars, the guard said, "There was someone looking for that Chinaman you met with."

"What did you tell him?"

"Nothing," the guard said.

"Did you get his name?"

"No."

"What did he look like?" the smuggler asked.

The guard rubbed thumb and forefinger together. More haggling, then a price was struck.

"A little over six feet. American. Well dressed. Good shape. Dark brown hair. Clean shaven."

The smuggler had contacts on both sides of the Green Line. It took him only a few hours to find out about the soldiers questioning "Mr. Graham." The smuggler called a number in Belgium that was his only way of reaching Willy Rose. He left a message. Three hours later, Rose called back. The smuggler told him what he knew.

"Thanks," Rose said when he was done. "I'll look into it."

"That will be another two hundred dollars," the smuggler said.

The line was silent. "Perhaps the best thing would be to get rid of the cutout," Rose said flatly. It took the smuggler a second to realize what he meant. The smuggler gulped.

"I had expenses," the smuggler whined.

"I'll send you a hundred," Rose said. "And I'll take care of this Graham for you."

"Thank you, thank you," the smuggler said. His hands were damp with sweat when he hung up.

Rose walked a few drizzly London streets to another red pay phone booth. He tried never to use the same phone more than once in a given day. He dialed a number and relayed what the smuggler had said.

"I'll check MI5 and the Canadians," the man at the other end said. "When I find out who it is, you will take care of him."

CHAPTER 16

Stark checked into Singapore's New Garden Hotel using another forged passport—Maher, a Seattle journalist. He inspected his room for bugs, even though he still wouldn't trust it to be secure. A proper debugging would take several hours and require a few thousand dollars' worth of equipment. He located fire doors, windows with ledges, and checked the lock on the door.

Then he took a three-hour nap.

On awakening, and doing a half hour of stretching exercises, sit-ups, and push-ups, Stark called the New York office.

Les Halliwell got on the line and briefed him on the latest business. Halliwell spoke in the vaguest terms, since Stark had made it clear he was calling from a hotel phone. Every hotel phone was assumed to be monitored.

"I'm going to be tied up with Mr. H's project," Stark said.

"You like playing cub reporter?"

"Call me 'Scoop.' Is Pedro available?"

"He's out doing a security check. On that thing you asked him to run. Fifteen possibilities. Scattered all over the globe. If we have to run them all down, it's going to go through his twenty grand retainer pretty quick. Oh, speaking of Mr. H, his sister's been calling here just about every day. Gets very hoity-toity when we refuse to give your whereabouts. Is she as foxy as she sounds?"

Stark ignored the question. "She probably wants to express her undying gratitude."

"Take it out in trade, buddy," Halliwell said.

"Of course I'll see you, Robert, old bean," Carl Witherby said. Witherby, who preferred to be called Chip—the nickname he'd earned at Eton—was a British army colonel turned arms dealer. Or so he led people to believe. He was a Chicagoan by birth, and a Brit by affectation. Stark didn't understand why, but many arms dealers put on a British veneer.

"Chip" had run into a pugnacious group of Irish sailors in a bar in Jakarta. One was holding a jagged bottle edge to his throat when Stark interceded. Subsequently, they'd crossed paths several times in Asia. "Chip" had provided weapons and intelligence to Stark.

Witherby's place was located near Jurong, the industrial center at the west end of the island. He had thrived in the pro-business atmosphere set by Prime Minister Lee Kuan Yew. Witherby didn't care that much of the old charm had been bulldozed under to make way for high-rises or factories. Yew had created a clean, relatively corruption-free city-state. Jaywalking, smoking in a nonsmoking area, being in downtown without a downtown permit—all earned stiff fines. Westerners with long hair were harassed. But if you had money, and were establishing a business, it was one of the friendliest places on earth. Singapore was Southeast Asia's greatest success story, rivaling Japan in its ferocious capitalist drive.

Witherby's warehouse was a one-story, cinder block building surrounded by a barbed wire-topped cyclone fence. Two guards armed with Ingrams, and struggling to keep German shepherds under control, patrolled the perimeter. It looked like a military base, right down to the signs for Royal Munitions Supply Ltd.

"Bobby, Bobby, Bobby," Witherby said, letting the monocle drop from his damaged right eye. He had injured it when he fell on a wicket during a cricket match, but credited the weakness to a fictitious battle. He was tall and lean with suberb military bearing and a slight tic in the corner of his mouth. "How can I help you? I just got in a load of H and Ks. Exorbitantly priced, but you can't beat that Kraut craftsmanship. You know I always give you what you want at cost."

"I don't need a gun."

"Have you changed your occupation?"

"No."

"And you don't need a gun?"

"No."

"Who is your insurance carrier?"

"I need information."

"Ah, the mother's milk of the intelligence trade. What piques your curiosity?"

"A young Japanese named Kenji Nakamura. I understand he was trying to buy a shoulder launched surface-to-air missile. A SAM-7 or a Stinger."

"The name is familiar," Witherby said. "Wait, isn't he the chap who was just shot in Thailand?"

"Yes."

"Never forget a name," Witherby said proudly. "He didn't come to me. I heard about him a while back. He made the rounds of a few dealers, offering a tidy sum for a rocket. He was laughed out of most offices. I gather one or two tried to fleece him."

"So he didn't get anything here?"

"Not that I know of. We do have certain ethical standards. If we sold sophisticated firepower to every jilted boyfriend or deluded loser who asked for it, the world would be a much sorrier place."

"I'm sure," Stark said. "Okay. How about a quick update on the arms trade."

"I hope you're not considering going into it. Business is tough."

"Really?"

"Quite. Many of the Third World countries now have their own plants. At least for the basic firepower. It used to be just Uncle Sam, the Russians, the Frogs, and Jolly Old England number four. The Krauts hard on our heels. Now you've got China, Italy, Brazil, Israel, Sweden, Egypt. We're cutting each other's throats."

Stark smiled at the imagery, and Chip frowned.

"The world needs us, Bobby. We supply freedom fighters and dictators with equal aplomb. It's like attorneys in the justice system. If your George Washington hadn't gotten guns, you'd still be forced to drink tea at 4 P.M."

"Chip, I know your background, so why the stiff upper lip?"

"After a while, you become the role you play."

"Okay, as long as you don't force-feed me crumpets."

"That's the only British matter I despise. Their food is vile," Witherby said. "Anyway, for the high ticket items, the superpowers still lead. But France's Mirages are always a staple. Most customers have to settle for surplus jets, unless your government deems them an ally worthy of strategic support."

"I know. The arms dealers are important as an instrument of defense policy," Stark said. "The government either licenses the sale, or the Defense Department buys from the manufacturer and sells it to the ally, tacking on a small administrative cost."

"Or they go through an arms dealer like myself. Deniability, old bean. I forgot, you just want an update. It's not often I get to lecture to an intelligent audience. Most times, I'm at a cocktail party, someone hears what I do, and I have to justify myself for hours. Usually, I just tell them I'm in heavy machinery export."

"Arms dealers are a poor, misunderstood lot."

"Spare me the sarcasm. It seems as if you've made use of my services more than once." The tic in Chip's lip was more pronounced. "Every government on this globe has employed private arms dealers, either as straw men or to fill in an emergency gap in supplies."

"Okay."

"Now a heavy ordnance deal—tanks, whirlybirds, aircraft—might take years to complete. By then of course the original model that was ordered is even more obsolete."

"How about some names?" Stark rattled off several, and Witherby gave him concise, cynical assessments. He didn't show much emotion until they got to Heinrich Mueller.

"An M.M. Munitions manipulator. A small-fry legal gunrunner, but ambitious. A Swiss, keeps his word. He got stung not that long ago. Someone tattled on a load that was passing through and authorities were forced to seize it."

"Any idea who snitched?"

"Several possibilities. The hot ticket rumor is that it was Gerard DeVille. An arms dealer, but a disgrace to the business."

"Why?"

"He lies, cheats, and steals. Even with fellow brokers. He also is a real up and comer. He's concentrated in small arms. A clever chap that way. Avoids the high ticket, high maintenance items like fighters or frigates. Mainly small arms, and certainly nothing larger than a tank or helicopter. Doing about $300 million a year in business, I'd guess. But he goes for volume more than markup."

"Where's he based?"

"Hither and yon. He's got an office in Paris but he's almost never there. Keeps a small staff. But he lives aboard his jet and runs the show like a one-man operation. Rumor is he's been stocking up through several front men, but no one knows where the guns are going. If it's true." Witherby paused, trying to decide if he'd told Stark all he knew. "He's most active in Africa and Southeast Asia."

"How is the territory divided?"

"Nothing as formal as all that. The biggies, like Interarmco, they'll go anywhere. Central America, the Mideast, Asia, Africa. If there's a trouble spot, they'll be there or have a local agent to put you in contact. But the days of building an empire are gone. Interarmco was lucky. They used to buy military surplus and convert it to sport rifles. Made a fortune in the U.S. But that's not done nowadays. I suppose Kennedy getting killed with a surplus Italian military rifle put a crimp in things. Damned unfair. He could've just as well been shot with a Remington 306."

"I'm sure if he had a choice, he would've preferred a domestic gun."

"Watch that tongue, Bobby. Not everyone is as thick-skinned as I am. I'm rambling though, and deserve a jolt. Anyway, in general we work where we have contacts or corresponding agents. It's a gossipy business, like most are. But deals can be cut in secret. At least initially. At some point, when you're moving tons of hardware around, people become suspicious no matter what the crates are labeled. Look how long Reagan was able to keep his guns to Iran deal under wraps."

"What about this DeVille?"

"If I were snooping around the business, he's the one I'd watch. He came out of nowhere with a few million in financing. No one's been able to figure out where it came from. He's given all different stories."

"What's known about him?"

"Used to be a merc broker. Got into handling weapons and pretty much let that drop. Though he does offer personnel from time to time. Supposedly he was in the Foreign Legion himself. Hard to believe to look at him. Looks sort of like Nero. All he needs is a fiddle."

"I'll keep him in mind. What about terrorists? Where are they getting their weapons? Anything like the Swiss Takeout Service?"

"Good God, that brings back memories." During the early 1970s, radicals looted Swiss armories on a regular basis, stealing weapons ranging from submachine guns, to heavy-duty "panzer mines" that could blow up a tank or a bank. "No. Nowadays most of it passes through places like Syria, Libya, Iran, Yemen. It goes to one country, who, for a nominal fee, ignores the end use certificates and sends it on to the bad boys. Frankly, terrorists place niggling orders. It's hardly worth the aggravation."

"Where's the buying and selling take place?"

"You'll probably find the biggest brokers based in Argentina, Brazil, Taiwan, Singapore, and Israel. Of course the

Israelis don't sell much to the Arabs. Though there have been a few deals where it passed through another country, and the Israelis were arming their enemies."

"I recall that. They had a missile deal with the Chinese, and the Chinese were selling to the Saudis."

"That was just one case. There're many others. The U.S. makes a weapon, abandons it in Vietnam, they sell it to Pakistan, who loses it to Afghanis, who use it against the Russians. There are Mausers from the early part of this century that have fought in every war in the Far East."

"If I wanted to track an arms shipment, how hard would it be?"

"Hmmmm. Difficult, but not impossible. It would be easy if you wanted a big item. F-14s or Hueys have a characteristic crate. But knowing you, you'll want something small. Also, it depends on the destination. Legitimate governments are easy to deliver to. Of course, they don't pay the high prices rebels or terrorists will."

"Everything's a trade-off."

"A catchy motto."

Witherby insisted on giving Stark a quick tour of his facility before he left. There were rows and rows of weapons, wooden crates piled high on the floor labeled Danger—Explosives—No Smoking—Handle With Extreme Care. Crates had English, Chinese, French, Russian, and Spanish written on the side.

"You can't be prejudiced," Witherby said. He passed a worker prying open a wooden crate with Belgian markings. Inside were FN FALS assault rifles. Holding twenty 7.62-mm NATO rounds, they could be fired auto, semi-auto, or in three-shot bursts.

"Overpriced and not suited to being lugged around hot, sticky climates by small people," Witherby said, taking one out and tossing it to Stark. Stark caught the matte black weapon, adroitly worked its action, and tossed it back.

They walked down the row. Above them security cameras scanned the workers, making sure the deadly inventory remained intact.

They were at another crate. Witherby popped the lid

himself and took out an H & K MP5. "A truly lovely piece of work. Less than twenty-seven inches long, and six and a half pounds with the thirty-round clip." Without the magazine in it, the submachine gun looked like a rifle with pistol grip attached and barrel cut down. A deadly sleek predatory animal, no excess fat, all teeth and muscle.

"Muzzle velocity of 1,312 feet per second on a 9-mm parabellum slug. Range of two hundred and twenty yards. A hundred rounds per minute on auto, forty on single shot."

"Very good," Witherby said.

"Favorite gun of German terrorists," Stark said.

"And police," Witherby responded, losing his pleased expression. "Terrorists are not big customers. They place orders in the dozens. By nature they're small groups. You know who's actually kept more than one dealer afloat?"

Stark shook his head.

"The dope cartels. They love the high ticket weapons. Money is no object. We're talking one hundred percent markup. As long as it's new and flashy."

"I'll remember that. Is there any way to get close to someone who supplies the terrorists?"

Witherby hesitated.

"What are you holding back, Chip?"

"This is not a business for amateurs. When, for example, the French found out who was supplying the Algerians, they arranged for him to have car trouble. The explosion took out half the windows for a block away. Every intelligence agency, out of work mercenary, and career criminal plays in the ballpark."

"I've been known to get in and out of rough spots."

Witherby sighed. "Well, the big deal is the Paris Air Show. That's in June and attracts the big money boys. But there're smaller gatherings all the time. It's the least dangerous way to get close. There's one coming up in a week or so in Belgium. The Flemish have always been arms merchants. Way back in the fifteenth century, Charles the Bold forbid Liege from making guns. They refused, since it was their main industry. He responded by slaughtering the residents and razing the town."

"A true peacemaker."

"Well, Fabrique Nationale, the Flemish arms company, is still among the most aggressive in the world. They were the first to get guns to Castro, they armed both sides in the Congo war. You won't find a skirmish anywhere without FN pistols, machine guns, or rifles. Ninety percent of Belgian arms manufacture is exported."

"You're a wealth of information, Chip."

"The show will feature the latest hardware, lots of junk surplus. Enough whores to service an aircraft carrier, a shooting competition, a——"

Stark interrupted. "What sort of shooting?"

"A few different small arms. Probably assault rifles, sniper rifles, combat pistol marksmanship."

"Can you get me in?"

"Not if you're going to go around making rude remarks."

"I'll be obsequious, servile, and polite."

"I doubt that. Just don't get yourself killed. Or jeopardize my business."

"I'm genuinely touched by your concern," Stark said.

CHAPTER 17

Arms dealer Heinrich Mueller hadn't wanted to see Stark. Mueller was still in a foul mood. His solicitor was fending off the Hong Kong authorities, who wanted to prosecute him for illegal arms transfer. And now this damned fool reporter wanted to talk to him.

"Does the name Gerard DeVille mean anything to you?" Stark had asked on the phone.

"I know the name. Why do you ask?" Mueller had demanded.

"I thought you might like to talk about him."

"I can spare you fifteen minutes later this afternoon," Mueller said.

"Thank you, Herr Mueller."

Stark found the office on the fifth floor of one of those overcrowded Hong Kong high-rises loaded with import/export businesses. In the small foyer, a plump Chinese secretary sat behind a beat-up metal desk and unenthusiastically pecked at a computer.

Mueller himself had a spacious office. On the walls were posters from H & K, Armalite, and Beretta. They featured guns and buxom women in tight T-shirts and bathing suits. There was a calendar from Bofors, Sweden's biggest arms maker, continuing the girls and guns motif.

An expensive jade desk set and a computer perched atop a

black lacquer desk. Other than that, the office had the run-down look of a movie set decorator's impression of a forties private eye's office. Light coming in through venetian blinds cast shadows like horizontal prison bars.

Mueller made a big show out of consulting his massive digital wristwatch and punching a button on it. "Fifteen minutes," he said.

"I can be quicker than that," Stark responded, setting a notebook on his lap. "Do you think Gerard DeVille was the one who notified authorities about your shipment of weapons?"

Mueller was a pale man and the red flush that began at his neck and rose to his thinning blond hair was as conspicuous as tomato juice being poured into a glass.

"Why do you believe that?" he asked, making a visible effort to keep from exploding.

"I'm working on a story on the arms trade," Stark said. "A profile of interesting personalities. DeVille was recommended to me."

"Interesting?" Mueller asked, the pressure building.

"Yes. I've heard he's put together a little empire for himself."

"So did Attila the Hun," Mueller said. "What have you learned?"

"Oh, only that he's an aggressive salesman," Stark said.

"Let me tell you about his tricks," Mueller said. "In one instance, a small African country was accepting blind bids to rearm their military. Dozens of bids were submitted, very confusing, especially to an inept government. DeVille swoops down, offers one recognizable bid, higher, but says he'll handle all the problems. They accept."

"And DeVille was the one who covertly submitted all the false bids and created the confusion," Stark said, pretending to take notes on his pad.

"Exactly. Another time, there was to be a big meeting in Saudi Arabia. A multi-multimillion dollar contract was up for grabs. Two men were considered serious rivals to DeVille. One was stopped at the border and they found hard-core pornography in his bag. Another had several bottles of liquor. Interestingly, it was Chivas Regal, DeVille's favorite brand. And the man who was stopped didn't even drink anything stronger than wine."

"How'd he plant the stuff in their bags?"

"He'd bribed the men's servants. Of course the delay at the airport was a setback to them. But DeVille had a copy of the Koran in his bag. Not that that *scheisskopf* ever read anything other than a balance sheet. Naturally, he got the contract. He's not even supposed to be operating in the Middle East."

"What about you? I understand your arms shipment was heading to the PLO?"

"On the advice of my solicitor, I cannot answer any questions."

"Who was your client for the arms?"

"No comment."

"Perhaps you could contact them and see if they'd talk to me."

"No."

It was time to crank up Mueller again. He was the sort who spoke more openly when he was angry. Otherwise, he was as cold and dignified as an Alpine slope. Stark needed to start another avalanche.

"How do you respond to critics who refer to you and your associates as 'merchants of death?' "

"Guns don't kill people, people do. Think how many children die each year from being locked in refrigerators. Does that mean we should outlaw iceboxes?"

"A gun is just a tool. Like a hammer. Except guns have only one use."

"Not true. There's hunting, target shooting, self-defense."

"Also murder, invasion, assassination," Stark said. "Do you ever feel guilty about what you do?"

Mueller had regained his flushed look. "If I didn't do it, someone else would," Mueller said.

"Someone like DeVille?"

"Exactly."

"I wonder if you could suggest any leads?"

Mueller looked at his watch. "In what way?" A few more minutes and he would be rid of this obnoxious American.

"Perhaps Mr. DeVille would like some publicity."

Mueller got a cagey expression. He rocked back and forth in his chair. Siccing this reporter on DeVille could be a way of getting back at him, Mueller decided. "You will tell no one who you heard this from?"

"Never." Stark lifted the notepad and pen.

"Okay. Examine Red Diamond Ltd."

"Great. Can you tell me about any specific activity?"

"If I were you, I'd go to the docks tomorrow and look for a shipment at Red Diamond Ltd."

"Going from where to where?"

"I've given you more than I had intended to. Good day," Mueller said.

"Good day to you, Herr Mueller."

"Oh, one last thing," Mueller said. "Be careful when you snoop around. Another reporter was killed doing the same thing."

The ultranationalist Sasaki welcomed the four members of the Japanese Diet into his home. Sasaki lived on the outskirts of the industrial city of Osaka. The house was gigantic by Japanese standards, about the size of a large American suburban home. It had every labor-saving gadget imaginable, even though Sasaki had a full-time domestic staff of five.

The members of the parliament were ushered in and settled down. Two were already in his pocket. He had given them several million yen over the years, a gift that could turn into a past due loan at any time.

The two unswayed members of parliament had already taken a step in Sasaki's direction by coming to Osaka from Tokyo. They were both conservatives, members of the inappropriately named Liberal Democratic Party which controls Japan.

For the first two hours of their visit, there was no mention of business. Sasaki had five geishas from nearby Kyoto entertain. The women were highly skilled, and highly paid, performers. Their fees for the night would total more than an ordinary salaried man would make in a year.

They played traditional tunes on the zither-like *koto*, the banjo-like *shamisen*, flute, and drum. They recited classical poetry. But most of all they made skilled conversation, flattering the men and refilling their sake cups with equal grace.

They slipped out of the room on signal from Sasaki and the industrialist got down to business.

"I want you to know you can count on my support in the future," Sasaki said. The financial implication was clear. "There is a matter that concerns me now. It's this rash of terrorism being blamed on our youth."

"Terrible, terrible," the politicians clucked.

"I have it from reliable sources that the Chinese Communists are behind it," Sasaki said, lowering his voice as he shared the confidence. "They see themselves as the dominant economic force in the Pacific in the near future. They want to disrupt our progress, disgrace us in the world community."

"How dare they," one of the sympathetic politicians snorted.

"How can you be sure of this?" asked one of the conservatives.

"It's not a secret that I have contacts within other governments," Sasaki said smoothly. "Read Musashi, the great swordsman. He makes it clear how important good intelligence is for any struggle. Business is a struggle. If I know which country will be in turmoil, or which needs steel, or has a growing unemployment problem, it's to my benefit."

"What can be done?" asked one of the pols who had already been bought.

Sasaki stroked his chin as if it were the first time the question had occurred to him. "I would like to subsidize a youth group. With the government's approval, of course. The group would instill traditional values, teach the martial arts. Provide discipline, patriotism, a sense of national pride."

"Sounds good to me," said the other corrupted pol.

The two respected conservatives exchanged questioning glances.

"How large an organization were you planning?" one asked.

"I would start small, and see how it's received. If the young people show as much enthusiasm as I expect they will, we would allow it to grow."

"You don't want any government funding?" one of the conservatives asked.

"No. I don't need official endorsement. Just allow it to happen."

"What will it be called?"

"Japanese Youth for Peace and Strength," Sasaki said.

"I like it," said one of the corrupted pols.

"Me too," said the other.

The two conservatives nodded acceptance.

Sasaki smiled. "I'll make arrangements."

Actually, he already had. A two-hundred-acre site he had purchased for a steel mill would be the base camp. Initially. For what Sasaki had in mind was an army. A private army.

It wasn't the first time a Japanese citizen had assembled his own army. Novelist Yukio Mishima had established his own elite militia. Then he tried rallying the Self Defense Forces with his call for ultranationalist militarism. His efforts had failed when the bulk of the SDF troops rejected his appeal. He had committed hara-kiri. This wasn't some medieval effort—it happened in 1971. Isao Sasaki disliked Mishima's florid writing, but he agreed wholeheartedly with his politics.

If the politicians were too weak to take action, then he would show them what had to be done.

CHAPTER 18

In the lobby of the Hong Kong Hilton, Stark used a pay phone chosen at random to call Halliwell-Stark in New York. Pedro Quesada picked up. "That Hancock chick's been calling here regularly. Les tried putting the moves on her. She put him down so hard he was quiet for fifteen minutes."

"I'll have to give her a call and find out her secret," Stark said. "Can you get me a T and R, forthwith?" The letters were shorthand for a transponder and receiver.

"Don't attach my mustache," Quesada said.

"What?"

"Isn't that Japanese for 'it's nothing?'"

Stark laughed. "It's *do itashi mashita.*"

"I was close," Quesada said.

"A little more practice, and they'll think you were born in Tokyo."

After hanging up, Stark dressed in a conservative suit and headed down to the cargo handling basin by Causeway Bay. He carried a Kevlar wrapped aluminum clipboard with forms attached. Designed for use by police in traffic stops, it was lightweight and bullet resistant.

He timed it to arrive during lunch break when there was the most traffic in and out. He was welcomed by the boom of a cannon, the famous Noon Day Gun fired at the nearby Hong Kong Yacht Club.

On the wharf, huge Mitsubishi cranes, capable of lifting nearly a hundred tons, traveled along crane tracks. The ground rumbled as trucks brought in forty-foot containers. The containers were unhooked from the truck bed, a spreader bar attached, and the cranes lifted and lowered them on freighters. The containers were stacked eleven across at the widest part of the freighter. After piling them up seven high in the hold, a hatch cover would be put on, and three more could be piled up.

Forklifts, hoists, and minitractors lugged tons of goods across the broad dock. "RoRo" vessels allowed vehicles to roll on, roll off; "LoLos" meant lifting on, lifting off. The names on most of the goods were Japanese, with the United States a close second, and the People's Republic of China third.

Huge brass propellers were stacked near the drydock. Everything was oversize, dwarfing the human figure. Nothing was measured in pounds; multiton weight was the norm.

Besuited Stark, wearing a hard hat he had swiped and officiously carrying the clipboard, walked around as if he owned the place. None of the workers dared, or cared enough, to stop him.

It took him a half hour of wandering to find the Red Diamond Ltd. holding area. It was at the end of a long wharf. An armed guard was patrolling and unlike the few other guards Stark had seen, this one was alert. He was a black man, tall and muscular. A slight slouch, but hints of a military bearing. He carried a Stoner 5.56-mm carbine with a thirty-round magazine, holding the weapon as though he knew how to use it.

Stark kept his distance, pretending to check concrete stanchions and making diligent notes on his clipboard. There was a cyclone fence topped with barbed wire. Impossible to get to the holding area without walking across a huge open space.

"Hey, what you doing?" a Chinese dockworker asked. He was a squat man with tattoos on his thick arms.

"Just routine," Stark said.

"Boss know about you?" the tattooed worker demanded.

"I'm with Lloyd's of London," Stark said imperiously. "We're considering providing insurance." He emphasized the word "considering." He waved a letter, with a forged signature by the dockmaster, authorizing him to inspect the premises.

Behind the tattooed man were four buddies. Two had long black hair knotted back with bandannas. They both held baling hooks. The other two were unarmed, but big across the shoulders and chest. They had a Neanderthal-like swagger.

"You come with us," the tattooed worker said.

"I'm too busy, old bean," Stark responded. "Check with your superiors."

In the distance he saw the merc guard, apparently indifferent to the confrontation.

One of the Neanderthals reached out to grab Stark. Stark sidestepped. The second one moved in, telegraphing a haymaker. Stark held up his Kevlar wrapped aluminum clipboard. The stevedore's fist slammed into it. The clipboard dented slightly——the dockworker broke two knuckles and screamed.

A worker swung a baling hook. Stark ducked under it and blocked with his clipboard. The Kevlar easily handled the hook. Stark caught the man's wrist and jerked forward, then shoved back, then twisted. The man was able to resist the first two movements, but they were just to set him up for *kotegaishi*, the third move. Stark twisted outward, hard, throwing the man, snapping his wrist, and making the hook drop to the floor.

The guard had hoisted his weapon, not yet aimed, but ready. He took a few steps toward the skirmish.

Stark dispatched the second bandannaed man by sidestepping his swing and striking his chin with a straight palm heel thrust. In the turmoil, Stark had dropped his clipboard.

The tattooed man and one Neanderthal remained. But the Neanderthal was backpedaling. He turned and ran. The tattooed man swung, clumsily, and Stark guessed his intent even before he saw the flash of the switchblade behind his forearm. It cut through the lapels of Stark's suit, but didn't reach his flesh.

Stark let the blade complete its arc, then pinned the arm against the man's body. He flicked his hand into the man's eyes, little more than a slap, but jolting. He spun the knife arm up and around, twisting it into a hammerlock behind the man's back.

The guard with the gun was aiming. He was about ten yards away. Stark held the knife wielder in front of him and dodged to the side. He managed to grab the clipboard and tuck it into his pants so it sat in the small of his back, under his jacket. The clipboard had his notes on the dock layout.

Stark backed up, keeping an eye on the carbine-toting guard.

The tattooed man wriggled. Stark increased the pressure on his arm. Stark backed down the dock, nearing cover.

The guard fired. The first shot went over their heads. The tattooed man shouted in Cantonese. The guard fired another warning shot. Again the tattooed man yelled back, this time the panic clear in his tone.

Stark dropped his human shield and began broken field running toward a stack of containers, only a dozen yards away.

The guard kept pulling the trigger. Stark felt something hit him, like a baseball bat across his spine. He staggered, then forced himself upright, and continued until he made it to the containers.

He weaved in and out between containers, dizzy, avoiding workers. A crane was lifting a container near him. He grabbed it. The container rose into the sky. The hoist was indifferent to his one hundred ninety pounds of weight.

Below him, he saw the armed guard prowling. Stark passed over a stack of containers. He let go, dropping on top of the containers with a resounding metal thunk. But the dock was so noisy the guard with the gun didn't notice.

Stark lay atop the container pile, catching his breath. He

checked his back for blood, and found none. The bullet had dented the Kevlar clipboard.

The guard advanced warily, right below him. He had no defense when Stark dropped on him. A strike to the ear and a blow to the temple and the guard lay unconscious on the floor.

Stark strolled off the dock as casually as possible. He hoped no one noticed the slash across his lapels, the scraped knees, and the bullet hole in the back of his suit.

The transponder, about the size of a walnut half, and a paperback size receiver were waiting in Stark's room. He tested them, found they both worked. Stark did his stretches and took a long hot shower. He urinated blood. The bullet would've driven right through a kidney if not for the clipboard. As it is, the impact was like getting punched by Mike Tyson. Wearing brass knuckles.

Gerard DeVille had rented a suite at the Royal Meridien Hotel near Hong Kong's Kai Tak airport. In the mezzanine were complete business facilities. He could fax, telex, xerox, hire a secretary, buy office supplies or computer time, get documents notarized or shredded, all without leaving the hotel.

DeVille used a resistance monitor to check that no one was listening in on the line. He had chosen the office space at random so none of his rivals could've planted a bug. Still, he checked over the room carefully. Assured that it was safe, he set up a five-inch-high ivory figure of the Virgin Mary on the desk and set to work.

He tried to keep his overhead down, recognizing the fragility of his operation. A government could default on payment, an arms load come in late, and his artfully built empire crumble. He thought of Adnan Khashoggi, at one point described as one of the world's wealthiest men. Now, that arms dealer had been reduced from yacht class to dinghy size.

DeVille began to work the two phone lines. Rocking back

and forth in a swivel chair, he kept calls balanced on three lines, making sales patter in French, English, and German. He stressed to his customers that the weapons were available at a cut-rate price for immediate cash on delivery.

There were escalating tensions between Kenya and her neighbors. When word of her increased military spending spread in the Organization of African States, her neighbors decided to respond in kind. The Sudan and Somalia had placed orders immediately. Since DeVille had known about Kenya's increase even before the announcement was made public, he had been able to get sales reps in prematurely. Although they had no apparent connection to him, the money ultimately was funneled back to his corporation. Kenya's other neighbors, Uganda and Ethiopia, were too impoverished to buy much. DeVille left them for other dealers to cultivate. Tanzania had declined to participate in the escalation. He made a mental note to prod them.

He quickly sold the SAM-7s to an Iranian arms broker. Shoulder fired rockets were in hot demand. The cash would be wired to one of DeVille's three Swiss bank accounts. Finding a market for the machine guns was harder. He had to split the order up between a mercenary supplier—who would probably ship them to South Africa—and an Israeli official. The Israelis had plenty of American hardware, but the current U.S. administration was playing games, and they always needed replacements.

He called General Grant at the DIA.

"The shipment of guns you wanted delivered to Thailand is going out soon," DeVille said.

"Yeah. And my check is in the mail. How's your other little project in Thailand going?"

"*Comme ci, comme ça,*" DeVille said.

"That means half-assed, right?"

"Better than half-assed. Perhaps three-quarters assed," DeVille quipped, but Grant missed his humor.

"I might just have a use for that stuff. It's all untraceable?"

"The provenance is murky."

"Good, we might just be able to do business."

"Perhaps you might tell me about any interesting transactions," DeVille suggested.

Providing information was part of Grant's payment. "Taiwan is getting a new load of assault rifles," Grant said.

"I knew that a week ago. Someone already has arranged to purchase their old Armalites."

"There's U.S. hardware that was passed on to the National Guard and they're dumping it."

"Anything worthwhile?"

"Nothing but a few tanks and Warthogs. They're all deactivated."

"How much work do they need?"

"A first-rate mechanic could make them combat ready in less than a week."

"Why are they selling them?"

"The latest rage is to use helicopters instead of fixed wings."

"Can you give me a lead?"

Grant put him on hold and came back on the line in a couple of minutes with a name and number.

Because the goods were technically deactivated surplus, there was no need for Congressional approval. DeVille was able to get a committment with just a few phone calls.

The Turkish Minister of Defense was pleased when he got the call.

"I can provide two reconditioned M-1 tanks, and four Warthogs," DeVille promised. He was eager to move the tanks and planes, preferring to keep smaller weapons in stock. "With a turnaround time of little more than a month."

"What are Warthogs?"

"Sorry, I thought you'd know," DeVille said, though he'd been pretty sure the Turk wouldn't. He wanted to put him in his place. DeVille was feeling cocky, confident. "A small plane formally called an A-10. The U.S. designed them for ground support in the Vietnam war. But by the time they were ready, the war was over."

"What does it do?"

"It's a low flying tank killer with a 30-mm automatic cannon in front. Flies comfortably at a mere three hundred to five hundred miles an hour, so it can be very accurate. It can deliver up to two dozen five-hundred-pound bombs. Or use the Maverick missile or smart bombs."

"If it flies so low and slow, what about antiaircraft fire?" the Turk asked.

"The pilot is protected by a titanium shell, the fuel tanks have built-in fire suppression mechanisms, and even if one of the engines is knocked out, it can perform like a ballerina with the second one. It's really a flying tank. And a bargain at the price I am offering."

"How much?"

"A hundred million."

The Turk snorted. "Not if you threw in an atomic bomb."

"The A-10s alone cost eighteen million dollars each for the U.S. to develop."

"And these have never been used? It sounds like the sort of aircraft that would take a lot of abuse. A used one will have many problems."

They haggled back and forth and agreed on fifty million, with DeVille throwing in several truckloads of 30-mm ammo and two Maverick missiles.

He got back on the phone to try and scare up the additional supplies he had promised. When the goods were delivered, the Turks would be angry that they weren't combat ready. DeVille would claim the seller had deceived him, and provide the upgrading at no cost. Customer satisfaction.

Two packs of Gauloises after he first entered the rented cubicle, DeVille left a happy man.

Stark bought a mask, snorkel, fins, wet suit, and a sixteen-inch stainless steel knife from a dive shop near Clearwater Bay. He tried to keep Saito's words in mind, doing everything with Zen clarity. It was easy to fall into old thinking patterns, aware only of security precautions and threats. He had to keep his mind clear, absorbing everything, fixating on nothing.

After picking up a can of heavy black grease from an auto parts supply store, he returned to his hotel room. He reviewed his notes on the dock and committed the layout to memory, then spent two hours exercising and meditating.

It was a little past midnight when he was ready.

CHAPTER 19

Willy Rose sat in the parked Lear jet reading the *South China Morning Post.* He had already been through the *Hongkong Standard.* The *Post* lay on a table, and his finger traced across the words, reviewing the briefs about skirmishes around the globe. Jets rumbled on the tarmac outside. Hong Kong's Kai Tak airport was one of the busiest in Asia.

He heard the heavy tread on the stair and his hand slid down toward his .45.

"What are you doing here?" Gerard DeVille snapped.

"A fine greeting that is, mate," Rose said.

"You scared me half to death," DeVille said. "You know we are not supposed to be seen together."

"I was careful. Your pilot knows who I am anyway. I recruited the chappie, remember?"

"What is it you want?" Seeing Rose had spoiled DeVille's good mood. Rose had the scent of death about him. To DeVille, shuffling munitions around the world was an abstraction. A skillfully arranged deal, the beautiful precision of a well-crafted weapon, the logistics of moving equipment through hostile territory, these were what DeVille liked to think of. Not people like Rose. The cigarette quivered as DeVille lit it.

"We had an intruder today by the Red Diamond Cargo

131

holding area," Rose said. "I stopped by to hoist a few with Mickey. He told me about it. The sod fit the description of the one who was asking about Nakamura in Nicosia."

"The description from Cyprus was hardly precise. Age, height, build, hair color, race."

"I got a hunch it's the same chappie. I don't think it's a coincidence."

"You worry too much, Willy."

"That's why I'm alive. Anyway, either we got one big problem, or two little ones."

"Let me handle the strategy. You stick to the tactics," DeVille said.

"Mickey said he shot the trespasser," Rose continued. "But no blood. And the sod didn't fall. No sign of a body."

"Are you getting superstitious on me? You think it's African mumbo jumbo magic?"

"More likely a bulletproof vest," Rose said. "I don't like anyone that well prepared. And Mickey said our visitor could really take care of himself. Dispatched a gang of local hoodlums without missing a beat. Mickey knows his martial arts. He guesses that the guy was a jujitsu expert."

"So? What do you want to do?"

"I don't know yet. But when a lion smells a cheetah sniffing around his water hole, he doesn't put his head down to drink."

"How colorful. I hope you're not going native on me."

Rose fixed DeVille with an emotionless look. Completely emotionless, as if DeVille were a piece of furniture to be discarded when his upholstery gave out. DeVille knew he had overstepped what was acceptable to Rose.

"We'll be more careful," DeVille said. "All we have at the dock is Russian junk I'm sending to Thailand."

"Double security on it."

"I do not want to call attention to it. I tell you what I will do. I will make sure we have only first-rate people down there. Will that make you happy?"

"I'll only be happy when we find the troublemaker."

* * *

Stark dog-paddled slowly under the dock, through a vile brew of oil slick, floating garbage, and murky water. There was a splashing sound in the shadows and Stark slowed his paddling. Sharks came into the water to feast on the garbage thrown from the boats. Then he saw the eyes glowing. It was a different sort of scavenger, a rat the size of a large cat. It was floating on a log, gnawing a piece of debris and trying to decide if Stark's head would be a tastier morsel. Stark hissed and the rat scurried off into the pilings.

Pole-mounted five-hundred-watt sodium lights threw an eerie yellow light that filtered down through cracks in the wharf above him. Rats watched his progress like spectators at a sporting event.

He shimmied up a piling, sliding back twice into the water as he lost his grip on a slick spot. His quarter-inch-thick neoprene wet suit was scraped through in several spots. His face and the back of his hands were smeared with black grease—for warmth and camouflage.

He chinned himself over the top. There was a guard a few hundred feet away, facing the other direction. Stark knelt behind a supply shed, peeled off his flippers, tied them together with a piece of polypropylene cord, and hung them over the side of the dock.

Water trapped between his body and the wet suit made little squishing noises as he moved. The guard turned and Stark pressed against the side of a container just in time. He concentrated on his breathing as the guard patrolled, at one point passing within a few feet of him. The air was hot enough to dry his footprints, but because it was so humid, the moisture wasn't absorbed. They glistened like a slug trail. If the guard glanced down . . .

The guard passed and Stark advanced. The building looked like a huge cargo container—a corrugated metal rectangle, about three stories high, painted blue, with scab-like rust. The door creaked as he opened it. He stepped in and pressed flat against the wall.

Many of the crates were military surplus, with German, Italian, and U.S. markings. Signs every few feet warned

Danger—Explosives—No Smoking in English and Chinese.

There were more than a thousand crates and containers to search through. He padded to the small office in a corner of the building. He slipped the lock on the door and made it in just as he heard the guard opening the outside door.

Stark ducked behind a desk. The guard turned up the lights on the inside and patrolled. His footfalls echoed off the worn wood floors. The guard lowered the lights and headed back out.

Stark began rooting through the papers. There were dozens of orders for military hardware. DeVille apparently had his major warehouse in Thailand, and many of the orders were reroutes from Bangkok to Hong Kong.

He picked the lock on a desk drawer and found ledger books inside. On the wood in the drawer was written a two-letter, ten-digit number. He jotted it down. People would write down safe combinations, telex codes, bank computer entry numbers, in what they thought were out-of-the-way places.

One of the invoices caught his eye. The packing sheet listed the contents as "Milling Machinery," due to be air shipped the next day to Bangkok. Why would an arms dealer be handling an order of milling machinery?

It took fifteen minutes of searching for Stark to find the crates in question. During that time, the guard made another circuit. Stark barely managed to duck in time.

Assured that the guard was a way off, he used his knife to carefully pry open crates. If the metal scraped on metal and caused a spark, he would go out with a blast.

Nails squealed as he pried open the boxes. He was disappointed. They did indeed hold milling machinery. At first glance. He lifted out the parts on top, removed the packing foam, and found a light board that also came out.

There were five neatly packed AK-47s. He went to a second crate from the lot and repeated the procedure. This one held five Skorpions, and a thousand rounds of 7.65-mm ammunition. The guns were in poor condition, with rust spots and nicks.

The types of weapons, their sorry condition, the method of shipment, the tiny size of the order, whatever unidentifiable instincts he had developed over his twenty years in the business, made him believe that the weapons were headed to terrorists.

Stark got pen and paper from the office, wrote down serial numbers from the weapons, then resealed the crates. Before closing the AK-47 crate, he activated the transponder and attached it inside. The mercury battery would last for a week, with the transponder emitting a signal every five seconds.

Stark made it to the edge of the dock seconds before the guard's next circuit. Stark slid into the water soundlessly and swam into the darkness.

CHAPTER 20

Stark booked a seat on an early morning flight from Hong Kong to Bangkok. From the airport, he called his business partner. It was sixteen hours earlier in New York and Halliwell was just returning from his usual two-hour lunch.

"Les, I need you to check phone numbers with my sister," Stark said.

Halliwell understood that to mean the figures were to be checked with the CIA.

"Any info available?"

"The first one, I know. Her name is Alice Kennedy, she's forty-seven, used to live south of Union Street in Brooklyn."

"Roger wilco," Halliwell said. The numbers were on Soviet manufactured AK-47s.

Stark rattled off strings of numbers.

Les read them back and asked, "Who should I bill this to?"

"Mr. H."

The cargo handling facility was at the edge of the Don Muang airport outside of Bangkok. There was the usual flurry of forklifts and small flatbed trucks, with the labor-intensive flock of workers typical of Third World countries. None had ear protectors or safety gear. The laborers had a languid grace. It was 6 A.M. and already beginning to heat up. No one survived in the tropics without learning to make the most of each movement, and rest whenever possible.

Stark sat in one of Asoke Car Rental's Toyotas about a quarter mile from the terminal where DeVille's crate was to be delivered. The cargo area was fenced in, guarded. He was still achy from the bullet bouncing off his back during his previous intrusion.

Stark was parked on a dirt side road that sprouted from the main service road route in and out of the terminals. He kept the receiver tuned low, a friendly beep at five-second intervals. An hour passed. Even though Stark had the windows rolled up, a tenacious mosquito from the wetlands bordering the airfield had made its way in. After brief sparring, Stark taught it the sound of two hands clapping.

Another half hour passed, and the beeping grew louder. A white Chevy van drove by and the beeping peaked with a Doppler-like effect. Stark waited a couple of minutes before starting in pursuit. The transponder receiver had a digital readout, which showed distance from receiver to beeper as well as position on a six-inch crosshatched screen.

The van was at least five years old but not sagging under the considerable weight of the guns. Reinforced shocks. The side windows, two on the back, were darkened. Writing on the side said the van belonged to the Amerasian Import Company.

He followed it southwest into Bangkok traffic. Street signs were largely in Thai, driving was on the left-hand side of the street, and Thai drivers were indifferent to the sixty kilometer per hour speed limit in the city. Traffic could sit for ten minutes at a light, then explode in all directions with drivers swerving into oncoming traffic. To focus on the van and not get hit by other drivers required every ounce of Stark's concentration.

They passed the Victory Monument, down Raj Damri Road, turned right, and got caught at the stop light at Patpong Road. Patpong, between Suriwongse and Silom—

famous among GIs and Asian sex tours—was quiet in the early morning hours. Police picked up drunks, garbagemen picked up empties. The go-go joints and nude bars looked pathetic and worn in the morning light.

In the city center, traffic was even worse. *Tuk tuks,* the Kamikaze-piloted three-wheelers vaguely similar to golf carts, darted through traffic. Motorcyclists, bicyclists, and pedestrians bent on suicide added to the ennervating brew. Doorless buses bulldozed down streets, with passengers hanging off the sides like streamers in the wind.

Though Stark hadn't seen his face, the driver of the van appeared to be a true native. He jumped red lights, didn't slow for pedestrians, and nearly sideswiped other vehicles a half-dozen times.

Inside the van, Nicky Webb cursed continuously. He had lived in the Orient since leaving the service in 1972. Webb was an ex-Green Beret sergeant, a combat veteran of the Vietnam war, who had that peculiar expatriate's love and hate of the Far East. He had been through three Thai wives, fathered six kids in and out of marriage, and was known in just about every bar on Patpong Road. He had been thrown out of many for brawling and had three-digit bar tabs at several others. When the infamous Lucy's Tiger Den closed, he'd escaped paying more than five hundred dollars.

Webb was forty-two years old and beginning to feel his age. There was a roll of padding around his once washboard flat waist. The tattoos on his arms had begun to blur. And for the first time in his life, the night before, he'd been unable to get it up. He knew tonight he'd hit the bars. With a vengeance. Find some young guy feeling his oats and kick the shit out of him.

But first he had to deliver the hardware. To a bunch of Commie bastard punks. He couldn't believe he was doing it. But he had to follow orders. He needed the bucks. With any luck, the punks would get themselves killed.

He'd taken a quick look at the guns when he'd picked them up. They were shit. A good chance they'd blow up in the face of whoever fired them. The buyers had to be dumb bastards to accept such a load.

Throughout Bangkok were the ornate *wats*, the temples that blended Indian, Chinese, Burmese, and Khmer styles for a beauty unique to Thailand. Brightly colored, glittering, with curved gables adorning multitiered roofs, they towered above the sleaze and clutter at street level.

Stark could pay little attention to the architecture. If the van got out of range, his transponder would be worthless. Using the device was the only way that one man could follow another with any certainty of not being caught.

The van circled blocks, zigged and zagged. Stark hoped it was a routine precaution, and not that the driver had discovered him. Stark hung a bit farther back. He lost the van twice, but was able to pick it up by using the beeper. He followed it west through Bangkok and across the greenish-brown waters of the Chao Phraya River.

Then the van doubled back and headed north. It took another hour to escape Bangkok congestion. As traffic thinned, Stark hung even farther back on the four-lane roadway.

They rushed by rice paddies and domesticated water buffalos. Lush swampy ground with two-foot-wide creeks cutting between green clumps. Smaller houses, more primitive. The road was lined with dense growths of coconut palms, banana trees, and sawgrass.

Then they drove into a modest size city. Even without checking his map, Stark knew where they were. Ayutthaya, the capital of Thailand from A.D. 1350 until the bloody takeover by the Burmese in 1767. The *stupa* and *chedi*, towers left over from the ancient city, gave a hint of its past grandeur.

The Amerasian Import Company driver got out of his van and walked among the crumbling brick walls. Stark went to a drink stand and paid ten baht for a Coke. He sipped and sauntered, keeping a safe distance.

The driver went into a temple where a twenty-foot-high, gilt-covered Buddha smiled down on worshippers. A man, with a sign saying Donations, played a xylophone-like instrument. Four Thai dancers clad in traditional high-spired headgear performed a classical dance. Their work had been paid for by a worshipper who wanted to gain the Buddha's favor by entertaining him.

While the dancing was going on, the Amerasian Import driver was off to the side. He leaned over and spoke briefly to a young Oriental man with greasy hair and a wispy beard. Then he headed out.

The Amerasian driver got back in his van and drove off. Stark waited a couple of minutes before following. The driver would be most alert, checking for tails. The beeper made any sort of lockstep unnecessary.

As Stark sat in his car, Wispy exited the temple and got into a Nissan pickup with two other people, a man and a woman.

Stark drove off after the van. He followed it until it turned off the paved road onto a smaller, packed dirt one. Stark made the turn, and slowed even more.

After a few minutes, the beeping became fixed in one spot. The van had stopped. Stark pulled off onto a patch of dirt that looked firm and managed to partially conceal the car. It might fool someone driving by quickly.

He began edging his way through the undergrowth.

The three gun buyers hovered about as Webb opened up the crates. He took out one of the AK-47s. It had been his favorite weapon during the war. More durable than the M-16. Besides, it made it harder for Victor Charlie to pinpoint friend or foe. The M-16 fired red tracers and had a certain whump and whine. The AK-47 fired green, and had more of a bark.

He did a little razzle-dazzle with the gun, twirling it like a cheerleader, snapping one of the curved thirty-round mags into the frame. It didn't fit as smoothly as a mag did into an M-16. The Russians just couldn't work precisely. But it held up better in the mud, grit, and humidity.

He snapped the mag out and passed the rifle to the

greasy-haired man with a wispy beard. The man handled it clumsily, unwittingly pointing it at Webb, and passed it to the second one. That one clearly had been a soldier at some point. He treated the gun with respect, holding it firmly, muzzle pointed away. He fingered a rust spot on the gun and looked questioningly at Webb.

"They're all in working order," Webb said. "Just not as pretty as when they come out of the factory."

The ex-soldier passed it to the woman. She regarded the weapon scornfully. A cold piece of work, Webb thought. Probably more balls than the other two. The first was probably the mouth, full of propaganda and yak shit. The second was a good trooper. The woman was the one to watch in a fight. Webb guessed there was a pistol under her loose-fitting shirt.

His own left foot was heavy with a .32 in a black canvas ankle holster. He cracked open the other crate and dug out a Skorpion VZ61. It had been a long time since he'd seen one. The three-and-a-half-pound weapon, without mag clip, was in even worse condition than the Kalashnikov. Which was real trouble in a finicky submachine gun. Webb played with it then respectfully handed it to the ex-soldier.

From the brush, Stark studied the Amerasian Import van driver, a white man with close cut hair and tattoos. American, Stark figured, though not really sure why. Of the three young Orientals, one man and a woman looked to be Thai. The third, Stark guessed, was Japanese.

The one who Webb thought of as the trooper, who Stark correctly identified as Japanese, walked to where a battered red four-wheel drive Ford pickup was parked in the thicket and backed it up to Webb's van.

Webb unloaded AK-47s from the box and into wooden crates in the back of the radicals' pickup. When he had emptied that crate, he started in on the Skorpions. All the while, he kept an eye on the woman.

As he was emptying the box, he noticed the walnut shell size brown lump in the corner. Webb had been in Southeast

Asia so long he felt he knew every type of mold or insect nest possible. He'd never seen a lump like that before.

There was one more Skorpion left. As he took it out, he banged the stock against the lump. He handed the gun over, then pretended to fiddle with the box. He didn't want the Thais to guess that anything was wrong.

The lump had popped free from the side, and looked like a baby turtle rolled on its back. Only instead of a belly, Webb saw electronic innards. As soon as he figured out what it was, he returned it to its original position. He casually turned around slowly, with apparently aimless movements, covering all three hundred and sixty degrees.

In the bushes, Stark saw the Amerasian van driver turning. Stark edged back a couple of paces, making sure undergrowth covered him sufficiently. The man's body language had changed. Always alert, it now bordered on tense. Stage One to Stage Two alert. Did he know something or had the Thais done something to make him wary?

The woman picked up on the change also. She shifted, stretched, loosened up. Her hand adjusted her shirt.

Webb didn't see anyone, but the "battle stations" bells continued to ring. He wanted to get out of there quickly. He had noticed the woman fiddling with the shirt.

"Payment?" he said harshly.

"Half has already been paid to your employer," the greasy-haired one said.

"I know that," Webb snapped.

The trooper bristled. The woman said something too low and quick for Webb to hear, but it calmed the trooper. The trooper had shifted so he was near the pickup and could come up behind it with gun drawn.

The greasy-haired one went to the pickup and reached into the cab. Webb's senses were humming. He plotted where he'd dive to and how he could come up with a gun. This setup was stupid. He should never have agreed to it. It showed how desperate he was for work. Which made him angrier.

But the man returned with a thin leather briefcase. He handed it to Webb and said, "Count it."

Webb did. It was tough to keep track of the amount, watch the brush, and watch the Thais. There was three thousand dollars in the case, U.S. currency. Webb wondered why his boss was involved with such a small-fry operation. There must be a lot more coming through.

CHAPTER 21

As he drove from the site, Webb reached under the dash and took out a Browning .45. He felt much better. The .32 just didn't have the knockdown power the .45 did. And having it right on the seat next to him, hidden under a rag, was reassuring.

The Thais wouldn't have placed the bug. They knew where he was going to be. If they wanted to set him up, it would've been easy enough. The deal had been completed without problems. He thought about the cold-eyed woman. Boy, he would've loved to put it to her, make her forget all that radical shit.

He watched his rearview mirror. Nothing. Of course it would be easy enough to tail from anywhere with that damned beeper in the box. Was DeVille checking up on him? Was some intelligence agency sniffing around? Or maybe a competitor out to cut in on his action. Webb's hands squeezed the wheel. He'd be having fun soon.

Stark knew he had a problem when he saw the conspirators transferring the guns into their own crates. That meant no bug. And their four-wheel drive vehicle could go places his rented car couldn't.

And it did. The trio took off through a narrow trail that

led into the jungle. Stark followed for two miles. He couldn't go more than thirty miles an hour, careful not to drive right up on the terrorists.

Then the terrain got too difficult. His rented car skidded on a mud patch and Stark just barely brought it under control, the front bumper kissing a bamboo grove.

Up ahead, it sounded as if the terrorist's car had stopped. He got out of his own vehicle and hurried through the bamboo grove. It would be too easy to be spotted on the narrow road.

He heard a throatier engine and pushed through the dense brush back to the road. He was running now.

By the time he reached the small landing strip, a plane was taxiing for takeoff. There were no markings on the vintage four-seater. It was airborne before he could even tell what kind it was. The terrorists' four-wheel drive was abandoned, the guns gone.

There was no license plate on the four-wheel drive. He opened the engine and jotted down the VIN number.

Stark returned to his car. He had to drive in reverse for nearly a mile before there was enough of a road for him to turn around. He switched the receiver back on to follow the white man who'd delivered the weapons.

The white man was nearly out of range. Stark drove until the blinking green dot showed again on the six-inch cross-hatched screen.

Webb had a small office in Thon Buri, the city across the Chao Phraya River from Bangkok. Thonburi, which was the capital before Bangkok took that title in 1782, had been swallowed into the Bangkok metropolitan area, becoming little more than a giant suburb to the six-million-plus person metropolis. But there were still many undeveloped patches.

Webb's office seemed even smaller since his second wife —who had an obsession with things British, and ultimately ran off with a British sailor while Webb was on a mission— had decorated it like a Victorian living room. Bric-a-brac clutter everywhere, red flocked wallpaper, elegant desk.

When she ran off, he'd been tempted to dump it all. But then he thought about how much it cost, and he decided to keep it.

Webb, aside from his mercenary skills, was good at coming up with artifacts, and arranging for them to be smuggled out of the country. He had teams scouting the countryside, looking for overgrown temples and abandoned grave sites. They'd swipe as much as they could, bring it to him, and he'd find suitable buyers.

He went to the office and slogged through paperwork. The Thai trio had given him the payment for DeVille, and he had to arrange to have it wire transferred to DeVille's Swiss account. Webb rooted in his desk, looking for the paper where he'd written DeVille's Swiss account number. Once he'd misplaced it, and had to have the boss resend him the information. DeVille had not been pleased. The only thing worse would be if the Frenchman felt Webb was holding out on him. Webb had to send all the money promptly to DeVille, who would then wire back his commission. Sometimes that could take weeks. It wasn't fair, but Webb couldn't do much more than bitch to drunken bar buddies who didn't understand any English.

He went through his whole desk twice looking for the scrap of paper. He had the habit of jotting notes to himself on whatever scrap was handy, then accidentally throwing the paper out. His third time through he found the scrap, right where it belonged. He stabbed it into the wall above his desk with a thumb tack.

Webb periodically peered out the window, looking for any strangers. No one. Whoever had bugged him was slick. But he was slicker.

After about an hour he walked out, got into his van and drove off.

Stark had strolled by the storefront twice, but he couldn't maintain a surveillance without being discovered. Like most of the Third World, the street teemed with life and he would have been spotted immediately. There were noodle vendors, children playing with a ball, old women haggling with fruit cart vendors, a couple of *tuk tuk* drivers smoking cigarettes and laughing.

Stark strolled around, browsing through carts, buying a few cheap lacquerware and teak items, nibbling pineapple slivers. He visited the *wats* in the neighborhood, enjoying the calm temple courtyards surrounded by Asian chaos. The smoky smell of sweet incense blotted out odors of food, sweat, and mildew. Saffron-robed Buddhist monks went amiably about their chores. They were young men fulfilling the Thai male Buddhist's duty to be a monk for at least a few months. Like the military service, Stark mused, right down to shaved heads and uniforms.

Stark had the receiver tucked into his waistband and an earplug in his ear. It looked like a hearing aid, but the constant beep let him know that the van hadn't moved.

Nighttime came and the beeping changed. He hurried back to his car and followed the sound. Suddenly, it stopped. The battery should've been good for days. It was possible the transponder had been broken by shifting cargo. Or given up due to moisture. Or been discovered.

Stark decided he'd check with Thanom, his government contact in the morning. Could he describe the three gun purchasers enough that they could be identified? Surely a woman activist was a rarity.

Back in his hotel that night, Stark couldn't sleep. Time zone changes, frustrations over the number of dead ends, made him get up and work out for an hour. He did all forty-five black belt *kata*, the stylized shadow boxing that was part of the jujitsu style. Blocks, kicks, punches, armlocks, and throws against single and multiple opponents. Each was done slowly, striving for perfection of technique. In reality, opponents were never as obliging as the imaginary assailants.

He was soaked with sweat by the time he finished. Calmer, but still edgy. Dressed in a dark outfit, carrying a penlight, six-inch titanium pry bar, and lock pick set, he headed out.

He parked four blocks from Webb's store. Not too close,

but not too far. Stark didn't want to have to do much walking carrying his burglary kit.

He strolled down the street. It was quiet. No one in sight. In ten seconds, he had picked the simple lock on the door to Webb's shop.

Webb heard the front door click open. He was hidden in an oversize cherrywood armoire. He had been there for three hours, barely moving, the door open a crack to let in fresh air. Webb rolled his wrist. The .45 was a soothing weight in his hand.

There was a thick curtain over the front window. Completely black inside. Stark sensed, rather than saw, objects around him in the darkness. He switched on the penlight, and was surprised at the Victorian drawing room clutter as all first time visitors to the shop were.

He made his way to the desk. The lock opened easily.

In times of stress it was too easy to develop tunnel vision, just use one sense. Stark had trained to develop total awareness. So while his eyes were focused on the papers in the desk, his ears picked up the slight creak of the armoire door.

He threw himself to the floor as the .45 boomed, a thumb thick slug crashing into the wall behind him. He hurled the pry bar in the direction the shot had come from, and heard a grunt.

Webb charged, gun in front of him, his right shoulder throbbing where the bar had hit.

"Come on out, cupcake, it's party time," Webb said, moving forward lightly in the darkness. He knew the layout of the office and easily avoided the obstacles.

Stark crawled across the floor. He held the flashlight in his hand, his arm extended away from his body. He switched it on, guessing where Webb's face would be.

Two shots exploded out, chewing up the floor right next to the flashlight.

Stark rolled and kicked out. Webb, temporarily blinded by the flashlight, couldn't see the low attack. The kick caught him in the knee and he went down. He grappled with Stark, swinging the gun at Stark's head.

Stark grabbed his hand. Webb tried to bite him. He was a ball of swinging limbs. The two men exchanged blows from knees and elbows, both trying to control the weapon.

They rolled around on the floor, crashing into small tables, knocking over vases, banging into chairs.

Face to face on the floor, Stark could hear Webb hissing with rage. Stark butted Webb's jaw with his forehead. The mercenary was momentarily stunned. Long enough for Stark to release the gun hand, and clap both hands on Webb's ears. Then a hook to Webb's jaw, and the merc relaxed. Stark grabbed the gun.

He had to move quickly. He fished Webb's wallet out and recorded his name and home address off the driver's license. Stark thumbed through the papers on the desk, taking a pile of coded telexes. Then he saw the note with the Swiss account number tacked above the desk and jotted it down.

Webb groaned. In the distance, Stark heard a siren. The boom of the .45 must've been audible for blocks.

He hurried out of the shop. Stark could see faces in the windows above the stores across the street. He kept his face turned down, concealing it from the spectators.

Stark called Langley and got through to CIA Chief Creange's top assistant. The deputy said he would arrange for Stark to have access to a secure line at the embassy in less than an hour. Stark had to do it that way, since official policy was to deny there even was a CIA station at the embassy. Which was like denying the President lived in the White House.

The American Embassy in Thailand is housed in a walled compound on Wireless Road in Bangkok. The Marine guard on duty at the wrought iron gate, a burly young black man in perfectly pressed dark blue uniform, checked his clipboard. He found Stark's name, then demanded photo ID. Stark produced a California driver's license. The guard allowed him in. He didn't change his expression or tone once during the entire conversation.

Stark was escorted by another Marine guard into the bowels of the embassy. The code encryption room was six by six, unfurnished except for a student size desk. On the desk was a device that looked like an old dictaphone machine, only it had numerous lights and switches, and a modern telephone handset.

"We're getting the new model in a few weeks," the clerk said apologetically. She was curious as to Stark's identity, but knew better than to ask.

Stark listened as she explained how to record and transmit. "Not much different from the one we used to use," he said.

"Were you with the Agency?" she asked.

"A long, long time ago," he said.

The connection to CIA chief Creange was as clean and crisp as a local phone call.

"You're getting your money's worth out of your tax dollars," Creange said. "Your partner contacted me and asked me to run some serial numbers."

"Were you able to do it?"

"Yes. And it turned up very interesting indeed. Those AK-47s were last recorded twenty years ago, in Vietnam. They were seized from a VC battalion in the Ia Drang Valley and supposedly destroyed by our troops."

"That large a load couldn't just be some GI's souvenir cache."

"Certainly not."

"I sense there's something you're not telling me."

"I've told you all I can," Creange said.

"Which means there's more."

"I have to get back to work, Robert," Creange said tartly before they broke the connection.

Creange felt bad about withholding information from Stark, but what he had learned was too disturbing to share until he had sorted it out. The name of the commander in charge of the unit that had seized the guns was then Colonel Todd Grant.

CHAPTER 22

Webb called DeVille's Paris office and left a coded message. Three hours later he was waiting at a pay phone in the lobby of Bangkok's Hyatt Central Plaza hotel. The phone rang right on schedule.

"We got problems," he said after DeVille identified himself.

"Pourquoi?"

"A guy broke into the shop. Swiped coded telexes. And the payment from the Thais," Webb said.

"Do you have any idea who it might have been?"

"A white guy. Good with his hands. At least six feet. Medium build. Clean shaven. Dark hair. Mid to late forties. No amateur. He had planted a transponder in the load of guns you sent. I think you got a leak on your end."

"Okay."

The line went dead.

Webb was furious that he had been bested. The three thousand dollars he'd claimed were stolen assuaged his feelings. He'd settle his bar tabs, pick up a couple of whores, and spend a month or so experimenting with new combinations.

"Yes?"

"We have a problem in Thailand," DeVille said.

151

"At the base?"

"No. With Webb. He's been blown. The money stolen. Telexes stolen."

"Any chance of leakage?"

"Non," DeVille said. "They were one-time codes. Unbreakable. He claims the burglar fit the description of our little problem. The visitor to the docks."

"What do you want me to do?"

"Webb is a weak link."

"I'll take care of it," Rose said.

CIA chief Creange and the other members of the National Security Restricted Interagency Group listened to reports about the world's turmoil.

The tension over Cyprus had plateaued. There had been hot rhetoric on the floor of the U.N. Violent demonstrations in both countries had left eight people dead. Both Greece and Turkey had ordered massive amounts of new military hardware. Each side had troops engaging in exercises, like macho competitors showing off their muscles. But it seemed as though war was not imminent and the RIG could move on to other matters.

"There've been signs of increased activity near the northern border of Thailand," said the CIA's leading Far East analyst. "A Marxist group has been agitating the hill people, notably the Yao. The agitators may be coming over the border from Burma, but we have not yet been able to verify that."

"I've got information on that too," Grant said. "We know exactly who is doing the agitating." He paused, milking the drama of the moment.

"Who?" the National Security Agency chief finally asked.

"Japanese Communists. Links to the old Japanese Red Army."

"My people haven't sent back any such information."

"Your people think the Shah of Iran is still in power," Grant cracked, and there were muffled chuckles around the table.

"Spare us your levity," Creange responded. "Do you have anything to document your claim?"

"Sure. A Japanese terrorist was found with a cache of weapons. AK-47s and Czech Skorpions."

"Did he make a statement?" Creange asked.

"Unfortunately, he was dead. My sources believe there was a falling out in the group. The weapons were inferior quality."

"That doesn't add up," Creange said. "I've never heard of terrorists abandoning a weapons cache."

"Maybe they were surprised. Thai troops apparently came on the body shortly after the shooting," Grant said, taking out a cigar and toying with it. "There's additional information, but it's eyes only for me and the President."

"That's ridiculous," Creange said.

"No. That's the way it is," Grant shot back.

For what seemed like several minutes, the only sound in the room was the humming of hidden machinery and the shifting of nervous bodies.

"The Thai government has approached us asking for helicopters to battle the terrorists," the assistant secretary of state said, breaking the long silence.

"How many?" the National Reconnaissance Office head asked, trying to ease the tension between the directors of the CIA and the DIA.

"Two dozen. We've got about ten reconditioned Hueys and a few Chinooks available," General Grant said. "It would be a good time for a show of support."

Creange turned to the analyst. "I'd like to hear your opinion."

"At this point, there are no signs of any substantial guerrilla movement," she said. "I think we should wait for more information."

"That's what Custer's scouts told him," Grant said. "They're asking for them pronto."

"How about we provide them saying it's for drug interdiction?" suggested the deputy secretary of state.

"That sounds reasonable," Creange said. He turned to an

aide. "See if you can get stats from the DEA on where the bulk of U.S. heroin is currently coming from. Let them know we want them to say the Golden Triangle."

"Yes, sir."

Creange turned to the CIA's Far East analyst. "Anything else?"

"The only other substantial political shift in the Far East is domestic. In Japan. A group called Japanese Youth for Peace and Strength."

"That's out of our ballpark, a domestic problem," Grant said, collecting the papers in front of him.

"The only reason I brought it up is that they are using the reputed JRA terrorist incidents as a rationale for their existence."

"How so?" the NSA chief asked. "Or should I say, ah so?"

"They're claiming the terrorism is caused by young people's frustration, being nurtured by outside agitators. They say the JYPS offers a healthy alternative."

"Like the Boy Scouts."

"Except instead of carrying knives, there's a movement afoot to arm them."

"What sort of weaponry do they have now?" the NSA chief asked.

"Wooden rifles," the analyst said.

"Probably pop guns too," Grant said. "Sounds harmless to me."

"Keep us posted," Creange told the analyst. "If there's nothing else, gentleman, I'm sure we all have work to do."

Creange got into the elevator with his assistant.

Grant stepped up before the doors could close and said to the assistant, "Why don't you take the next elevator down."

The staffer looked at his boss. Creange nodded. The staffer got off and Grant released the door open button.

"I heard you made inquiries at ATF on a load of AK-47s and Skorpions."

"Correct," Creange said stiffly. "Perhaps there's a connection with this supposed Japanese terrorist."

"The matter you're nosing about comes right from the top." Grant was standing close, whispering. The elevator was considered a secure area, swept daily by antibugging experts, but Grant was a cautious man.

"Do you mean there's a covert operation I'm not aware of? Perhaps I should take it up directly with the President."

"It's best to let it drop. Why did you ask about those guns anyway?"

"Just curious," Creange said with a tight smile.

"Curiosity killed the cat," Grant said.

"But satisfaction brought it back," Creange responded. The elevator door opened and Creange walked away briskly. He felt weak in the knees.

What was Robert Stark into that one ranking U.S. government official would issue a veiled threat to another senior official?

Stark decided that Webb was worth another visit. From Webb's driver's license, he easily found the three-story, gray concrete building where Webb lived. Clothes hanging on lines providing the only color. The apartments opened onto a central courtyard.

As Stark lounged in a doorway up the block, a thin white man with a gaunt face hurried out. He walked right past Stark. He had the kind of eyes that could cause a chill even in a tropical clime. The man looked at Stark as if he were trying to place his face, but continued his brisk walk away.

Stark waited until he was out of sight to go up to Webb's third-floor apartment. He stuck his pick into the lock and tensioned it. He twisted the knob and it opened easily. Not even locked. That wasn't consistent with the kind of operative who would lie in wait for hours in the dark.

Stark edged the door open. The smell of cordite was still fresh. The door wouldn't open all the way.

It was banging against Webb's foot. He had been shot once, in the forehead, with a large caliber gun. Stark slipped in and pulled the door shut. Blood still trickled down Webb's face. That meant his heart had only just stopped pumping. Stark took Webb's pulse and confirmed he was dead.

Moving quickly, he checked the obvious—the small

writing desk, night table, the dresser, then the most common hiding places: inside the toilet tank; under the mattress; in the freezer. He found nothing of value. There wasn't time to do a thorough search.

Stark hurried out and to his hotel. He packed his bags and made reservations on the next flight to Los Angeles.

CHAPTER 23

Interesting, but frankly not as dramatic as I'd hoped for," Edward Hancock said as Stark recounted the events in Thailand. "I wonder if there's any way to go higher up the chain."

"Find out who Webb was working for?"

"Exactly. Unfortunately, a dead man doesn't make as catchy a villain as a live one."

They were seated in Hancock's office in the grand Los Angeles Post building in downtown Los Angeles. It was sixty years old, making it among the oldest office buildings in town. The building had an eclectic mix of styles: heavy gray Greek columns; orange Spanish tile roofs; and Colonial windows and shutters. Hancock's penthouse office, with a spectacular view of City Hall and the civic center, was lined with framed front pages recounting major news stories of the twentieth century.

"What do you think that number is that you found in Webb's office?"

"A Swiss bank account. It has the right combination of letters and digits. It matches one of the sets of figures I got during my visit to the Red Diamond docks."

"There's an old newspaper axiom. Follow the money."

"Swiss accounts are tough to crack and there's a good chance that the effort will be detected."

"Do you have other paths of inquiry?"

"Yes. If you want to keep funding the investigation, I'm game," Stark said.

"What do you plan to do?" Hancock asked.

"I'd rather not say. You're protected if I do anything illegal. You can say you had no idea."

"And you don't have to worry about me accidentally blurting out your plans to someone."

"Exactly."

"Very good. By the way, Diana would never forgive me if I didn't ask you to call her," Hancock said. "I think she has a crush on you."

Waves crashed on the rocks, sending plumes of spray into the air. A hundred yards out, three wet-suited surfers tried to get their balance. Stark and Diana had been watching them for close to a half hour. What the surfers lacked in ability they made up for in determination.

About twenty feet off on either side of the couple stood muscular young men wearing loose Benetton shirts over gun-bulgy waistbands. Bodyguards, hired by Diana's brother, they trailed Diana the way Labrador retrievers followed their owners on the Malibu beach.

The warm midday sun was tempered by cool breezes off the Pacific. Gorgeous men and women paraded back and forth, wearing minimal amounts of skimpy, but expensive, clothing. For those who wanted to go a step farther, there was the nudist beach by Paradise Cove. But most preferred the barest illusion of modesty. There were a few minor celebrities on the beach, costars of TV shows, the director of a moderately successful film, a former Rams end. The big names were in the big houses in the hills above them, enjoying the same sun by the side of their swimming pools.

A strikingly beautiful blonde who resembled Christie Brinkley strutted by. She was wearing a skimpy maillot bathing suit, and her tanned skin was covered with goose bumps from the cold.

"Am I as pretty as she is?" Diana asked Stark.

"No. But I'm not as good-looking as the jock over there,"

Stark said, indicating a perfectly proportioned weightlifter sunbathing on a towel that said Gold's Gym. "They're bred to be like that. From all over the U.S., pretty boys and girls are told they'll be a star in Hollywood. They come here, fail, but spawn, and their children become beach gods and goddesses."

She grinned. "I'm glad I convinced Eddie to hire you."

"It was your idea?"

"That bum took credit? He was ranting and raving after I got back how he wanted to do something. I said hire you to investigate terrorism. Then he backed off. I told him I would if he didn't. I bet he's glad now he changed his mind. How about you come with me to dinner tonight?" she asked abruptly.

"Any place special?"

"There's a big dinner tonight. All kinds of political heavyweights. I can't do it without a friendly face."

"Okay."

"Super! You know what I'd love to do now?"

"What?"

"Practice aikido."

"Show me your stuff," Stark said.

She made as if she were going to undress, laughed, then went into a *hanmi*, an on guard position.

She did a forward roll, a backward roll, brushed the sand off, and did a few basic exercises.

"Not bad, not bad at all," Stark said, moving into a T-stance, feet at right angles, with one pointed forward, the other to the side. "Stance is the foundation. You need to be mobile." He moved back, forth, and sideways. "Also, able to protect yourself." He held his hands up, open, covering his center line.

He advanced, sliding his foot in the sand, showing her *irimi* (entering) and *tenkan* (turning) techniques.

"If you combine awareness with good evasive movements, you're halfway there." He blocked imaginary punches and kicks so smoothly and effortlessly he seemed to be gliding.

As he spoke, he did a *kata* form, based on two imaginary

assailants attacking. There was a flurry of kicks and punches, an armlock, spinning one opponent into the other, followed by a throw and a wristlock.

"Wow. That looks different than what I've been shown."

"It's jujitsu."

"I thought they only taught that in the back of comic books."

"It's what the founder of aikido studied. He softened it and added a spiritual component. The founder of judo was also a jujitsu man, who adapted it for sport."

The couple worked out slowly. Diana was clearly a beginner, but a talented one. He guided her through several moves.

The two bodyguards stared in fascination.

"Okay," Stark said to her. "Throw a slow right punch at my face."

She did. He leaned back, simultaneously brushing the hand aside with his left and giving her a little push on the shoulder. She stumbled and nearly fell.

"See. I don't need to use any strength," he said.

She swung again, with her left. Again he deflected gently, and nudged her.

She launched a flurry of spirited punches and kicks. Stark slapped them all aside. She tried to kick him in the groin. He caught her leg and lifted up a couple of inches, and she fell to the sand on her backside. He threw himself in the air, looking as if he would land on top of her, but broke his fall with his arms and knees. He planted a gentle kiss on her forehead.

Assured that she was uninjured, the bodyguards discreetly looked away.

"You've got a lot of spunk," Stark said to her. He had the same half smile on his face that he had had when the lesson began.

"You're not even breathing hard," she said.

"I only breathe hard when I'm making obscene phone calls," he said.

"I'll wait by the phone."

He kissed her again, this time on the lips.

"Reach out and touch someone, right?" he asked.

"Let your fingers do the walking." She pressed her body against his momentarily. He could feel her heat, smell her perfume. "Can you show me some more moves?" Diana asked.

"I think you've got all the moves you need," he said.

"Not those kinds."

"Okay. Just a few basics."

She clapped her hands like a little girl, then rose and got into a T-stance.

General Todd Grant folded the report he had withheld from CIA director Creange. He leaned against the railing, looking out over the East River. The tram to Roosevelt Island swung across the river toward the Yuppie-infested condos that dotted the narrow island.

With the general was a trim and dapper Japanese man, the defense attaché from the Washington embassy.

"You understand that me and the President are the only ones who have seen the completed analysis," Grant said.

"I understand." The Japanese, whose English was as perfect as his tailoring, found it painful when Americans mangled the language. He nearly corrected Grant to "the President and I."

Grant handed him the paper like a principal reluctantly presenting a diploma to a troublesome student. The defense attaché bowed slightly as he accepted it. He began reading.

Grant gazed out over the river.

"Is this true?" the defense attaché asked.

"Yes."

The attaché folded up the paper and slipped it into his jacket. "I will immediately see that this information reaches the prime minister. My country is grateful to you, General Grant."

"What are allies for," Grant said.

The defense attaché hurried off. Grant took out a cigar, went through the preparation ritual of dampening, slicing, and poking it. He lit up.

Mission accomplished, he thought.

Joggers regarded him contemptuously as he puffed contentedly on Cuba's finest.

Diana Hancock threw out her chest and patted the back of her head like Mae West. "You like what you see, big boy?"

She wore a low cut, black silk evening gown with red décolletage, revealing a generous amount of freckled flesh on her front and back. Her high hem bared long legs leading down to black high heels. She wore white gloves that rode all the way up to her elbows. A low slung beret covered her bad ear. She mixed youthful liveliness with womanly sophistication.

"You look stunning," Stark said.

"You're not so bad yourself," she said.

Stark wore a custom-made black tuxedo. The cummerbund had a Kevlar lining, making it bullet and knife resistant.

She looped her arm through his and tried grabbing his hand in a *kotegaishi* wristlock he had shown her. He let her grab, then countered, throwing her back onto her couch. Her dress hiked up high.

"Don't you know any groundwork?" she asked.

"I'll show you advanced techniques later," he said. "C'mon, we don't want to be late."

She got up and adjusted her outfit, pouting. They walked out to the limo. She flirted with Stark shamelessly while the two bodyguards trailed a few feet behind. She had the rich person's ability to completely ignore the help and act as if she were alone with Stark. He was more aware of the guards and the reason they were there.

Diana Hancock snuggled against him in the back of the limo. Her hand brushed across his groin, and he throbbed under her touch. She pretended it was an accident, but they both knew it wasn't.

He'd have to work hard to keep lust from clouding his awareness.

CHAPTER 24

The President stared out the window at the Rose Garden. His hands were clasped behind his back. It reminded CIA director Creange of photographs he had seen of JFK.

It was the middle of the night, the only time the President had free. There were bags under his eyes and the few wrinkles that he'd had at the beginning of his term had deepened. Sometimes when he moved, it seemed like the weight of office would crush him.

"You know, Teddy Roosevelt used to sneak out of the White House and jog," the President said. "He was the first to have full-time Secret Service protection. Of course he came into power because McKinley was shot."

When the President started telling historical anecdotes, Creange knew he had serious business on his mind.

"Dan, I heard you've been asking questions that are best not asked," the President finally said.

"What do you mean?" Creange asked respectfully.

"You know what I mean. I have to request that you drop it. General Grant knows what he is doing."

"I'm your director of Central Intelligence. Are you saying I'm not trusted enough to hear it?"

The President sighed. "There were certain systems put in operation before I came into office. Certain systems that can't be dismantled. They have a momentum all their own."

"Are you saying you can't control them?"

"I can. To some degree. But to some degree I'm like the boy riding the tiger. There's no getting off."

"Fire Grant. Clean house."

"Not so easy. You remember what happened when predecessors did that at the CIA. Rogue elephants like Wilson and Terpil. Disgruntled agents cranking out memoirs. Leaks to the press. Valuable expertise lost. The entire national security apparatus was jeopardized."

"Fire them," Creange repeated.

"Did you ever hear that quote from LBJ about Hoover? When asked why he didn't sack him, Johnson said 'I'd rather have him inside the tent pissing out, than outside pissing in.'"

"You're willing to let whatever it is go on?"

The President just stared out the window.

"Please, answer me," Creange said.

The President turned to face him. He looked on the verge of exhaustion and tears. "You can't understand what it's like being president. The power everyone sees. But there are restrictions no one talks about."

"What restrictions?"

The President fiddled with his tie pin.

"Is keeping information from your CIA director par for the course?" Creange asked, struggling not to raise his voice. "What's going on with this report Grant has about Japanese terrorism?"

"It's best this way. Surely you understand compartmentalization and need-to-know limitations."

"If I don't know what's going on, how can I give you proper advice?"

"It has to be that way, Dan. If you can't accept it . . ."

"You'll have my resignation on your desk in the morning."

"I'm sorry."

"I'm sorry too, Mr. President," Creange said coldly and marched from the room.

* * *

"If someone were to wipe out this room, the government of California would collapse," Diana Hancock whispered to Stark.

"I see a half-dozen important federal people too," Stark said, counting a supreme court judge, two congressmen, a junior senator, the FCC chairman, and the secretary of defense.

The party at the Bonaventure Hotel—which had been used as the backdrop for sci-fi films because of its ultramodern cylindrical glass towers—had taken over the largest ballroom. The gathering brought together a combination of glamour, big bucks, and power. Film stars, high-powered agents, financiers, politicos, studio execs, coke dealers.

Hancock moved smoothly through the crowd, wielding power, making money, as attractive as any actor.

"Look at him," Diana said admiringly. "Isn't he slick?"

"Very."

Edward would shake hands sincerely, exchange a few bon mots, and move on. The party was ostensibly to honor the venerable head of Universe Studios, who was retiring after fifty years. He had known most of the legends of Hollywood, and could recall the peccadillos and perversions of most of them. Rumors that he was writing his memoirs had frightened many old-timers.

Edward returned to his seat on the dais, all smiles. His wife, who had remained dutifully seated, spoke with him briefly. His fixed smile remained in place.

Right before the waiters began bringing out the meals on wagon wheel–size silver trays, Hancock was buttonholed by General Todd Grant. Hancock's pleased expression cracked. Shock, anger, and fear passed across his face before he composed himself. Stark was too far away to hear what was being said.

During the meal, Hancock was restless, fidgety. The speech he gave afterward—the dinner was in the form of a "celebrity roast"—was lackluster.

"I wonder what's wrong," Diana commented. "Usually Edward has more charisma than a revivalist preacher."

"Have any of his papers done exposés on the military recently?" Stark asked.

"I don't think so. Why?"

"Just curious."

The studio president's speech was a rambling diatribe against MBAs turning Hollywood into pure business and losing the sense of fun that he and the other ruthless studio heads had. He received hearty, insincere applause. Then the frenzied table-hopping resumed.

Stark sidled within a few feet when he saw Grant accost Hancock again.

"Remember what I told you," Grant was saying.

Hancock bobbed his head.

Grant continued, "DeVille must—"

"Darling, it's so great to see you. I've been meaning to talk all night." A corpulent agent with a thick beard had pushed his way to a woman right near Stark. Stark recognized the woman as the mistress of a drug czar in a recent cop film.

The agent was blathering so loudly, Stark couldn't hear a word Grant was saying.

"You deserve better billing," the agent said, after gushing about her last performance. "Leave William Morris. Their film people haven't gotten off their butts since D.W. Griffith. We'll make better deals. I know two studios who would love to have you on a multipicture deal."

The actress looked distinctly unimpressed. "That's nice."

Stark shifted positions to get nearer to Hancock. But there was no way to do it without being obvious.

Hancock slunk back to the dais, working the crowd. But clearly his mind wasn't on it. Stark followed Grant as he made his way to the coat check room. Grant stopped for a minute and spoke with one of the congressmen, a hawk on the Armed Services Committee who always gave the Pentagon what it wanted. The two men vowed to go fly fishing soon.

As Grant handed in his claim check, Stark moved in.

"A pleasure to meet you, General Grant," Stark said, offering his hand. "My name's Robert Stark."

Grant shook his hand and smiled a noncommittal political smile. "Nice to meet you."

The girl behind the counter handed Grant his tan coat. He gave her a wink and a generous tip. She smiled and pocketed the money. Grant turned to go.

"We have a mutual friend," Stark said. "Jerry DeVille."

Grant stopped and turned back to Stark. "What makes you think I know DeVille?"

"Everyone in the defense industry knows Jerry," Stark said. "Of course some people know him better than others." Stark winked at Grant. Grant looked around nervously. "I don't know what you mean. Who are you, Mr. Stark?"

"Just a concerned taxpayer. DeVille's exploits interest me. I've been looking into them."

"What have you found?"

"You'll have to wait and see. I'm going to be selling my story to Hancock. It might even sell as many papers as the story 'Elvis's UFO Love Slave Finds Cancer Cure.'"

Grant frowned. "You should clear your writing with my office. There are matters of utmost importance to our national security."

"How about your personal security?"

Grant's wife appeared at his elbow. "Honey, we're waiting."

Grant nodded. "Mr. Stark, be careful. For the country. And yourself."

He turned and marched away.

CHAPTER 25

A fine date you turned out to be," Diana Hancock said as Stark returned to the table.

"Business before pleasure."

"Well, at least you weren't talking to any of the actresses here. Have you ever seen so many face-lifts in one room?" Diana asked. "I don't want to go back to my brother's house. Let's do something wild."

"Tweedledum and Tweedledee won't approve."

One bodyguard was at their table, on the far side. The other was one table away. Considering that none of the government officials, corporate leaders, or film stars had security people with them, the guards seemed to be overkill. They had enjoyed themselves spotting stars. If any celebrity had tried to attack Diana, they would've been right on top of him.

Stark and Diana sauntered out. White stretch limos picking up passengers were three deep at the curb. The valet took Stark's ticket and retrieved his four-year-old Toyota.

"Hey, man, what do you got under the hood?" the valet asked admiringly.

"A few little modifications."

They climbed in. Stark flipped open the hidden electronic sensor panel under the dash and checked that no one had added any bugs or bombs. The LEDs blinked all clear. He drove off. The bodyguards trailed in their Camaro.

"How about we get rid of my chaperones?" Diana suggested. "Can you outrace them?"

"Without shifting into second gear," Stark said. "But I've got a better way."

They drove up to Mulholland Drive and pulled into a spot near Coldwater Canyon overlooking the San Fernando Valley. The lights of thousands of tract homes twinkled in the darkness. In the distance, the mass of the Santa Susana mountains was blacker than the night sky.

Stark shut the engine. Diana slid to the edge of her leather bucket seat and put her hand on Stark's thigh. "I like your idea, but they're still there," she said, peering out the back window.

He had positioned his car near the edge of the lot. He shut the switch to the dome light. It was dark. Around them parked cars were steamed up and gently rocking on their suspensions.

He exhaled heavily a few times. The windows began to fog. Diana did the same. On the fogged glass she traced "DH & RS", and encircled it with a heart. She giggled and swiftly wiped it off.

The windows were quickly fogged over.

Stark's side of the car was away from the bodyguards. He opened his door a couple of feet and slid out to the pavement. "Follow me."

She climbed over the seat and crawled out. Bent double, they hustled away. Once they were in a grove of trees, he stood upright.

"You feel like walking?" he asked.

She kicked off her high heels. "Where to?"

"One of the fire roads leads near my apartment."

The fire road was a dirt trail, just wide enough for a vehicle. It was a moonless night but city lights reflecting off the clouds providing more than enough illumination. Traffic noises were muted by the trees.

"I feel like Adam and Eve," she said.

"Oh, that reminds me, watch out for rattlesnakes."

She froze.

"Just kidding. As long as you don't go rooting in crevices or walking quickly and quietly in the brush, you're fine."

She put her shoes back on and stayed even closer to him.

She chuckled. "I was just thinking of what those goons will do in the morning when they discover the empty car. You know, one of them came on to me."

"Very unprofessional. But understandable."

She turned to face him. They kissed, long and slow, bodies pressed together. The warmth of their contact made her realize how chilly a night it was.

"How far to your place?"

"Just over the ridge."

Stark's Los Angeles pied-à-terre was a one-bedroom cottage tucked into the Hollywood hills. It had a narrow swimming pool for doing laps, weathered cedar exterior, and a large living room with a working fireplace. The cottage looked larger than it was since he had few furnishings.

Stark shut off the alarm and gave her a quick tour.

"What about those advanced mat techniques?" she asked.

He picked her up and carried her into the bedroom. He laid her down gently on the king-size platform bed.

"Mnnnnnn," Diana said, arching and stretching out on the bed. "If I had known you could do that I would've left the dinner hours ago."

"You mean it was more fun than listening to recycled Friar Club gags?" he asked.

She nipped his shoulder.

"Or eating rubber chicken?"

She bit down harder.

"What's the matter, kid, they don't feed you at home?" he asked.

"I'm starving," she said.

"Let's see what I've got left over."

"Not for food," she said.

"I know what you meant," he said, taking her mouth from his shoulder and pulling it up to his.

Keeping Saito's admonition in mind made their lovemaking that much more overwhelming. He focused completely on his pleasure, and hers, performing the most basic of acts with an intensity that shut out all else.

"All right, now I'm starving for food," she said, panting. An hour had passed though neither of them were aware of the time. Her tanned body glistened with a dew-like sheen of sweat.

"I'll see what I can scavenge up." Since he never knew when he'd be in the house, his cupboard was relatively bare. He put a couple of TV dinners in the microwave, chilled a bottle of chardonnay, and set candles on the table.

"I think I saw this on a TV dinner commercial," she said as she came out of the bedroom, gloriously naked.

"Was the actress dressed quite the way you are?"

"No."

"I suspected as much."

They ate, sipped the wine, and made postcoital silly talk.

"Is this a service you provide all your clients?" she asked.

"It's in the contract. Lots of lovemaking and TV dinners. Wait until Edward sees the bill."

They sat on the sofa that faced the big picture window. The sun was beginning to glow over the ridgeline.

"Do you feel like talking?" he asked.

She burrowed against him. "I'm done whining and wimping out. For a while there, I was really pitying myself. I felt as if I were doing good and had no right to be punished." Knowing you were around got me through a real dark time."

He put his arm over her shoulder and squeezed. "When you had to function, you provided the key clues that allowed me to identify Nakamura."

She lay back and beamed. "I hadn't really thought about it. That was pretty tough, wasn't it?"

"Damn straight. Now, if you're up to it, I'd like to review the whole incident."

She stiffened. "I've been through it so many times."

"I know. One more debriefing though. I think you might be more relaxed, better able to recall details. Like exactly what happened before the raiders came. Did it seem as though anyone at the camp was directing them?"

"No."

"Fine. What I want you to do is lean back on the sofa. Half shut your eyes. Think of your body immersed in warm water. Relax."

"Are you trying to hypnotize me into being your sex slave for life?" she asked. "Because you don't need hypnosis."

"More of that later. Just relax. You're safe here."

"I know that."

"Okay. Think of that warm water. It's lapping at your toes. You're in complete control. The soothing water is rising over your calves. Now your knees."

Stark continued softly repeating soothing words until she was nearly dozing. Then he began gentle questioning.

"Did you overhear anything as to why you were chosen?"

"No."

"Ever any mention of who they were working for?"

"No."

"Japanese Red Army?"

"No."

He rattled off a dozen names of terrorist groups active in Asia and then all over the world. He got a groggy "no" each time.

"Was there ever any mention of other terrorist acts?"

"Uh, yes. Kenji said something about a bombing a few days earlier."

Cyprus, Stark thought. He asked a few questions along that line, but she didn't have any additional information.

"Did you hear anyone else's voice while you were blind-folded?" he asked. "Anyone bring them supplies, orders, food?"

"No. Wait. That's right. There was someone else. He sounded British. No. More like that actor who plays 'Crocodile Dundee.'"

"Australian?"

"Yes. He was the boss. Kenji didn't like him but he obeyed him. Kenji was scared of him. The Australian was the one who actually cut off my ear."

She shuddered. She was wide awake, bolt upright. Stark hugged her as she trembled.

"I can feel his hand holding my head. There was a slight smell of cologne or aftershave. Sweet, like roses. Then I felt pressure on my ear. No pain, just pressure. Then warmth. I realized it was blood. Then I felt the pain." She sobbed. "Oh, my god, oh, my god."

He held her until she stopped trembling. The sun was nearly up when she regained her composure.

"I'd better get dressed," she said.

"What about all that talk about being my sex slave for life?" he asked.

"I, I don't know. I feel kind of weak."

"Well, let's see if a little distraction works."

He extended a hand and pulled her down to the thick Oriental carpet on the floor. He held her tenderly for a few minutes. Then affection turned to passion, and they both let go.

CHAPTER 26

Stark spent the morning playing with the computer in his Century City office. He had programmed it to search for an Australian or New Zealand-born sniper, still active in terrorism, the mercenary world, or organized crime. There were about thirty entries.

While he was on the computer, he read through the wire service reports.

A load of AK-47s and Skorpions had been found cached in southern Thailand, near Songkhla. There had been terrorist activity there in the past from Muslim separatist groups who had bases just across the border in Malaysia. But this time a dead man found at the scene was identified as a suspected Japanese Red Army member.

Stark used his secure line to call CIA headquarters in Langley, Virginia. He was told that director Dan Creange had quit to pursue private matters.

He called Creange at home.

"I don't know what you're involved in, Bob, but watch your posterior."

"Does this have anything to do with your sudden retirement?"

"Yes."

The abrupt response made it clear Creange did not care to elaborate.

"I wanted to know about that load of equipment I asked about," Stark said. "Something turned up in the news that seems similar."

"I saw a report before I left. It was the same."

"That news is worse than being stung by forty-seven scorpions."

"Huh? Oh, yes."

"Do you have any job possibilities?" Stark asked. "HSA could always use someone with your expertise."

"Thanks, but no thanks. I've got a few offers. But for now I'm going to catch up on fishing upstate."

"Stay in touch."

"Again, Robert, this is a matter of national security. I think we're in trouble. The country, that is. Some people have the President's ear and are feeding him dangerous garbage.

"I'll do what I can."

"But do it carefully."

His secretary buzzed him almost immediately with another call. A furious Edward Hancock was on the line.

"You're fired," Hancock bellowed.

Even though the voice was coming through a phone receiver, it had a powerful resonance. Stark held the receiver away from his ear.

"What you did last night was grossly irresponsible," Hancock said. "Those guards were to protect my sister. If anything had happened to her, it would've been entirely your fault."

"What I did was unpredictable. Which is the best defense against any attack."

"I don't care. You're fired."

"You said that already."

"I don't like your insolence."

"Whose insolence do you like?"

"I can make it very hard for you to get work, Mr. Stark. Perhaps I'll commission a series on antiterrorism consultants, the good and the bad."

"Don't forget the ugly," Stark said.

Hancock slammed down the phone.

Stark buzzed his secretary. Gina was a stunning blonde with a knack for faking voices. She could be a British secretary or a Parisian model, a German clerk or a Brooklyn housewife, with equal ease. She had been a successful con woman before her arrest and subsequent employment with HSA.

She sauntered in and perched on his desk, revealing a dazzling stretch of perfectly sculpted legs.

"You've already gotten three calls today from Diana Hancock," Gina said, holding up a sheaf of papers and speaking in a stiff, upper crust voice. "Buffy and Muffy at the country club will begin to talk." Gina switched back to her regular voice. "Is she why you have that smug expression on your face?"

"Diana and I have a purely physical relationship," Stark said. "Cheap sex in motel rooms on Sunset Boulevard. Orgies up in the hills. You know how it is."

"No. How is it?"

"Can you ring up Les in New York for me? And I need a final bill for Edward Hancock. But before you do"—he handed her the list of snipers. "See how many of these can be eliminated."

She took the paper. "Just when the conversation gets interesting. This is a lot of people."

"But they're all in a high risk category. Half of them have probably gone to that great big Outback in the sky."

"No problemo," she said. "And if you and Diana want a threesome . . ." Gina bounced away.

One of these days, Stark thought, I'm going to take the bait. And probably regret it for the rest of my life.

His connection to Halliwell cut short his musings.

"What did you do to piss Hancock off?" Halliwell asked over the phone.

"It's a long story, Les. But don't worry. I'm not giving up."

"What does that mean?"

"I'm going to continue investigating."

"Who's paying? Let me guess. It's another one of your *pro bonos,*" Halliwell said. "We need you around the office.

There're a half-dozen clients who want security surveys. Business has picked up. We're stretched thin."

Stark didn't say anything about Creange's concern.

"Shit," Halliwell said. "I know what a stubborn SOB you are."

"If you prefer, I could go back to Japan."

"No, no, no. Just don't piss off too many people."

"Me? I'm the very pillar of politeness. You know I make friends wherever I go."

CHAPTER 27

Even before the 1960s bloodshed in the Belgian Congo, Belgium was a center of mercenary activity. Several of the top merc and arms brokers were based there. It's got a central European location, with embassies from virtually every Third World and Eastern Bloc country in Brussels, and there are excellent transportation, manufacturing, and communications setups.

Belgian bankers are as discreet as the Swiss. Most residents speak at least three languages. Antwerp, the fifth largest port in the world with ninety kilometers of docks, claims the fastest cargo turnaround time. The state-owned arms company—Fabrique National, better known as FN—not only manufactures weapons, but provides shipping and handling of other manufacturers' weapons. FN's aggressive salesmanship makes them preeminent in the field.

It was a fitting country to host the show. Everything from P-38 can openers for C rations to armored personnel carriers (APCs) and rocket-equipped helicopters. There were no vendors of the really high ticket items—long range bombers, AWACS, or naval vessels—in attendance.

The show was held in two converted airplane hangars near the international airport on the outskirts of Antwerp. From the distance, it looked like any other convention or trade show. Only on getting closer could a visitor see that it was machine gun equipped jeeps and antipersonnel mines, and not RVs or antiques that were displayed.

There were booths selling subscriptions to *Soldier of Fortune, Jane's* and *Aviation Week* and *Space Technology,* other publications with full glossy pictures of the latest carbines from FN. Models in skimpy outfits demonstrated how to field strip an Armalite AR-18 assault rifle. The Russians, with the new *perestroika* slickness, had equally striking young women touting Tokarevs. Third World generals in gaudy uniforms climbed over Sikorski helicopters like insects on a fresh kill.

But the real feverish deal making went on away from the main exhibits. When General X bought a new load of Walther submachine guns, he could unload his old stock of Soviet PPS submachine guns, which dated back to World War II. The old guns would be designated as scrap and the general would take possession for pennies on the dollar. He would then sell them to another, poorer nation, and keep the profits, or maybe split them with a corrupt minister or two.

There was a lucrative market in spare parts, and like American automobiles, the parts totaled up could cost more than a new weapon. Countries like Iran, rich with American gear left over from the Shah but unable to get spare parts, would pay dearly for every strut and firing pin.

Attendance at the smaller shows had increased steadily over the years. The Paris Air Show, which was the premier armament event, had grown too big. The Lockheeds and Interarmcos had squeezed out the small dealers. Third World potentates could go and drool like boys at a luxury sports car show but, with a few notable exceptions, unless the superpowers funded the buying spree, they'd have to stick to cheaper items.

In the corner of one of the hangars was a partitioned-off section where hourly lectures were offered by manufacturers and military experts. The theme of the show was "Small is Better," and the keynote address was by noted military tactician Paul McCarthy.

"A present day platoon equipped with the proper armaments can put out as much firepower as most World War II battalions," McCarthy said to the crowd of nearly one hundred who had chosen to leave the selling floor frenzy for an hour.

"Small terrorist groups have shown how effective they can be against larger, better armed countries. Recent history has afforded a number of more conventional military models as well. The Vietcong guerrillas versus the best-equipped fighting force in the world."

"Fuckin' right," piped up a former Marine captain who now served as a security consultant in Saudi Arabia.

"And there was Chad's blitz on Libya, where Toyotas equipped with machine guns outfought the expensive firepower that Qaddafi had accumulated." He continued to cite examples, including the success of small Iranian gunboats and the failures of supercarriers.

"It is my belief that this trend will continue, and the smart military leaders will adjust and adapt. For example, guns using lighter ammunition. What you sacrifice in knockdown power, you pick up in the number of rounds your soldiers can carry.

"And shoulder carried missiles will continue to be a determining factor. Look at what the Stinger did to the Soviets in Afghanistan. Prior to the shoulder launched rocket's introduction, the Russian HIND helicopter controlled the landscape. Due to the exposed nature of the Afghani terrain, *moujahadeen* were picked off like sitting ducks. Shortly after the CIA began passing out the Stingers, the Soviets decided to abandon ship."

"No balls Commies," the Marine captain muttered loudly. It was clear he had had too many beers. A couple of GRU men a few seats away glared at him. He gave them the finger.

The session ended, and was followed by naval tactician John Clark, who offered his analysis of "Trends on the High Seas."

Robert Stark and Pedro Quesada rose from their seats and drifted toward the door.

"Don't get me wrong, I'm having a good time, but I don't really understand why we're here," Quesada said.

"The sniper who killed Nakamura in prison was a world-class shot. Of the snipers currently working, five are going to be competing. Plus I hope we see some of the players in the arms to terrorists business."

"You sniff around the right people long enough, and something's bound to happen. Right?"

"Right. If nothing else, you get to compete."

Quesada, who was a crack shot and better than Stark with a long rifle, had entered the competition. As the two men headed toward the door, they picked up sales brochures as they ambled along.

"Les will love this," Quesada said, holding a full color pamphlet with a picture of a state-of-the-art infrared detection system. "I already sent him a postcard with a picture of the new minigun."

"He's liable to be on the next flight over." The two old buddies made amiable chatter, all the time scanning surrounding faces. They recognized several front men who purchased weapons for the black market, forging end user certificates when necessary to get governmental approval. They logged in who was talking to whom. Was the Libyan overly friendly with the Turk? Did the Chinese seem more than casually interested in the French helicopters?

Gerard DeVille was also present, but he had skipped the lecture. He too was deal making. Like a crapshooter with a hot set of dice, others were gravitating to him.

As Stark and Quesada rounded a corner, a moonfaced, pale man with a cigarette dangling from his lip sidled up. Stark slipped into a fighting stance before the man was within arm's reach.

"I know you," the smoker said to Stark. "You're Alex O'Dell."

It was the cover name Stark had used during a CIA assignment in Malaysia.

"That was a long time ago," Stark said truthfully, relaxing a little when he recognized the smoker. He was a small-time hustler, always on the fringes, looking to make a big score. Although there was no physical similarity, somehow he reminded Stark of Peter Lorre.

"I'm Nance. You looking to buy something? Or sell?"

"Just looking. What's your interest?"

"Deals. I know everybody. I've lived in Belgium for five years now. Would you like a tour?"

Stark turned to Quesada, who shrugged. They had a few hours before the shooting match.

Stark introduced Quesada as Juan Sanchez.

"Bay of Pigs, right?" Nance asked.

Quesada didn't respond.

"Okay, okay. No questions."

Nance led them toward the door. As he passed each table, he cited the limitations of each gun: which jammed, which took too long for delivery, which was inaccurate. He built up his qualifications as someone who could get a variety of quasi-legal or illegal jobs done.

Nance's car was waiting outside. He donned dark Carrera sunglasses and black pigskin driving gloves. The glamorous accessories didn't match his battered, eight-year-old Fiat. Nance drove around the city, keeping up a well-informed spiel.

"The town's famous for diamonds, the docks, and the painter named Rubens who had a thing for fat ladies," Nance said. "We can go look at paintings. Or go to the Maritime Museum at the Steen." Nance pointed to a fortress-like building in the distance. "The zoo. Twenty-five acres. They try not to use cages. They keep the pythons in by blasts of cold air. And the birds by clever use of lighting.

"If you'd like another kind of wildlife, they've got friendly girls working the hotels near Central Station. I can guarantee you a clean, good time."

"You're not just doing this as part of the local welcome wagon," Stark said when they stopped for cappuccino and pastries at a sidewalk cafe.

"No. I thought it a good way to get you away from those vultures," Nance said. "What are you really looking for? AK-47s, I can get those. If you prefer, Ithaca shotguns, or Steyr Mannlichers, or H & Ks. TOW missiles, Blowpipes, Sam-7s. Seventy-two hours notice, no more, I promise.

Armored vehicles take longer, as do the helicopters. More people have to be bribed to get them through the channels."

"Honestly, I'm just here to watch my friend shoot," Stark said, nodding toward Quesada. "Do you know anything about the competition? Who's the smart money on?"

"It will be close this year. Schick, Palumbo, and Golan are considered to be the three top shots. But there's a guy named Rose who has surprised people in the past."

Schick and Golan were purely target shooters, whose names did not turn up on Stark's list of guns-for-hire. Palumbo was a former U.S. Army Ranger who had worked for several years in the Mideast, training guards for the oil company pipelines. "No one knows too much about Rose," Nance said. "He travels a lot. I've heard he's done merc work, some munitions supply. Never any big deals."

"What's his nationality?" Stark asked.

"I think British. He's vague about his background and no one presses him."

"He have a left or right bias?" Quesada asked.

"No. He works for Communists or Fascists without prejudice."

"I meant in his shooting?"

"Not that I know of. As I said, not much is known about him. He was in SAS. A real cold-blooded one."

"What sort of gun does he use?"

"A customized XM-21."

"How about Palumbo?"

"A Remington 700."

Stark glanced at his watch. "We better head back. You haven't made any money off of us," he said to Nance.

"Not today. But tomorrow is another day. People will have seen me talking to Alex O'Dell of the CIA. It will be good for my reputation."

"I prefer to keep a low profile," Stark said.

"Of course, of course," Nance said.

Stark had no doubt that his cover name and history would be known by half the attendees within a short time.

* * *

The target competition was held in a large field about ten miles out of Brussels. The field was shrouded from the road by a cluster of trees. At the far end was a low cliff with a stone quarry cut in the side. The targets were set up with the cliff as a backdrop.

Small tables were provided for the shooters to rest their elbows on. Some used small sandbags, monopods, bipods or tripods. The rifles were as diverse as the competitors, with most major manufacturers represented. All the guns had been custom modified, making them worth thousands of dollars.

There were fifty men and eight women signed up. In the first elimination round—where competitors had to put three slugs inside a four-inch circle from two hundred yards—more than half the competitors were knocked out. Quesada made the cut, but was eliminated in the next round, where it was three slugs in a two-inch circle at three hundred yards.

He dolefully cleaned his weapon—an M-21, the sniper rifle issued to U.S. Special Forces—while he and Stark watched the rest of the competition.

Soon it was down to the four men Nance had named: Schick, Palumbo, Golan, and Rose. Now the crowd was whistling and humming approval after each shot. Spectators watched the shooter for his form, then used spotting scopes to see where the shot had pierced the target even before the judges announced it.

Palumbo was eliminated at six hundred yards, Golan at seven hundred. At one thousand yards, Schick placed three in a two-inch circle. Rose had two in the circle, and one nibbling the edge.

"I've got an idea," Stark said, edging away from Quesada to where Nance was trying to charm a squat Belgian man. Nance gave him a big welcome, the ubiquitous cigarette dangling from his lips.

"I thought of something you can get me," Stark said, as the Belgian drifted away and he and Stark were alone.

"Diamonds? You have a girlfriend who'd like?"

"No. Can you get me the bullets and targets of the four finalists?"

Nance regarded him quizzically.

"I'd like to give them to my friend. As a souvenir."

"I know one of the judges. Maybe. But I don't know how much it will cost."

"You get it and I'll settle with you. One thing. Make sure each target and bullet is carefully marked."

Nance nodded and bounced away.

"What was that about?" Quesada asked when Stark returned.

"I saw the way you handled your weapon," Stark said, as the two men walked back to where vans waited to take them into town. "And the other pros. Lovingly. Would you compete with any other gun?"

"No."

"I'm thinking that if one of the shooters is our killer, he used the same rifle that he did on Nakamura. I'm betting it's Rose."

"Why?"

"I recognized him."

"From where?"

"Outside the apartment of the gunrunner who was murdered in Bangkok."

"No shit?"

"Another thing. Diana said the man who lopped off her ear was Australian. His accent isn't very thick, but I'd bet you a Vegemite sandwich he was born within a kangaroo hop of Sydney."

CHAPTER 28

"Bloody bastards, you should've won," the former SAS sergeant said as he downed his sixth pint of Newcastle Brown Ale. He had been a handsome youth, but barfights and too much alcohol had wrecked his features.

Willy Rose shrugged. Normally he left immediately after competing. But several old mates from his SAS regiment were at the show. They dragged him along as they went drinking and whoring. Rose, who prided himself on being a loner, had to admit to himself that he enjoyed seeing them.

They caught up on old times and badmouthed the winner of the shooting competition. The ex-SAS sergeant had been a judge, and he said it busted him up to have to give the award to someone else.

"It doesn't mean anything," Rose said, though the five thousand dollars in gold would've been nice.

"Righto," the ex-sergeant said. "Whether you can put a bloody hole in a piece of paper don't mean diddlysquat. It's can you look down the barrel at a bloke and pull the trigger." The ex-sergeant mimicked holding a rifle, aimed it at a noisy German a few tables over, and pulled the imaginary trigger. The ex-sergeant belched. "Damned Krauts." He slouched over and toyed with his drink.

"You did the Regiment proud," another SASer said to

Rose. "Remember Captain Duncan. He was one crack shot, wasn't he?"

"Sadistic bastard," the drunk piped up. "What a bunch of lunatics. Just like those here. Like the nut who wanted the targets."

Rose perked up. "What?"

"This little twit slipped me a hundred pounds to swipe the targets for him. And the bullets from the backstop. Said he wanted them as a souvenir."

Rose's gaze was so intense it was like a blast of cold water on the drunk. He straightened up.

"Would you recognize him?" Rose asked, his tone as cold as his eyes.

"I suppose so."

"Let's find him."

"Lemme finish my drink."

Rose grabbed the drunk's arm and pulled him off the seat. The other SASers watched as Rose double-timed their former sergeant away.

An hour later, the drunk spotted Nance and pointed him out to Rose.

"What's this about?" the former sergeant asked.

"Just don't mention it to anyone else. Or that I know."

"Why not?"

Rose smiled at him. The teeth-baring expression ensured the sergeant's silence. The grin had nothing to do with mirth.

Rose drifted over to where Nance was trying to hustle a dashikied black.

"I can get end user certificates forged," Nance was saying. "You pick the country you want. It'll take only a couple of days."

"I don't need them," the black said imperiously.

"Sounds interesting," Rose interjected.

"Who are you?" Nance asked, turning to Rose. The black drifted away, glad to escape Nance's relentless sales pitch.

"I represent South African interests," Rose said. "We've been having a problem getting what we need."

"You're embargoed."

"That's right. But I've got a suitcase full of Krugerrands that I'm ready to open. If you can provide the goods."

"I can get whatever you need," Nance said, glad at last his luck had changed. The conference thus far had been a bust. His best deal had been the four hundred dollars he'd hustled off Robert Stark.

They went back to Rose's hotel room. The Australian locked the door behind them. While Nance was gazing around the room, Rose slid a flat, six-inch steel knife from his hidden forearm sheath.

"About that——" Nance began.

Rose slammed him against the wall and put the needle-sharp tip to his throat.

"Who did you give the targets to?"

When Nance regained his breath, he gulped, "No, no need for the knife. It's no secret. O'Dell. Alex O'Dell. CIA. His friend was competing. He gave them to him."

"Who was his friend?" Rose asked, the point drawing a pinprick of blood on Nance's Adam's apple.

"The big Mexican with one arm. Juan something or other."

Rose sensed Nance was telling the truth. He let up the pressure. Nance clutched his throat.

"Get out," Rose growled. "And if you warn O'Dell, I'll have your eyeballs for breakfast."

Nance raced from the room.

DeVille was closing a few final deals. There was a certain desperation on the final day, with many suppliers willing to unload goods at half the price they had initially asked for. He bought medium-size loads from several sources, rather than take a large load from anyone. As in any industry, gossip traveled quickly. He tried to make it seem as if he were buying and selling, not buying and accumulating for his Thai warehouse.

Rose spotted him talking to a florid faced salesman for Omnipol, the Czechoslovakian arms company. DeVille was casually animated, the Czech sullen. After a few minutes, they shook hands and the Czech stomped away.

Rose strolled by DeVille.

"We need to speak," Rose whispered.

DeVille nodded acknowledgment. Rose wended his way toward the men's room. DeVille followed a few paces behind, pausing occasionally to greet people.

Rose was combing his hair in the bathroom mirror when DeVille entered.

"We've got a problem," Rose said, rapidly outlining what had happened.

A man came in and used a urinal. Rose and DeVille didn't speak until he exited.

"Describe them," DeVille said.

"A big Hispanic, used the name Juan Sanchez. A good marksman, he was in the competition. About fifty, 180 centimeters, sixteen stone, mustache. His friend was mid-forties, about 185 centimeters tall, fourteen stone, clean shaven, dark hair, well built. Named Alex O'Dell. Nance said O'Dell had been CIA."

"I have several contacts I can check."

"Let me know."

"I told you not to enter that competition," DeVille said as he strode from the room.

It was true. But Rose had wanted the visibility. His relationship with DeVille had taken a downturn. If he had to, it wouldn't be easy finding a new employer. His work for DeVille was such a tightly guarded secret, and Rose had been doing it for so long, that he couldn't offer much in the way of credentials.

Rose was the perfect man to go in, supply the underdog and stir up trouble. DeVille would approach the reigning powers and offer hardware to suppress the insurrection. There were always two parties ready to war with each other, long-standing hatreds festering under the surface. Tamils and Sinhalese, Hindus and Sikhs, Muslims and Jews, Greeks and Turks.

They had quarreled previously over the Nakamura setup.

DeVille had been angry that the Japanese held the girl so near to the hidden base. Rose pointed out that it was a hundred kilometers, most of it jungle, between Chiang Mai and the arsenal. Not that Rose even knew exactly where the underground base was. DeVille was a secretive sod.

Rose had always been convinced that the Frog would go far. Now he was being rewarded. Rose was very close to becoming a millionaire himself. He'd put up with DeVille for a while longer. But he'd be sure to get out before DeVille decided to fire him.

One of Rose's first tasks had been to terminate his predecessor. With a .45, not a pink slip. With what Rose knew about DeVille's operations, he had no doubt he'd get the same retirement bonus.

DeVille used the scrambler phone in his jet to call General Todd Grant at the Defense Intelligence Agency.

"There was a CIA man named Alex O'Dell. I suspect he is the one who has been making a nuisance of himself," DeVille said, offering the description of Stark. "He was with a one-armed Hispanic who used the name Juan Sanchez." DeVille gave the brief description of Quesada.

"I'll have them run it by the brain," Grant said.

The massive Cray supercomputer took less than a minute to review the hundreds of thousands of intelligence community players logged into its memory. It spat out Stark's and Quesada's names.

Grant got back the eyes only report, read the information, muttered a curse, and fed the paper into his office shredder.

Stark called Japanese Police Captain Okada while waiting for his New York flight at the airport on the outskirts of Brussels.

"Would your lab people be willing to run a ballistics test on a few bullets?" Stark asked.

"This relates to the matter you left Japan for?" Okada asked.

"Yes."

"Perhaps it would be best not," Okada said. "The case has

become quite controversial. Sasaki is using it as an example of weakness."

"How?"

"His front men say Nakamura was a Japanese citizen murdered before any proof of terrorist activities was brought forth. They claim the Thais are deliberately slandering us at the behest of the Communist Chinese. His politicians are calling for aggressive financial retaliation." Okada cleared his throat. "Your own FBI actually is much better for such matters. We don't have as many problems with firearms here as your country does."

FBI agent Steve Hodel made it clear that he wasn't thrilled to see Stark. Hodel, known as a prima donna, but good enough that the Bureau put up with it, had met Stark ten years ago, on a kidnapping case. Stark had rescued a hostage by illegal means, and allowed Hodel to take credit for the safe return. It had been mutually beneficial. Since then, they had cooperated on several cases. Hodel was currently assigned to an organized crime squad in New York. The two men met down by the waterfront, near where Hodel had a stakeout on a restaurant favored for meetings by a corrupt longshoremen's union official.

"Son of a bitch sits inside eating steak tartare and I got to piss into a bottle in my car," Hodel complained.

"But you know you're fighting for truth, justice, and the American way."

"Give me a veal scallopini with a big bowl of pasta and I'd be half inclined to join the mob," Hodel said cynically. "You must want something or you wouldn't be slumming like this."

Stark took out the slug from Rose's gun. "Can you get a match on this with a bullet the Thai government has?"

"Sure. Simple as pie. I'll just fly over there, fly back, get them to run it through the lab without a case number, and have the answer for you in an hour."

"I know it's not easy."

"That's putting it mildly."

"But you can do it?"

"This damned physical surveillance is taking up all my time. We've been trying to get a bug in there for weeks. A couple of times we got telephone repair people inside, but the wiseguys had it swept within hours."

"Let me guess. Then you tried health inspectors."

"Building inspectors," Hodel muttered.

"Your imagination astounds me. Were they wearing white socks?"

"If I want comedy, I'll listen to Garry Shandling. We've tried making like customers, but they watch any stranger like a hawk. I'm about ready to say fuck it."

"I didn't think FBI agents were allowed to curse."

"Fuck that. Think you can do it?"

"Call your bugger."

The electronics whiz was a nondescript man who would easily be mistaken for an insurance company clerk.

"How long do you need?" Stark asked.

"Three minutes," the agent said confidently.

"Let's do it."

"What are you going to do?" Hodel asked.

"Have a drink," Stark said.

It was dark inside the bar and it took a few minutes for Stark's eyes to adjust. The place was furnished in mahogany, with brass rails and plushly upholstered booths. No California ferns here, it was a real meat and potatoes joint.

Stark went straight to the bar and ordered a Rob Roy. He hated the drink, which made it easier to sip slowly.

The bugging specialist entered and sat a few seats away at the bar. Both he and Stark were watched carefully by the staff.

Stark swayed slightly on his chair, pretending to be tipsy. The bartender eyed him, but served him another drink. Stark managed to covertly spill most of it on the floor at his feet. He took a mouthful of the free peanuts from the bar and chewed them.

He spotted the longshoremen's union official being attended to by servile waiters. The official was eating with an elderly man who Stark recognized as the boss of the Queens crime family. He had a "who me" kind of smile, and looked like a kindly grandfather. In his younger days, he was believed responsible for the deaths of fifteen individuals. Nowadays, he just ordered murders, and raised tomato plants.

Stark got up from his seat and wandered toward the table. He carried half a drink and had a slight stagger.

"Hey, I know you," Stark said to the union official.

"No, you don't," the official said. "Get outta here."

Stark swayed back and forth. He clumsily spilled his drink on the union official.

The official jumped to his feet. "This is a thousand dollar suit, ya fuckin' drunk."

"Excuuuuuse me," Stark said.

The official grabbed his lapel.

"Haven't I seen you someplace before?" Stark asked, his words slurred. He still held peanuts in his mouth.

"No way."

The Queens crime boss told the official to calm down. The union man relaxed his grip on Stark's lapel.

"Sure. At the Ramrod," Stark said, naming a notorious rough trade gay bar. "You said you'd lick any guy in the place. Then you did."

"Sonofabitch."

The official grabbed Stark's lapel and swung a haymaker. Stark, appearing woozy, ducked under it. The official swung again, but the jab was telegraphed, and Stark could avoid it easily.

One of the union official's bodyguards jumped up from a nearby table. He grabbed Stark and spun him around. Stark leaned in close before the man could swing, and pretended to gag. He spewed the chewed peanuts in his face.

The bodyguard pulled back in disgust.

Stark had studied the *tai chi chuan* form known as "drunken monkey." His moves were far from classically pure, but he was able to evade blows and still look like he was inebriated. He swayed woozily, but instead of toppling, he would tug his opponent off balance.

The union official charged and Stark pretended to fall forward, butting the official's nose with his forehead. The official's nose gushed blood. The bodyguard threw a few punches. Stark let them graze him.

Then the bartender came out and grabbed Stark from behind. The bartender was a big man, who easily lifted Stark. Stark didn't resist.

"No trouble," the bartender said to the mobsters. "The cops are looking for an excuse to barge in."

The barkeep dragged Stark out and threw him in the alley behind the restaurant. Stark took the fall on the garbage cans. He got up drunkenly as the bodyguard came racing out of the place with murder in his eyes.

Stark staggered to the street, knocking over a garbage can so that it tripped the bodyguard. The goon got up and kept coming.

Stark reached the street. A police car happened to be cruising by. The thug, who was about to grab Stark, froze. The officers stopped and watched the scene.

The bodyguard launched a long stream of curses in English and Italian, then marched back into the restaurant.

The cops eyed Stark. "Get yourself a cold shower and a cup of coffee," one of the cops shouted without leaving his car.

"Right you are, ossifer," Stark said, saluting.

"You got more balls than brains, you know that?" Hodel asked.

"I ought to bill Uncle Sam for the suit that got ruined," Stark said.

"Jesus H. Hoover. You oughta hear what those mojos said about you."

"So your bugger got the device in place?"

"You were one first-rate distraction. He put it right under the lip on the bar," Hodel said happily. "We're picking them up as clear as a compact disc."

"You'll be able to run that bullet?"

"A deal's a deal. But what would you have done if I hadn't gotten a squad car to do a pass?"

"If there hadn't been a police car outside? I'd have waltzed around with him some more. How long until you get an answer on the bullet?"

"A few days," Hodel said. "I hope you're getting big bucks for this case."

"It's for my own curiosity."

"Just like I said. More balls than brains."

CHAPTER 29

Diana Hancock stepped into the office in her brother's Bel Air home. Edward was visiting his Toronto newspaper, which had steadily been losing money. She had gained admittance by telling her brother's security chief that Edward had left her papers to pick up. There were indeed papers he needed her to sign, involving the tax status of the Hancock Foundation, but they were far from urgent.

The security chief didn't trust her and he tagged along. He stood in the doorway, watching as she walked around the room.

"Now, he said he'd leave them right on his desk," she said, casually flipping through pages.

A bell suddenly began ringing and a light near Edward's desk blinked.

"What's that?"

The chief drew his gun. "Perimeter security breach," he shouted over his shoulder as he ran from the room.

Diana hurried to the office door and locked it. She raced to the safe and attached the cigarette pack-size device Stark had given her. The suction cup leeched on and activated the buttons. A minimotor spun the dial while a supersensitive contact mike picked up the sound of tumblers clicking into place. The green LED on the device blinked and she opened the safe.

Ignoring several gold bars and a bag of precious stones, she grabbed a sheaf of papers. Edward had a small photocopying machine in his office. She didn't even need to use the Minox camera Stark had given her. She copied the documents without reading them, ears straining for the security chief's return. In the distance, guard dogs barked and men shouted. The alarm bell continued to ring.

She shut the photocopier just as she heard the pounding feet. Then there was banging at the office door.

She hurried to the safe and shoved the papers back. She locked it.

"Who's there?" she shouted.

"It's me," the security chief said.

"How do I know it's you?" While she spoke, she composed herself, and hid the photocopies under her dress.

"Open the damned door before I shoot the lock off," the chief said.

She did. He stormed in.

"Why'd you lock me out?" he demanded.

"I didn't know what was happening. I thought I'd be safer," she said. "What is happening?"

"Someone cut the fence on the far end. They were a few dozen yards inside the property when they tripped a sensor."

"Did you get them?"

"No." The chief scanned the room. Nothing appeared to be displaced. "Are you done?"

"Why, yes. And I'll make sure to mention your hospitality to my brother." Diana Hancock hurried out. She prayed that Stark hadn't been injured while creating the diversion.

Five hundred young Japanese men in dark blue uniforms marched back and forth in perfect formation. The ultranationalist Sasaki watched through binoculars, a quarter mile away. He tried to avoid drawing unnecessary attention to himself. He turned his head a bit to focus on young men rappeling from a tower. He could hear their *kiai*, energizing shouts, even at this distance. All that was missing was the sound of gunfire. But that would be coming soon.

His Japanese Youth for Peace and Strength had been an unqualified success. The waiting list was several hundred names long. At least that's what he led the members of the press, and public, to believe. He opened a second, and then a third, camp. The mixture of military discipline, challenging martial arts, and patriotic rallies, drew youth from Hokkaido to Kyushu. Thousands of young supporters flocked to Japanese Youth for Peace and Strength rallies.

The political education classes were carefully structured, calling for the return of the Kuril islands from the Russians, charging Chinese expansionism in their takeover of Hong Kong and Macao, and challenging the U.S. right to keep bases on Okinawa. His representatives called for abolishing Japan's strict gun control laws.

Sasaki's success was watched nervously by the members of the Southeast Asian Treaty Organization (SEATO) as well as the Communist countries. Pressure was put on the Japanese prime minister to speak out against the movement.

But Sasaki had already lined up too many members of the Diet and powerful editors at *Asahi Shimbum* and *Mainchi Shimbum* newspapers. The criticism was blasted as outsiders meddling in Japan's business and even those who didn't support his ideas resented the intrusion.

In reality, he hadn't gotten the overwhelming response he'd expected. But with skillful manipulation of the press and politicians, he'd created an atmosphere of success.

The first step had been the organization. Then came getting the guns. It would be a sign of their seriousness, a gauge of his power. Then he would infiltrate his people into the military. And then he could control the Self Defense Forces.

He watched the vigorous youths go through their paces and his chest swelled with pride.

Stark spent days reviewing the papers Diana had swiped. Diana stayed by his side, telling him what she knew about the various corporations. At first she had felt that the stolen papers would convince Stark that her brother was not involved in anything criminal. Then she'd felt guilty over betraying Edward. By the end of two days, she was as absorbed as Stark in trying to pierce the corporate veil. Edward had created a murky network of subsidiaries and holding companies, and many of the papers were cryptic or in a homemade code.

Stark called Janet Kaye, the Los Angeles *Wall Street Journal* bureau chief. She and Stark had cooperated in the past. He had tapped her for information—she had gotten story leads from him. She was able to use her paper's database, and her own expertise, to help him.

Stark continued to slog through the papers. He had eliminated some as useless, and narrowed the more interesting paperwork down to a couple of sheets. One held initials that corresponded to the names of the corporations, and had what looked to be multimillion dollar amounts written in. The second sheet was covered with numbers and a few apparently random letters. TXC 356473. VCT876934. GPR453627.

The buzzer hummed and Gina told him Mr. Hoover was on the line.

It was Hodel. "Those bullets are a matchup. What are you going to do about it?"

"Would it earn you Brownie points to tip the Thai government to who killed Nakamura?"

"Could be. Though the chain of evidence has too many weak links," Hodel said.

"The bullets came from a sniper rifle fired by Willy Rose. I'm pretty sure he also committed a homicide in Thailand of a gunrunner named Nicky Webb." Stark recounted what he had learned.

"It wouldn't make a case in U.S. courts," Hodel said. "I don't know about over there. I wonder if I can cadge a trip to Thailand outta this. Best trip I've ever gotten was to Cleveland in the winter."

They exchanged friendly jibes and hung up.

The break in concentration allowed Stark to shift mental pathways. The letter/numbers were suddenly clear. Swiss bank accounts and various balances. He scanned the list, knowing that the Rosetta stone which had let him break the code was in there. He had seen it and not immediately recognized it. VC-768432. The account number that had turned up at Nicky Webb's. Edward Hancock was somehow connected with the dead gunrunner.

Edward Hancock returned from his Toronto trip and his security chief told him about the attempted break in.

"Well, you nipped it in the bud," Hancock said.

The chief hadn't told Hancock about his sister being alone in the office. It would mean admitting his own failure.

After the chief left, Hancock opened the safe. All the vital papers were in place.

A half hour later, Hancock needed to photocopy a profit and loss statement he had picked up in Canada. He opened the machine.

Inside, someone had left a sheet of paper. One of the papers that should've been inside the safe.

CHAPTER 30

Hancock called his security chief back in. After a few minutes questioning, the chief admitted that Diana had been left unsupervised in the office. Hancock fired him immediately. As soon as the man was escorted off the premises, Hancock called Grant.

"My sister has been seeing the man who I had sent off on the terrorism series."

"Robert Stark," Grant said through gritted teeth.

"Right. He's still up to something. My sister broke into my office while I was away. I'm sure she did it at his behest."

"He will be taken care of," Grant said coldly before breaking the connection.

There was a knock at the door to Diana Hancock's apartment. The bodyguard had been sprawled on the sofa, reading *Strength and Health* magazine. He glanced at his watch. It was nearly 11 p.m. Expecting one of her flaky friends, the bodyguard opened the door on its chain lock.

"Who is it?" he asked, peering out. He couldn't see anyone. He was about to close the door when the silenced .32 was shoved in the gap and two shots fired into his face.

Willy Rose kicked the door, wrenching the chain lock from its moorings. He pushed the heavy body of the weightlifter aside, then dragged it into a closet. Rose checked the house for other staff. All clear. Rose wiped the blood droplets from Hancock's hardwood floors.

Stark and Diana worked out at a friend's *dojo*. The school, ornamented with traditional rich woodwork, had no classes that night. They had the mat to themselves. Diana was making admirable progress.

"ABC," Stark told her. "Awareness. Expect nothing, be prepared for anything."

He feigned a punch at half speed, and she knocked it aside.

"Balance." He moved to push her. She sidestepped and went into a stance.

"Coordination." He threw another punch, letting her grab his arm and apply a *shihonage* throw, folding the arm back on itself and pulling down.

"Use your hips and lower body more. Not just your arms. Otherwise, excellent."

"But you attacked so slowly."

"You study martial arts for self-development."

"What about self-defense?"

"That comes later. If you want to just learn how to protect yourself, go for a simple self-defense class. They'll show you how to gouge eyes, knee the groin, shove car key into the throat."

"What do I get from this?"

"You learn about yourself. How you handle a crisis. Do you have a strong foundation? Do you overreact? Do you think quickly? The idea is to be relaxed, harmonize. Let the aggressor do all the work. And don't fear getting hurt. Or death. That's the only way to live."

"I don't know about all that."

"Neither do I. It's something to strive for."

There was a small shower stall in the back of the *dojo*. They showered together. Midway through soaping each other, he took her into his arms. He lifted her up and slid into her.

The couple had made love at every chance they got. For Stark, who had been celibate for nearly six months, it was like a Muslim feasting after Ramadan.

When they both were spent, and very clean, Diana suggested they pick up a couple of *bento* box dinners and go back to her apartment.

Diana Hancock's apartment was located on the south edge of Brentwood, a Yuppie enclave just north of UCLA. She lived on a tree-lined side street where her modest one-bedroom cost two thousand dollars a month. It was an older area, without parking. They found a space up the block.

"That's a clear sign of good luck," she said, leaning against him as they walked the few steps to her door.

"Why are you so alert?" she asked, noticing him scanning the boxwood hedges and the street.

"This is when you're most vulnerable. Getting in and out of your car, going in or out of your house. Your actions are predictable. Most people are distracted."

"Are you ever not on?"

"Only when I'm off," he said.

"I don't know about this violence stuff. Ever since I met you, I feel as if I moved to West Beirut." She sighed and twisted her key in the lock. "Being with you is a trip, I'll say that much."

She pulled the door open. Stark smelled the cordite and the sweet scent of roses even as she turned on the light switch. He grabbed her by her shoulder and shoved her backward. She toppled onto the lawn, yelling, "What the hell?"

A silenced shot whizzed past. Stark threw himself to the floor.

"Sodding son of a bitch," Rose said as he ran toward them. At just the right moment, Stark kicked the door. It caught Rose's arm, knocking the gun hand aside. Stark dove in on top of him.

The men scuffled. Diana Hancock screamed.

A Los Angeles Police Department squad car was a block

away. Hearing the scream, they raced over, screeching up just as Stark wrenched the gun from Rose.

"Police! Freeze!" the cops shouted. One was a rookie and his hand trembled as he aimed his service revolver. His more experienced partner had her 12-gauge shotgun pointed at Stark.

Stark obeyed. Rose moved behind him, then dove over the hedge. He took off running. The cops, seeing the gun in Stark's hand, kept their weapons on him.

"The other one!" Diana Hancock yelled.

"Go after him!" The experienced cop shouted to her partner. The rookie took off after Rose.

Within five minutes, the police helicopter was circling overhead, shining its "night sun" spotlight in backyards. A half-dozen police cars clogged the street, their revolving lights painting bands of red and blue. The neighbors who came out to gawk were shooed inside.

The rookie couldn't catch Rose. But at least Stark was no longer under the gun. Diana Hancock and Stark had produced ID and explained what happened. Police found the body of the guard in the closet, sealed off the area, and called detectives.

Diana and Stark were kept apart for the first hour and asked to repeat their story several times. When they were allowed together, Diana threw herself into Stark's arms.

"That man, the one who tried to shoot me, I recognized the voice," she whispered to Stark. "He was the one who ordered Nakamura around. He was the one who cut off my ear."

"Did you tell the police?"

"No. I wanted to check with you."

"Tell them. It's okay."

"I want you with me when I do. I never want you to leave me."

"I have to. I have to find him."

"But what if he comes back and tries to do it again."

"You weren't the target."

"How do you know?"

"He could've shot you easily when you opened the door. It wasn't until I stepped in that he opened fire."

"But why would he want to kill you?"

Before Stark could answer, a detective came over and said, "We need to ask a few more questions. If you have any coffee around, young lady, you might want to put it up. It's going to be a long night."

CHAPTER 31

Sasaki and the two politicians paused by the *koi* pond on the grounds of the Imperial Palace. It was more than just a pond, almost a lake. The fish too were larger. After all, they belonged to the emperor, the living symbol of Japan.

Sasaki stared at a leaf, floating on the water. The red and yellow colors of the huge fish swimming beneath the surface echoed the colors of the leaf. He thought it would make a lovely haiku.

The three men had said little during their stroll, nothing more than pleasant commentaries on the weather, the scenery, and how well a favored sumo wrestler had done during a competition the night before. The tension was building. The pols knew they had been summoned for a reason.

Sasaki smiled, and the curtain went up. "My plan for strengthening our country is ready for its next step."

"It has gone very well to date," one pol said.

The other nodded and added a few words of agreement.

The two fawning pols spoke the truth. The program had been a bigger hit than the Tokyo Disneyland. Sasaki had more than fifteen thousand young men and close to a thousand women enrolled in his youth organization. The "troops" had participated in parades, holiday festivals, and martial arts competitions. They had been written about in every newspaper and magazine, filmed by every TV station.

"The swordsman begins his training with a *bokken*," Sasaki said, using the name for a wooden sword that was designed to feel just like a real one. "But then the time comes when he must feel a true blade in his hand, know what it's like to parry, to slice, to slash, with perfect steel."

The politicians nodded, unsure what he was getting at.

"I have arranged for the Japanese Youth for Peace and Strength to receive weapons," Sasaki said.

"There are strict laws regarding the importing of firearms," one blurted out.

Without answering, Sasaki walked over to a small wooden bench and sat down. The two pols followed. They stood before him, shifting from foot to foot, unsure whether to join him on the bench. The industrialist sat perfectly erect, a shogun with a couple of low-level samurai at his castle.

"We currently have some of the toughest gun control laws in the world. All weapons are restricted, even the ownership of swords, which are the very symbol of the samurai. Aren't our current laws based in part on the American constitution?" Sasaki asked rhetorically.

"*Hai, so desu,*" the politicians responded, nodding.

"Are you familiar with their constitution?"

They shook their heads. They both knew more about the American constitution than the average U.S. high school student, but they didn't want to lose face if Sasaki asked an esoteric question and they didn't know the answer.

"The first ten amendments are called the Bill of Rights, and they are as important for the rights of citizens as the constitution is for arranging the administrative nature of government. The second amendment is the citizen's right to bear arms. Modern Americans have interpreted this to give the individual the right to carry guns. Legal scholars say it is providing for the formation of a militia. The home guard. Each able-bodied man should be ready to defend his home and his country if the need arises."

The two pols nodded along.

"My group is nothing more than a militia. We are seeking to exercise our right to bear arms."

"Will the Americans allow it?"

"We are not children who need a parent's permission," Sasaki said, his voice as hard as a slap to the face. "We are an independent nation. I want you to introduce a measure to the Diet. We shall start by allowing the import of weapons for use by a sanctioned organization, such as the Japanese Youth for Peace and Strength. I will pay for the weapons myself. It will cost the government nothing and provide greater security."

The two pols were silent.

"As for your concern about the Americans, many of the weapons I will be getting will be coming from them," Sasaki said. "They're not yet ready to openly endorse our rearming, but they will not stop it."

"I do not know if there will be enough support in the legislature," one pol said.

"Don't worry. I've made arrangments. The right people have already been contacted. The measure will pass. One of you should introduce it. The other will second the motion. And you will be heroes. I've made sure of that."

The two pols bowed.

"Domo arigato gozai masu, Sasaki-san," they said.

He brushed aside their thanks with a wave of his hand. "I'm an old man. I will sit here and relax while you return to your business."

The pols bowed again, repeated thanks, and hurried away. They began bickering over who would introduce the bill, and who would second it.

Sasaki returned to his attention to the pond. He took out a scrap of paper and a thick gold Montblanc pen and began to work on his haiku. The chill wind that blew leaves onto the water didn't bother him. He pulled his collar tighter and scribbled.

CHAPTER 32

"Edward was distinctly bizarre on the phone," Diana said as she hung up. She rolled over in bed to face Stark. "But he agreed to meet me."

"Good," Stark said. "Now I suggest you not be there."

"What?"

"Your brother and I have some things to talk about," Stark said. "You might not want to hear them."

"Does it involve the attempt on us last night?"

"Yes."

"Then I have a right to know, don't I?"

She stood up and stretched. Naked, her smooth skin stretched over gentle curves. But they hadn't made love. She had needed holding more than physical satisfaction. She had twice awoken during the night with nightmares and snuggled against him.

"I want to know," she said.

Willy Rose had just arrived at the basement parking lot when Stark's car came down the ramp. Rose had gotten there a half hour before Stark was due, to set up the ambush. Stark wasn't due until 11 A.M. But the counterterrorist had beaten him by also coming early.

He'd get Stark when he left. Rose had a limpet mine—ideal for attaching to metal surfaces and capable of blowing a hole in six-inch steel—in the trunk. But he suspected that Stark's car would have elaborate alarms that would go off if he went too close. And Rose knew of systems that put out an electric field that would detonate the mine even as he installed it.

From the back seat of the BMW he took out a LAW rocket—a disposable Light Anti-tank Weapon—and positioned himself so he could lift and aim the khaki tube easily. He would fire with the LAW out the window to avoid injury from the back blast.

His car faced away from Stark's, but he had a clear view in his rearview mirror. He settled into the leather seats and put himself into the semi-relaxed state of an experienced predator.

The gym was on the top floor of the Westwood high-rise. Twenty stories up, with glass walls and a 360-degree view that, on one of L.A.'s few clear days, allowed those on the Lifecycle stationary bikes to see everywhere from Santa Monica and the Pacific Ocean to the Hollywood sign.

It was a gym for people who didn't need gyms, beautiful bodies in Spandex designer exercise outfits, with individual trainers who looked so perfect they seemed to be from a different species. High fashion faces and Olympic athlete bodies. Music with a heavy bass and drum line—varying from rock and roll to Big Band to classics—thumped out of six-foot-high Altec Lansing speakers throughout the five thousand-square-foot facility.

Stark and Diana were guided through the forest of chicly sweating and grunting bodies to Edward Hancock.

The multimillionaire was on a multifunction computerized exercise machine that was equipped with a voice simulator. It called out his reps, and if there was too long a pause, would say "Go for it," or "Feel the burn," or "No pain, no gain" in an electronic warble. To back up the machine, a lithe blonde stood nearby, counting along with the machine and telling him how good he was doing on his overhead presses.

"You can go now, Ellen," Hancock commanded and the

210

lithe blonde bobbed away. Hancock finished his set and adjusted the machine so he could exercise his deltoids. "What do you want, Diana?"

"Robert needs to talk to you privately," she said.

"I have nothing to say to him. And almost nothing to say to you," Hancock said coldly.

She looked surprised, opened her mouth to speak, and he cut her off. "You left a paper in the Xerox. It wasn't hard to figure out what happened. Your latest lover boy convinced you to steal from me." Hancock continued doing his reps, the machine warbling electronic encouragement. "You've abused my trust," Hancock said to Diana, not even looking at her. "I'm cutting you off. You know how the will is structured. You'll always have a few thousand coming in. But no more jet setting."

Diana bit her lip. She didn't know whether to cry or yell at him.

Stark had said nothing. He had intended to subtlely question Hancock, not confront him. He gently put his hand on Diana's shoulder and pulled her back. She was as brittle as a pane of thin glass.

Stark stepped in and leaned forward over Hancock, withdrawing a paper from under his jacket like it was a weapon.

Willy Rose checked his watch. He was hoping to catch a plane in two hours.

He heard the footsteps approaching and turned casually, just enough to spot the figure out of the corner of his eye. A rent-a-cop, his belly rolling over the belt of his pants, was waddling over.

"You waiting for someone?" the cop asked.

"Yes."

"Lemme see your license and registration." The cop had no authority, but Rose couldn't take a chance on him calling the real police.

Rose switched on his deadly grin. The rent-a-cop took a step backward and patted his nightstick.

"I don't have it on me, officer," Rose said sweetly. "I just came by to pick up my wife. She's already ten minutes late. She works in the bank." Rose was confident that every high-rise had at least one bank in it.

"Uh, okay." The guard walked away.

Rose debated letting the guard live. The mercenary was wearing tinted glasses, and had been inside the dark car during the conversation. Still, the guard might be able to identify him.

"Excuse me!" Rose shouted. The guard turned. "I found my paperwork," Rose said.

"That's okay," the guard responded, staying about thirty feet away.

Rose got out of the car. He was committed now. He glanced both ways, making sure there was no one about.

"I want to show it to you," Rose said.

The guard backpedalled. He withdrew his nightstick.

Rose smiled, holding his wallet out in front of him like someone offering a biscuit to a dog. "C'mon, mate, don't want to give you a hard time. You got a job to do."

A car drove into the garage. Rose turned so his face wouldn't be visible. It was a monthly tenant and they just breezed up to the machine, stuck a card in, and the gate opened. The car drove up the ramp.

Rose had to move fast. He had to be back at the BMW before Stark returned.

He drew his gun and held it low. "Put the bat back on your belt and come with me."

"I didn't see anything, Mister."

"You're going to come and keep me company, that's all."

They walked to the BMW. Keeping the gun on the guard, Rose opened the trunk. Another car passed by. Again Rose positioned himself so all they could see was his back.

"Climb in," Rose ordered.

The trunk was half full, and the clumsy guard had to wiggle to get in. "I won't be able to breathe in here," the guard said.

"Trust me," Rose said, and shot the guard twice in the head with his silenced Beretta. Rose slammed the trunk and hurried back to sit in the car. He repositioned the LAW rocket and checked that it was still armed and ready.

"What's your connection with an arms dealer named Nicky Webb?" Stark demanded.

"Never heard of him."

Stark lifted the sheet of numbers that Diana had taken from the safe. He read off the account number he'd gotten in Thailand. "I found that account number in Webb's office and the same number on papers in your office."

Hancock stopped doing his reps and grabbed the paper. "This is stolen property. I could have you arrested."

"Do *you* realize the enormous interest the IRS has in Swiss accounts?"

Hancock peered at the sheet.

"Any problems, Mr. Hancock?" Two of the Adonis types were standing behind Stark. He had been aware of them since a few seconds after they began heading over. They were poseurs, no real threat.

"No. Leave us alone," Hancock snapped.

The muscle boys exchanged whispered remarks and swaggered away.

"This account belongs to Gerard DeVille," Hancock said reluctantly. "He's an international businessman."

"An international arms dealer to be specific."

"I don't have anything to do with the arms trade," Hancock said.

"What was your connection?"

Hancock returned to his reps. "That's none of your business."

Stark hit Hancock with a rapid-fire account of what had happened, throwing out names and places, everything from his first trip to Cyprus to his encounter with Webb in Thailand. Edward Hancock was connected to Webb by the Swiss account number. Webb was connected to Gerard DeVille. Webb had apparently been killed by Willy Rose. Rose was tied to Kenji Nakamura's murder by a ballistics report. Nakamura had kidnapped Diana.

"Circumstantial links don't prove anything," Hancock said pompously.

"Did you ask DeVille to kidnap and torture your sister?" Stark asked.

"That's outrageous. How dare you even suggest that."

Diana stepped close to her brother. "Rose tried to kill us last night."

"Nonsense."

"Your rivals at the *Times* will think it's a great story," Stark said.

Stark and Diana walked toward the door. They were conspicuous, dressed for the street, surrounded by the Spandex-clad muscle-seekers. And most of those present had been aware of "the scene" with Edward Hancock.

"Wait!" Hancock called out.

"Keep walking," Stark whispered to Diana.

"Wait!" Hancock shouted again.

Stark and Diana were a few feet from the door. Hancock jumped off the machine and ran to them. He reached to grab Stark's shoulder to spin him around, but Stark had already spun to face him.

"Wait! Please," Hancock said. "I don't understand what it all means."

They stood in the reception area, which was lined with plants and posters on the wall showing perfect bodies.

"What's your connection with Gerard DeVille?"

"A few years ago we were involved in a joint real estate venture. It didn't work out. DeVille held me responsible, tried to get me to reimburse him for more than three million."

"The same amount as Diana's kidnappers wanted?"

"Omigod," Hancock said, as he realized it was. He stepped back wiping his hand across his forehead.

"What's General Grant's role in this?"

"He told me to drop the terrorism investigation I started you on." Hancock spoke stiffly, numbly. "He didn't want you looking into Diana's kidnappers. Claimed U.S. national security interests were involved. I had no idea there was any connection between Diana's kidnapping and DeVille."

"So you fired me, but it wasn't because I spirited your sister off," Stark said.

"No."

"When Grant spoke with you at that dinner, you looked like someone who was having his short hairs pulled," Stark said. "He threatened you, didn't he?"

"I'll pay you for all the time you've invested," Hancock offered.

"Of course you will," Stark said. "But you'll also answer my question."

He hesitated. "I've been involved in several deals that could bring me a certain tax liability. Grant threatened to blow the whistle. I didn't know how he knew. DeVille must've told him."

"I was kidnapped, had my ear cut off, and was nearly killed, because of you and sleazy business deals," Diana growled.

"I'm very concerned for her well-being," Hancock said. "You're not really going to show the IRS those papers, are you?"

"Somehow, I get the feeling you're more concerned about that than you are about your sister's suffering."

"Of course I care. But there's nothing I can do about that now. If the business is destroyed, she'll suffer too. As well as my family. And thousands of employees."

"How noble of you," Stark said. "Tell me what DeVille is up to. What are his assets and liabilities?"

Hancock rattled off everything he knew. There was nothing of value in the information. "It's been a few years," Hancock said apologetically.

"Where is he now?"

"I don't know," Hancock insisted.

"Take a guess."

"His pet project has been a facility in Thailand."

"Exactly where?"

"I don't know."

"What does he have there?" Stark asked.

"He's building a huge arms storage depot. Fortified. He figures Thailand is secure, but every country around it isn't.

He can make quick deliveries to Burma, Laos, Cambodia, Vietnam, China, Malaysia. India's not that far away. Indonesia is a good customer, he told me. He'll be able to offer fast delivery and reduced shipment costs."

"What's his relationship with Grant?" Stark asked, changing tack to throw Hancock off.

"I'm not sure."

"You can do better than that."

"Well, Grant was involved in some of the Defense Department's major purchases. He's well connected to several large arms manufacturers. That's all I know."

"One final question," Stark said. "When you discovered the paper in the photocopier, who did you call?"

Hancock hesitated. "No one."

"You're lying," Stark said.

"How do you know?"

"I'm like Santa, I know when you're being naughty or nice," Stark said. "C'mon, Diana."

"Wait. Okay. I called Grant and told him."

"That explains our visitor to Diana's apartment last night." As Stark and Diana turned and took a couple more steps to the door, Hancock said, "So you won't be showing those papers to the IRS, right?"

"Right." Stark was at the swinging glass door. "I won't. However, I'm giving them to your sister to do with as she sees fit."

Diana grinned broadly. "Isn't there a federal office here in Westwood?"

Hancock ran after them. They were out in the carpeted hallway.

"Wait, Diana, don't. You'll suffer too. All the family assets will get tied up."

"I can live cheaply," she said.

He grabbed her arm. She peeled his hand off with a simple aikido spin, then faced him, hands raised in a defensive position.

"Don't touch me," she said.

A couple of passing businessmen eyed the trio. The Hancocks and Stark were silent, waiting for the spectators to move on. The elevator came, disgorged people, and the businessmen got on. When the elevator passengers were gone, Hancock said, "Listen, it's not just for me and the business. And the family. It's for the good of the country. A national security matter."

"What is it?"

"I don't know. It's too classified for anyone to know."

Diana glared, angry words in her mind, but none made it to her lips. She spun and walked to the elevator. Stark followed.

Hancock sagged, watching them, a man forced to admit a secret he had held dearly, bested by his baby sister, and unsure what his future was going to be.

"Diana, I'm sorry," he said.

She faced him, on the edge of tears. "I could hear you better if I had both my ears, dearest brother."

Diana punched the button for the parking garage lower level.

Stark punched the button for the third floor.

"Why'd you do that?"

"We shouldn't go back to your car. No doubt your brother told Grant we were meeting. We could easily be ambushed."

The elevator door opened, they got out, and walked down the fire stairs to the lobby.

"Is the IRS office nearby?" she asked.

"I'd hold off on that."

"Why?"

"It's possible your brother was telling the truth about its affecting the country. Maybe he's telling what he believes is the truth, but he was lied to."

"Sure. It wasn't your ear that was chopped off. It wasn't you who was kidnapped and tied up and abused. And what about those poor brave men who tried to save me at the refugee camp? Or the bodyguard? I owe them something."

"It's your decision. But I'd ask you to hold off a few days until I can see if the story is legit."

"Screw this country if they're cooperating with people like DeVille and Rose."

"Our country, every country, does. When we need arms delivered somewhere but want deniability, we go to an arms dealer. The more unethical, the better it serves our purpose. At some points, we've armed both sides in a conflict. Like the Iran-Iraq war."

"So gun dealers can make money?"

"Partially. And so we have allies no matter who wins. I'm not defending it. If there is some legitimate national security project, then it might be best to hold off. We'll find another way to teach Edward a lesson."

"What if Edward was lying? What if it isn't a national security matter?"

"I'll find out. And then I'll walk you over to the tax men myself."

CHAPTER 33

Willy Rose waited another half hour in the parking garage. It was nearing 4 P.M. and more people were exiting the building. Too many witnesses.

He drove the BMW to Hollywood. The area had more glitz than glamour, more junkies than stars. It was dangerous to stand on the corner of Hollywood and Vine when the sun went down. Leaving the body and the LAW rocket in the trunk, he ditched the stolen BMW on a side street in East Hollywood. He hoped that the car would be stolen by someone else, complicating tracing it. Rose caught a bus, rode a couple of miles, then hailed a cab.

"It's best if you stay at my friend's house for a few days," Stark suggested. "He's just about the only person I'd trust my life to without hesitation."

"I'm safer with you," she said.

"Not where I'm going."

Stark convinced Diana to stay with Pedro Quesada. Quesada's wife—a nurse who hated her husband's violent, high risk occupation—welcomed Hancock with such hospitality that Diana felt right at home.

What was harder was convincing Quesada that he couldn't come along.

"I need you to watch over her," Stark said, nodding toward the other room where Diana and Carmen were. Carmen had a couple of dark-haired wigs, left over from previous females they had sheltered. Diana was trying them on and the two women were laughing.

"You're going to Thailand solo?" Quesada asked.

"This is just a scouting mission. If I'm not back in five days, you call in the bombers."

"It doesn't seem like such a great idea to me."

"I have to see what's there, then decide. This is nothing more than recon."

"If you stumble on something, you're not going to wait before you go kicking ass and taking names."

"This might just be a washout," Stark said. "Anyway, I need you here to watch over Diana."

"You love her?" Quesada asked hopefully. One of his goals in life was to see Stark happily married and the father of several children.

"I care about her."

"That's a start. *Vaya con dios,*" Quesada said.

"*Hasta mañana.*" Stark responded.

Pedro gave him a hug. Diana did too, but hers included a long slow kiss. Then Stark hurried back to his house and packed. He called Gina at the L.A. office, and had her do a computer run on a few mercenaries. She came up with the names of two who had died recently. He could use their names as references.

It took Stark a while to pass through the usually perfunctory customs in Bangkok. They were suspicious of his black and camouflage outfits.

At 10 P.M., he met Thai official Thanom on a street corner a couple of blocks from the Oriental Hotel. It was a touristy area and Stark only drew attention from cab drivers who tried to hustle him to visit a massage parlor.

"You missed a wonderful fight at Lumpini Stadium last night," Thanom said by way of greeting. "Our welterweight champion was in top form."

"I need your help."

"I assumed that is why you called."

"A man named Webb was murdered."

Thanom made a clucking noise. "Do you want me to intercede with our minister of justice?"

"I didn't do it. I saw the man who did."

"You wish me to relay information anonymously?"

"Later. For now, I want to get background on Webb. I want to interview his neighbors and my Thai is more suited to ordering food than interrogation."

"You want me to be your translator?"

"Yes. But you have to swear what you hear will go no further. Until I tell you."

"Why should I do this?"

"Because it's in your country's interest. Having *farang* murdering each other does nothing for the tourist trade." Stark also knew Thanom couldn't resist a little adventure.

"Okay. I will be your Kato, Green Hornet. Where to?"

Stark gave him Webb's address in Thonburi. They hailed a cab. Thanom bargained with the driver, got them a fair price, and they set off in Bangkok traffic.

They questioned three of Webb's neighbors before they got a lead.

"He had many woman," the neighbor said. "But there was one who lasted several months. She worked in a bar on Patpong. I spoke to her once. Her name was Chittiwong Soon. She had a specialty act at the Spicy Lady Nightclub."

Patpong Road is one of the Orient's major vice centers. It's surprisingly small, not much more than a long block lined with four-story buildings. Different bars cater to different nationalities. There's an Arab section, a Japanese section, and a European and American section. Thais favor cheaper places off the well-known strip.

Neon lights flashed names like "The Thigh Club," "Pink Pussycat," "Geisha," "Sahara." Barkers touted the pleasure inside in broken English, the universal language. Heavily made up young women in short skirts swung their hips as they tottered along on ridiculously high heels. Cab drivers every few feet accosted males and asked, "You want Thai lady?"

"It's hard to believe that prostitution is as illegal in my country as it is in yours," Thanom said. He smiled, a sign of embarrassment rather than amusement.

"Every city has its red light district," Stark said.

"The police know. Everyone knows. But to stop the trade would be like your southern states stopping tobacco growth. More people have been killed by cigarettes than sex," Thanom said defensively.

They entered the Spicy Lady. A pair of hostesses swooped down, grabbed their arms, and guided them off to a vacant table by the side.

"Two beers," Thanom ordered.

"What about for us?" one of the hostesses asked.

"Just get us a couple of beers."

One of the hostesses muttered in Thai that he was a "sticky shit," cheapskate.

The girls brought back the beers and sat down. They instantly had their hands on the men, stroking and patting and commenting on how good-looking they were.

A teenage girl, no more than sixteen, came out on stage. She carried a pack of cigarettes. She was naked. She lit a cigarette and placed it in her vagina. Then a second, a third, and a fourth. She used her vaginal muscles to puff on the cigarettes. The crowd cheered.

"Do you enjoy the show?" Thanom asked Stark through clenched teeth.

Stark found the show as erotic as a circus sideshow. "Ask about Chittipong Soon," Stark said.

Thanom fired off a burst at the bar girl caressing Stark.

"You policeman?" the girl asked Thanom.

He shook his head.

The smoker left the stage and was replaced by a woman with a handful of Ping-Pong balls. She began swallowing them into her vagina. The crowd counted out as each ball went in.

"Two!"

Thanom kept asking the bar girl questions.

The girl folded her arms across her chest and looked off into space. Stark set five hundred baht, about twenty dollars, down. She reached for it. He pinned it to the table with his fingers.

"Three!"

"You don't need her, I much better," the girl said in halting English.

"I want her," Stark said.

"Four!"

"She not work here anymore," the bar girl said.

"Where is she?"

The girl lapsed into Thai and Thanom picked up the questioning.

"Five!"

After a few sentences back and forth, Thanom said, "Let's go."

As Stark and Thanom exited from the smoky bar, the crowd shouted, "Seven!"

Even the humid nighttime air seemed sweet after the smoky, sweaty, lusty closeness of the club.

"I have a daughter not much younger than the women in there," Thanom said.

Stark patted his shoulder.

"If my daughter ever did that, I would kill her," Thanom said. "And myself."

They found Chittiwong Soon in a three-story guest house in the Din Daeng area, overlooking the murky Sam Sen canal. Soon was behind the desk, watching a variety show featuring a transvestite, a fat man, a dwarf, and a Don Juan with grotesquely large teeth that pointed in different directions. She was laughing and rocking a baby in her arms.

Thanom and Soon spoke for a few minutes. Then she turned to Stark. "I knew your friend in a past life," she said in English. "What do you want to know?"

"Webb was murdered. I'm looking for the people who did it."

She took the news without any sign of emotion. "He had dealings with bad men. But he was not a bad man. He never beat me. He was generous. His money helped to buy this building."

Stark nodded. "We need information about where Webb traveled to in Thailand."

"All over. The beach at Phuket, the hills around Chiang Mai. He liked my country. Most of the time."

"Any place more than others? Or that seemed to be business-oriented?"

"He didn't talk with me about business."

"But you are a smart lady," Stark said. "I'm sure you heard things. Maybe a man named DeVille."

"Nicky did much work for him."

"Yes. Where?"

"All over. Thailand. Malaysia. Sneak into Burma some-time."

A man came out of the back and questioned Soon in Thai. She answered, then he went back behind a curtain.

"My husband," she said.

"Is it okay to talk?" Stark asked.

"He knows about my past life. It's what has paid for this and allowed our children a chance to go to a better school. It was only my body. My mind was never touched."

She bent down and rooted through a drawer under the counter. She came up with pictures.

"This one time, he very secret. He wouldn't tell me where he went. But he left these pictures behind. I think they are where he went."

The photos showed dense foliage, a few rolling hills, a creek that was nearly a river. In the background was a thatched hut with crosspoles forming a V where they met. In the distance was a mountain.

"Helpful?" she asked.

"They can be. May I keep them?"

"I don't know why I was saving them," she said, waving them over to Stark.

"Khob khun khrapb," Stark said.

"You are welcome."

When Thanom and Stark were back on the street, Thanom asked, "Those pictures could be anywhere in Southeast Asia."

"Not quite. Look at the building. The poles with the V. Isn't that supposed to represent a water buffalo? That's a trademark of northern Thai architecture."

"You're right. I took it for granted."

"And the foliage doesn't seem that tropical. It looks like what I've seen in the northwest. So I'm guessing it's a cooler climate."

"Like around Chiang Mai."

"Right."

"That mountain," Thanom said, peering closely at the picture. "I think it is Doi Suthep. Just outside Chiang Mai. But why did he take these photos?"

"They're no snapshots. I'm taking a guess, they might be reconaissance photos. I wouldn't be surprised if Webb helped DeVille pick out the sight of his fort."

"What do you do now?"

"Catch the next flight to Chiang Mai."

The Thai Airways flight landed at Chiang Mai an hour and fifteen minutes after takeoff. The small airport included a bank, post office, two snack bars, and a bar housed in an old Air Force plane permanently parked at the near end of the tarmac. A half a dozen hustlers—cab drivers offering tours, drugs or women, and vendors of fresh antiquities—rushed up to the *farang* tourists.

Stark waved them away with a gruff air and some pidgin Vietnamese, playing the role of the Ugly American vet. Moving with rigid military bearing, he hailed a cab, refused the various and sundry deals, and rode downtown to the Garden Flower Hotel. It was middle of the road, but on the decline. No air conditioners, TV or phones, and the ceiling fans moved listlessly. Stark had an upscale room, with a private bath that had been cleaned at least once during the past month.

He unpacked, making sure to set a few indicators to warn him if anyone visited his room while he was out.

"Where do the Americans hang out?" Stark asked the young man behind the front desk.

225

"American tourist go everywhere. You want to see hill tribe show? Craft factory? Hidden temples? Maybe you want Thai lady? Special massage?"

"No." Stark mimicked someone shooting. "Those kinds of Americans. Or Brits."

The young man lowered his voice. "You want opium? Best in north Thailand?"

"No dope."

"Girls. Dancers. Very pretty."

"Not tonight, I have a headache." Seeing he was getting nowhere, Stark asked "Okay, where do the dopers hang out?"

The young man began puttering with some papers. Stark took out a hundred *baht* note, worth about five American dollars.

The young man flirted with the bill, but continued to look coy.

"Listen, Bub, I'm sure it ain't a secret where the smart money boys play. If you don't want my money, I'll find someone who does."

The clerk snatched the bill and pocketed it. "Try Tha Phae Palace or Asia Best. Late at night, they go to Casablanca."

Stark strutted out and began his night of barhopping. The first bar was dark, with a band blasting mixes of Thai pop tunes, tepid jazz, and sixties hits. Hostesses tried to hustle patrons to buy drinks while young men in sunglasses sold opium and marijuana in quantities from a single bowl or joint, to pounds. Most were police informers who made their living turning *farangs* over to the cops. The police would fine the aspiring drug buyer five thousand dollars, a princely sum, and the informer would get a ten-percent kickback.

The hangout was so dark that waiters used flashlights to show people to their seats. Stark sat at the bar. A young woman plopped herself down on his lap. She weighed less than ninety pounds, small boned, with a big smile and sad eyes. He drank his beer, fondled her, and paid for her overpriced champagne—which probably had about as much liquor in it as apple juice.

The crowd was clearly small-timers, the dregs of the counterculture who had come to Thailand to score a big drug deal, and wound up staying.

He moved on, disappointing the hostess, who had mentioned several times how near the bar she lived.

The second bar was a clone of the first, only the band was better. Stark could recognize most of the tunes they played. There were a few legit tourists mixed in with the crowd, and the hustlers were more polished.

At Casablanca he found what he was looking for. The bar was done up like the movie, only the cracks in the wall were real. Half the ceiling fans worked, swirling, but not dispelling a cloud of cigarette smoke.

Stark was searching for a certain kind of customer. He spotted the man, back to a rear wall, eyes half closed but alert. He was about forty, wiry, white but sun bronzed. There were tattoos of hearts and arrows partially visible on his bicep. The man was drinking Mekhong Whiskey, seventy proof rice whiskey that was one quarter the price of imported liquors.

"Mind if I join you?" Stark asked.

The man looked up and shrugged.

Stark sat and offered a Marlboro. The man lit it and puffed contentedly.

"What's your name?" Stark asked.

"Call me Tex."

"I'm Bob." Stark stuck out his hand. Tex shook it without enthusiasm.

"You look like someone who's been around," Stark said.

"If you're from the government, go fuck yourself."

"I ain't."

"You look like a fucking narc."

"Then don't sell me dope and you don't have to worry. I just need a little advice."

"Do I look like fucking Ann Landers?"

"No. More like Dear Abby."

Tex rolled his shoulders as if he were about to get up and take a swing at Stark. Stark shifted, ready to block, but not intimidated.

Tex laughed. He waved to a hostess. She came over and he ordered a glass for Stark, and another bottle. His Thai was rough, but fast. The girl didn't try and hustle him. Tex was clearly a regular.

Stark filled his glass and lifted it. "Lemme guess. Special Forces?"

"How'd you know?"

"The steel Rolex."

Tex looked at his watch. "You got it. And you?"

"Rangers."

"They're okay," Tex said condescendingly. "So what're you doing here?"

"Looking for action. I've bounced around since Nam."

Tex was a little drunk. He had to make an effort to keep from slurring his words. "You ain't the first. I never went home. Knew I wasn't fit for the world. Got me a cute little Thai wife and a nice hooch a few miles out of town. I lead tourists on treks. See genuine hill tribes. Smoke opium with the headman. You interested?"

"Nah."

"Didn't think you were."

"I'm looking for a different kind of action."

Tex waited him out.

Stark used the names of the two dead mercs Gina had dug out of the computer. "Then there was a guy named Nicky Webb in Bangkok. He told me there were people hiring up here."

"You talk the talk. Can you walk the walk?"

"Can't dance." Stark took out the photos he had gotten from Chittiwong Soon. "You recognize this spot?"

"That heap bad juju, white man," Tex said with an exaggerated black accent.

"It's near here?"

"Not far. But you don't want to go there."

"Why?"

"Put it this way, I've seen SAC bomber bases that are less fortified."

"Can you take me there?"

"Not for all the Twinkies in San Francisco. You couldn't see anything anyway. The hot ticket rumor is the whole shebang is underground. All they got up top is mean, ugly motherfuckers with guns."

"How can I get in?" Stark asked. He took his wallet out and put it on the table.

"You don't need to pay me to tell you how to get killed," Tex said. "They can probably use fresh meat out there. Got any specialties?"

"Hand-to-hand combat."

"Not much call for that. Everybody's a Rambo. Big guns, little dicks." Tex laughed at his own joke.

"I can handle most small arms. I won't blow my balls off if you give me a Claymore."

"You want to play jungle warrior? The Karens need help going into Burma. Pay sucks, but you get free malaria pills and all the rice you can eat."

"I'm not interested in hill tribe bullshit."

"Shan Army?"

"I ain't guarding dope. Unless the pay's great. I heard those fuckers don't like white guys anyway."

"They don't trust 'em. DEA tried to slip an agent in on them. They're still finding pieces of him in the Ping River."

"So what about getting into that underground gig?"

Tex finished his glass. "There's a bar outside of town. Take the road to Chiang Rai and turn off onto the dirt road about three klicks north. You'll hear it before you see it. You can try selling yourself there."

"I owe you one."

"Just pay for the bottle," Tex said. "Watch your ass there. If they think you're anything but a good grunt, they'll make you wish your daddy had worn a rubber."

CHAPTER 34

The cabbie initially refused to take Stark to the bar Tex had recommended. But by paying twice as much as he should have, Stark got the ride. The cabbie dropped him off and pulled away hurriedly, leaving Stark at the junction of the main road and the dirt road.

Country and western music drifted through the night air. During lulls in the music, Stark could hear the breeze rustling through the coconut palms, and insects and frogs chirping and croaking. There was a struggle in the brush, small animals fighting or feeding. Kraits and cobras slithered out for their night hunting. Stark stayed in the middle of the dirt road. The moonlight showed him a clear path.

The bar was eight teak posts with a corrugated tin roof and a sign saying "Officers Klub." Bare light bulbs hung suspended by wire. A generator grumbled in the background and gave off a faint smell of gasoline.

Burly white men lounged on beat-up stools. Skinny Thai women lounged on top of them. Behind the bar—thick planks resting on empty crates—a Thai man with a pencil thin mustache mixed drinks and changed the cassette in the big radio. Syrupy sweet, high-pitched Thai pop music came on.

"Gimme a Singha," Stark said.

He could feel the eyes of the other patrons on him.

"This private club," the bartender said.

"Oh, yeah? A friend of mine named Tex said I could get a brew here. Is that a problem?"

The bartender called out in Thai to a fat Thai man sitting at a table near the bar. The fat man sized up Stark and signaled okay with a wave of his hand.

Conversations resumed, but Stark still felt the patrons' wariness. This was a place where violence was the norm. He sipped his beer.

He covertly eyed the two dozen or so men drinking and fondling hostesses. Every now and then, one of the men would disappear out back with a woman. He'd return fifteen minutes later, inevitably fiddling with his fly.

A big, ruddy man, with close set eyes and short cut dirty blond hair, came from the back draped over a woman more than a foot shorter than him. His muscular chest stretched the fabric of his red and yellow T-shirt. It bore the Marine Corps logo and the words "Semper Fi."

The woman patted her hair into place. He leaned on her and cupped a small breast. He had a happy, dopey grin.

"I gotta take a whiz," the man said, and stumbled away.

Stark followed the man in the Marine T-shirt. He caught up with him as he urinated against an Indian rubber tree.

"You look like someone who might be able to help me," Stark said.

"If you're a fag, better get outta here before I break your dick off and stuff it down your throat."

"I got three wives and a girlfriend that'll vouch for me," Stark said.

"What's your scam?"

"I heard there's people who could use a guy who's been around."

"Yeah?"

"I've kicked around since Nam. I was in the Marines. Saw action in Au Shau Valley with the 39th."

"Yeah? You know Jimmy Dixon?"

"No."

"Good. He wasn't with them. I was with 11th Battalion, Third Division." The man was relatively relaxed from a healthy mix of postsex endorphins and liquor. But he still had the hard edge of a merc.

"No shit."

They compared notes on battles they had been in, rattling off the names of outposts on the DMZ like Cam Lo, Con Thien Gio Linh, and Dong Ha. Stark, who had served with the CIA in Vietnam, was able to bluff it through.

"So what've you been doing since then?" the ex-Marine asked.

"Little a this, little a that," Stark said. "Did some work guarding oil fields for the Saudis. Too fucking hot and you can't get booze."

"Tell me about it. Same thing in Kuwait."

"You know anyone got an opening? I can handle communications, demo. I taught hand-to-hand combat."

"Lemme talk to a couple people. Come back tomorrow night."

"Semper fi," Stark said.

"Fucking A," the ex-Marine responded.

Midway through the day, Stark had the feeling he was being followed. He made his tail as a white-shirted Thai man, fairly professional. When Stark came back to his room after lunch, he found that it had been adeptly tossed. If he hadn't put a wedge of paper in his door and memorized the alignment of his clothing in the dresser, he never would've known.

A message had been left at the hotel desk. "Be at the Casablanca at 2100 hours." Stark did a complete set of stretching exercises and a few *kata* to loosen up. Then he headed over to the Casablanca.

The President toyed with a book on the shelf in the Oval Office. He fingered the binding without reading the title, then slid it back into place.

"Okay, let's take it from the top," he said.

In the leather upholstered chairs were the acting head of the CIA—the former number two man who understood he held the position temporarily—as well as General Todd Grant, and the President's national security advisor.

"We're facing a major problem with Japan," the national security advisor said. "It began as a backlash to the terrorism. Reports say the ultranationalists have received a large push, cash from slush funds."

"I've read the reports," the President said. "Japanese Youth for Peace and Freedom movement, correct?"

"Yes, Mr. President," the acting CIA chief said. "There're plans to integrate them into the military within a few months."

"What is Japan's military status?" the President asked.

"Currently, more than a quarter million troops, about five hundred aircraft, and sixty destroyers," the chairman of the Joint Chiefs volunteered.

"Not very much," Grant muttered.

"The Japanese spend one percent of their GNP on their military," the chairman of the Joint Chiefs said. "We spend six percent. To put it in a global perspective, the USSR spends fifteen percent. Though Gorbachev is working to reduce that."

"Why don't the Japs pull their own weight?" Grant asked.

"Their 1947 constitution, which we helped them draft, effectively renounced war as a policy," the National Security advisor explained.

"Then how come they got a Self Defense Force that sounds like a military to me?" Grant asked snidely.

"By 1950, they had decided that an army of sorts was necessary," he responded.

"I don't see why this is a crisis," the President said.

"The SEATO countries are very upset," the acting CIA chief said. "So are Peking and Moscow. They're demanding that we, as Japan's strongest ally, make them cease and desist."

"Screw 'em all," Grant said. "Let them worry about the Japs. With any luck, we can sell 'em the hardware."

"We're talking a serious escalation of tension in the Far East," said the National Security advisor.

"The immediate problem is arming the Japanese Youth for Peace and Strength," the acting CIA chief said. "If we allow that to go ahead without taking any action, I've no doubt the Chinese or Soviets will respond. Perhaps with a troop buildup. Which Japan will perceive as a threat and become more militaristic."

"Nervous nellies," Grant said.

"Our best analysts have come to that conclusion," the acting CIA chief said.

"A bunch of college kids who don't know shit from shinola," Grant responded.

The CIA chief was about to respond, then decided against it. He had yet to learn how far he could go in challenging the other power players.

"When do I have to decide?" the President asked.

"Unfortunately, we suspect the movement of the guns is imminent," the National Security chief said.

"Where are they? Can we covertly interfere with it?"

The CIA chief looked down at his papers. "Uh, we're not sure where they're coming from."

Grant snorted in disgust.

"I'll let the prime minister know that we don't approve," the President said.

"Unless you go public, it won't do any good," the National Security advisor predicted.

"I can't do that," the President said. "We can't risk jeopardizing our relations with Japan."

The acting CIA chief sighed. "Then we're in for trouble, sir."

Stark felt dozens of eyes on him as he walked into the bar. It was as if everyone knew.

"I heard you were looking for a job," said a short, dark-skinned Mediterranean man with a Roman nose. He had appeared at Stark's arm silently. Stark guessed he'd be a skilled knife-in-the-back artist.

"That's right."

"We checked you out, you're hired." From his intonation, Stark guessed he was Corsican.

"Great," Stark said.

"Come with me," the Corsican said, walking out through a back door. As Stark followed, they passed Tex. Tex mouthed, "Watch out." Stark winked.

Stark pushed the door open hard, so it would strike anyone waiting on the other side. Nothing. A tuk-tuk was waiting at the mouth of the alley. The Corsican had already climbed in.

They rode to the jungle bar, the "Officer's Klub." Stark recognized a few of the faces. This time there was no silence when he entered.

The Corsican took Stark around to a few tables, introducing him. Only first names were used. The patrons were hard drinking soldier types, military flotsam and jetsam from a dozen different armies, and a hundred different battles. He was obliged to join in toasts at every table.

Stark remained on the alert. He held his drink in his left hand, ready to throw it in the face of an assailant. His right hand was prepared to block or strike. He kept in a balanced stance, and wary of those around him. He tried to drink as little as possible, pouring dollops of liquor to the dirt floor whenever no one was watching. Stark feigned being more affected by the liquor than he was.

Was it this easy to be accepted into this ragtag bunch of mercs?

Stark sat in a chair and covertly dumped another load of beer on the floor. The Corsican was huddled at a table, laughing over a comment one of the mercs had made.

A barmaid, no more than twenty years old and quite attractive, came over and plopped down on Stark's lap.

"You new here?" she asked.

"Yup."

"I give you special treat," she said, wiggling around to straddle him. They were face-to-face. She ground her hips into him.

"You like?"

Stark nuzzled her neck as an answer. As he did, he peered

around the room. A couple of customers seemed to be watching. What did they think he was, a vice cop? The thought struck him as funny and he chuckled.

"Why you laugh?" the girl asked.

"Just thinking of an old joke."

She wiggled some more. "You want to go back in woods?"

"I'm tapped out."

"What that mean?"

"No money."

"This freebie. You first time."

Stark imagined the limitless ambush possibilities in the dark. "Maybe tomorrow."

"You homo?" She patted his groin. "You no feel like homo."

She wiggled again and wrapped her legs around him. She hugged him and nibbled his ear.

Suddenly her arms were wrapped tight around him. Her legs had locked around him as well. She was surprisingly strong. A head butt would've loosened her grip enough for him to free his arms and counterattack. But he hesitated, unable to strike a woman with the same cool confidence he'd dispatch a male assailant.

Four men with guns ringed him. They snapped handcuffs on his wrists and hoisted him up, the barmaid still clinging to him. They clicked shackles on his legs. The girl slid off.

She reached over and grabbed Stark's testicles, squeezing hard enough to make him wince. "Too bad," she said, then gave him a peck on the cheek.

There were raucous cheers and guffaws from the customers. The girl took a slight bow. The Corsican handed her six hundred baht, about twenty-five dollars. She bowed again and walked off.

Stark was forced into the back of a beat-up Datsun station wagon. They rode for a half hour. Stark breathed deeply, struggling to compose himself and let the adrenaline in his system negate the alcohol.

He was pushed out of the vehicle and led for fifteen minutes into the jungle. He counted a half dozen men.

Stark stumbled several times from the shackles. They

picked him up and prodded him on, guzzling beer and laughing. The jovial, casual mood was more like a brutal fraternity hazing than an execution party.

"Nice piece of work that sheila back in the bar," a burly Australian said, giving Stark a hard nudge with an elbow. "The only bird I know who can literally break your back."

They came to a clearing. It looked like a bomb had hit it, with signs of charring on the foliage. A four-foot chain was looped around Stark's shackles, then padlocked to a thick Indian rubber tree. The cuffs were removed.

Stark stood ready for their assault.

The Corsican had been carrying a small parcel that Stark assumed was more liquor. The Corsican unwrapped it and threw a switch. The other men backpedaled.

"You have five minutes to defuse this," the Corsican said, carefully setting down a shoe box size package in front of Stark. "It's packed with ammonium nitrate."

The plastic box was khaki green, with a military coding stamped on the side that Stark didn't recognize. The package hummed slightly. It weighed about ten pounds. Twelve screws were set in the top.

A small digital clock on the side counted down.

If it had been a conventional piece of ordnance, he would've had a chance. But he couldn't defuse an unknown device. He'd need tools and a lot more time than they were giving him.

He glanced around the clearing. He could toss the box, but there was a solid wall of bamboo forming a ten-foot perimeter around him. There was a good chance the box would bounce back on him. And it might be wired with a mercury switch that could make it explode from rough handling.

Stark dug a coin out of his pocket. It was too small to turn the screws on top.

Precious seconds ticked by.

He felt his captors watching from just beyond the bamboo.

Stark tugged at the chain and his shackles. No luck.

He began digging. The earth was soft and moist. Both

hands scooped and tossed the dirt. He checked the counter. Two minutes left.

He dug furiously, like a dog desperately searching for a misplaced bone.

One minute. The hole was about two feet deep and a foot wide.

He heard laughter in the brush.

Thirty seconds.

He dropped the bomb into the hole and shoved dirt back on top.

Fifteen seconds.

He ran around to the other side of the tree and tucked himself into a ball.

Whump!

A muffled explosion. Too weak to be ten pounds of explosive. Could there be a second blast, like the IRA bombs designed to draw a crowd with a weak explosion, so the killer blast could claim more victims?

But his captors were coming back.

His feet still shackled, Stark stood in a modified fighting stance.

"Good job," the Corsican said.

Someone tossed something at him. He caught it. A beer open, spilling fluid.

Another man undid his leg shackles.

They all lifted beers.

"Vive la mort! Vive la guerre! Vive le mercenaire!" they shouted, gulping their drinks. It was the French Legionnaire's toast to death, war, and mercenaries. Stark took a sip. The drink appeared safe.

"What the fuck was that about?" he demanded.

"We get too many pretend hotshots," one of his captors said. "Guys who think a subscription to *Soldier of Fortune* means their shit doesn't stink. You passed the test."

"What if I hadn't buried it?"

"There were just a few large firecrackers in there," the Corsican said. "And several pounds of water buffalo dung. You did well. And didn't even wet your pants. Congratulations. You're hired."

CHAPTER 35

After stopping at the hotel and picking up his bags, Stark climbed into the back of a Toyota Land Rover and was blindfolded by the Corsican.

The Corsican drove like a native, that is, with a casual disregard for human and animal life. He sped through flocks of chickens with the same vigor he raced through clumps of people. Stark heard the fowls' terrified squawking, the occasional shouts of a narrowly avoided pedestrian. Miraculously, everyone got out of the way in time. The Toyota took the bouncy road with vigor and special shocks. Stark swayed from side to side, nearly tumbling over during a couple of particularly enthusiastic turns.

Stark heard a waterfall twice. Judging by the pitch and timbre, it was the same fall.

The Corsican was probably circling.

The road got narrower, bumpier. Stark heard branches thwacking against the side of the jeep. The engine groaned and whined as they sometimes battled forty-five degree inclines.

They forded a few streams, bounced over boulders, and once nearly got stuck in sand.

Suddenly the air was cool and dank. And the sound of the Toyota echoed off hard walls. A cave.

They were descending deeper into the earth.

"Who goes there?" a voice shouted.

"Marcel," the Corsican responded. "With a new recruit."

There was a hydraulic sound, Stark guessed some sort of barrier gate being lifted or slid aside.

They rode deeper into the tunnel. All around were the sounds of men and machinery working. Shouts, grunts, curses, mixed with whines, hums, and rumbles.

"You can take off the blindfold," Marcel said.

Stark removed it, squinting. It was fairly bright underground, with fluorescents lining the walls. Stark had been inside the NORAD facility at Cheyenne Mountain, so it wasn't the most impressive underground fortification he had ever seen. But it came close.

The cavern was enormous, several stories high. The stone floor, which was longer than a football field, was lined with tanks, armored personnel carriers, and heavy trucks. Stark estimated there were more than two hundred vehicles. A mix of Russian, Chinese, American, Japanese, and German hardware.

"Quite a sight, *n'est ce pas?*" Marcel said.

"What's it worth?"

Marcel gave a Gallic shrug. "Follow me. I will show you the barracks."

They got out and walked to a side tunnel, then climbed down a ladder to a lower level. Stark memorized details— the way ducts were built into the wall, the bamboo used as conduit around electrical wires, the twists and turns the tunnels took.

Through a narrow passage to the barracks lay a dimly lit long room about twenty feet wide. It had a typical military layout, but military tidiness was not enforced. Half the bunkbeds were unmade, the footlockers open, shoes and dirty socks scattered about, a smell like an unventilated locker room. A dozen of three dozen bunks were occupied.

"We run twenty-four hours a day here," Marcel said. "You will share a bunk with someone, sleeping in shifts, so there is no space wasted."

Stark found an unoccupied bunk on the end and Marcel disappeared.

"You're the new meat, eh?" asked a huge Canadian with the broken blood vesseled nose of a heavy drinker. He had swaggered over with the exaggerated shoulder bob of a bully. No doubt few people challenged a man who was six feet, six inches, and more than three hundred pounds of muscle and ugly.

"Right."

"Well, that's my bunk you put your bag on."

Under normal circumstances, Stark would've removed the bag and avoided the confrontation. But he knew what was coming. Several of the slumbering men had half risen on their beds to watch. It was a ritualistic welcome, establishing Stark's place in the pecking order.

Before the Canadian could say another word, Stark kicked him in the groin. As the man folded he kneed him in the face and rapped him on the head, sending him to the floor.

Stark hopped into bed and stretched out. He feigned sleep. The Canadian got up and staggered away. There was rude snickering from other bunks.

Over the next couple of days, Stark managed to meet most of the workers. They were about one-third white, one-third Thai, and one-third blacks, other Orientals, and Hispanics. The racial and ethnic groups usually clustered with their own kind. The vast majority were hard-core mercenaries, with an aura of barely repressed violence. All were combat veterans; most had technical skills. Stark watched them work on the assembled armaments. They were competent, careful, whether welding, cleaning, painting, or testing the gear.

Stark was put to work on a small arms assembly crew. DeVille had several thousand rifles, pistols, shotguns, and machine guns. Most were new or in perfect condition. Firearms would be field stripped and test fired in a hundred-yard range. All the work was done underground. Without his wristwatch, there was no way of knowing night or day.

Recreation consisted of watching porno movies in the lounge, working out in the gym, or reading in the library. Actually, it was more looking at pictures in the magazines for most of the men.

The men were allowed out once a week, escorted by one of the officers. Marcel, Stark learned, was a captain. There were three lieutenants, four sergeants, and six corporals. The Canadian was a corporal.

During their trips, the men were allowed into Chiang Mai where there was an arrangement with one of the whorehouses. They would get drunk and laid and then return. No liquor was allowed in the underground bunker. Anyone who got involved in a brawl in town had his visitation privileges suspended for a month. As a new man, Stark had to wait a month before being allowed out.

"What if I quit?" Stark asked.

"You don't." The rules were explained to Stark by Fleming, a burly South African with bad teeth and worse breath. He was a sergeant. He told Stark, however, that no one addressed officers by their rank.

"Like in the SAS," Fleming said. "You call a fella by his rank, it makes him a better target."

"Got it."

"Good. Now, there's a crate of Garands over there that need your loving care. Get on it."

DeVille arrived at his fortress and immediately went to his office. It was in a part of the compound that was cave rather than excavated earth. The stone walls had been cut flat and etched to look like castle walls. A large window had been set in the wall, with powerful lights on the other side. A gauzy curtain was always pulled down. It made the office seem as if it were above ground.

DeVille hated working out of his fort. He felt like a gentleman forced to spend time in a Hun camp. He relied on a strict chain of command, going through his two captains, to avoid contact with his workers.

He sat in his office and switched on the radio, which was connected to an antenna that traveled up two hundred feet through the dirt to pull in radio waves. He tuned in the BBC and half listened while cleaning up paperwork.

The announcement that the Japanese government was permitting Sasaki's Japanese Youth for Peace and Strength to arm itself shocked the world. His organization had grown to ten thousand, a small army in itself.

The SEATO countries filed a formal protest at the U.N. Tales of World War II atrocities filled Southeast Asian newspapers. The Soviet Union and the People's Republic of China both joined in the uproar, claiming the arming was the first step in a Japanese program of capitalist expansionism and imperialist aggression.

All the countries vowed not to supply weapons to the Japanese, and to impose economic sanctions on any country that did. Israel and South Africa put out secret feelers, but the deals were discovered and blown apart by a combination of threats and promises.

The United States issued a half-hearted condemnation, then nothing. The silence was taken as a sign of support in Japan. There was talk of incorporating Sasaki's troops into the Self Defense Forces, using it like a private ROTC.

Which was what Sasaki wanted. There was no point in trying to motivate the Japanese military from the outside. But with his troops infiltrated into the army, it would be easy to sway opinions, to weed out those who didn't have the proper loyalties, to control.

Despite all the weapons being worked on, ammunition in DeVille's fortress was strictly guarded. Every bullet had to be accounted for and any handheld weapon was never worked without supervision. Many of the men, however, had armed themselves with homemade shanks. There were occasional rapes in the shower room and frequent brawls. It was like being trapped in a huge, underground prison. Violence hung in the air like humidity in the tropics.

Frenchmen had to work side by side repairing tanks with Germans. American Vietnam war veterans crawled down tunnels with former North Vietnamese sappers. Irishmen who had fired at British troops for the IRA tested weapons under the eye of English supervisors. Black former Army Rangers took orders from South African officers. It was no melting pot. The hate was palpable.

Stark tried to stay neutral, but being white and American immediately made him certain enemies. And it didn't guarantee him any friends. He kept his conversations to a minimum, limited to "Pass the salt" or "Gimme that wrench."

The men were more restless than ever. As in any institution, there was a fast and partially accurate grapevine. They knew DeVille's stocks had to be prepared immediately, that they were being shipped out within a few days. Most of the rumors said it was to Japan. Apparently someone had seen paperwork involving the Japanese diplomatic pouch. And a few Japanese had apparently inspected munitions at some point. It was all very vague.

Crews were working double shifts. Then the next scheduled leave had been cancelled. Security had been increased. And shortly after DeVille arrived, the heavy metal door at the mouth of the cavern had been slammed shut.

Despite hundreds of tunnels and side passages, Stark found only two ways out. One was through the main portal, the entrance where tanks could pass without even touching the walls. The other was a man-size passage, an emergency exit, guarded at all times by two men armed with submachine pistols. It was considered status duty, and reserved for the most reliable.

A Thai worker was caught trying to escape to see his family. He was shot dead. A second man was caught fiddling with the main door. All the men were ordered to watch his punishment. He received twenty lashes with a cat-o'-nine-tails.

Fleming happened to be standing near Stark during the flogging.

"Still thinking about walking out?" the South African asked with a chuckle.

CHAPTER 36

The ex-Israeli paratrooper discovered a red swastika painted on the side of his trunk. Everyone denied doing it. Then the Israeli saw the red spray can, stolen from the shop, in one of the German's duffel bags.

There were shouts and curses, shoving and wild swings, but no one was hurt.

A few hours later, one of the Americans found that his prize Zippo lighter was swiped while he was in the shower. It had his Vietnam unit's name engraved on it and had been his good luck charm through every battle. He tore through the barracks, and found it under one of the Asian's pillows. He used his homemade shank and lay in wait for the man, stabbing him repeatedly before he was pulled off by other Asians. He was beaten by them. Attacker and victim wound up in the infirmary.

There were numerous incidents of sabotage in the shops. Power cords were cut, parts disappeared, sand was put in truck gearboxes. "KKK 4 Ever" was spray painted in one of the hallways. A few of the blacks blamed a particular redneck, who chuckled. They attacked him, his buddies responded, and four more people wound up in the infirmary suffering concussions, stabs, and broken bones.

The infirmary was quickly filled, and the crews were short

staffed. Everyone had to work longer and harder to meet the deadline.

The timing on the arms shipment was crucial. Opposition was building in Japan. But if it was a fait accompli, it would generate its own momentum. Otherwise, DeVille could be stuck with a massive inventory that he couldn't pay for.

He left the personnel problem to the care of his chief aides. The captains were both former French Foreign Legion. The ex-Legionnaires decided the only way to control the brutality was with worse brutality. Two of the men they deemed troublemakers were executed.

Security was increased.

Due to the long shifts, when men did get to sleep, they collapsed. Stark feigned sleep, then crept out of bed. His one-man crime wave had been successful, creating more tension in the brutal environment.

Stark snuck down a hall with the small jar he had stolen from the kitchen. As he made his way through a dark tunnel, he spotted a few roaches scuttling along. The tunnels had problems with rats and roaches.

Stark collected the roaches in his jar.

"What're you up to?" It was the huge Canadian Stark had fought his first day.

"Collecting bugs," Stark said. "I was thinking we could race them. A little betting, a little fun."

"I see."

The Canadian stepped in closer. He was loose-limbed, too casual. His hand was folded back on his arm.

The arm swung forward, the blade hidden behind the forearm slicing through the air. Stark had anticipated an attack, and stepped back. He let the arm go past, then pushed forward, pinning it flat against the Canadian.

The man tried to swing with the other arm. Stark's free hand blocked it, then snapped under the man's chin with a palm heel strike. Stark grabbed the arm with the knife and pivoted, taking it up into the air in a painful *sankyo* grip. He twisted the wrist, and the knife dropped to the floor.

The Canadian pulled free, then swung again. Stark ducked under the blow and drove a punch into the man's abdomen. The Canadian was so pumped up on adrenaline that he barely responded.

As he swung another time, Stark blocked and slid in. He delivered two hard elbow strikes and then launched an *osoto gari*, sweeping out his leg and throwing him hard to the floor.

As the big man went down, he cracked his head against the stone wall. He didn't get up.

Stark hung back, waiting for a trick. A minute passed. He picked up the fallen shank and advanced. The man still hadn't moved. He felt for the pulse at his neck. There was none.

Stark picked up the jar of roaches and headed back to the barracks. Halfway back, he got an idea. He went to where the corpse lay. He took the shank and pounded the hilt in a dozen spots around the man's calves.

The body was discovered in an hour. Without the heart pumping, the calf bruises had grown to the size of half dollars. The overworked medic guessed that they were Kaposi's sarcoma.

"What's that mean?" his assistant asked.

"AIDS."

The assistant jumped back and refused to touch the body, even with gloves.

Word spread quickly. Since the men shared the same women when they went whoring, there was near panic. By the next meal, everyone knew. Many were unafraid of dying in combat. But the idea of dying slowly, from a disease that bore a social stigma, set everyone on edge.

In the middle of the meal, several men suddenly discovered roaches swarming over their feet. They didn't notice Stark's open jar on the floor. The long tables were overturned, the food, which was at best merely palatable, was thrown at the men behind the counter.

The rioting mercs swarmed out of the lunchroom. Those who got in their way either joined them, or were beaten and trampled. The guards at the ammo dump fired shots at the charging mob, but they were quickly overwhelmed. The men broke into the ammo room and the gun room and charged the entrances. The remaining guards quickly joined the mob.

The gates were lifted and everyone charged out. It had been less than seventy-two hours since Stark had begun his covert campaign of harassment.

Stark stood in the main chamber, staring out at the rows of tanks, armored personnel carriers, and trucks under bright work lights. The main chamber no longer echoed with the sound of men's voices. Only the grumble of the generators and the ventilating turbines.

Stark made his way down the tunnel and up the stairs to DeVille's office. The heavy steel door was locked. A video camera mounted above the door focused on Stark.

"What do you want?" DeVille asked through a speaker.

"They're all gone. You're going to need a new top dog. I thought I'd volunteer." Stark stood with military bearing and just the hint of cockiness in his tilted shoulders.

"That's very ambitious."

"Yeah. Well, I want a thousand dollars, American, a week." It was twice what he was getting as a regular staffer.

"C'est possible."

"I guess mosta the rest'll be straggling back soon enough," Stark said. "We gotta decide if you want them punished or what."

The heavy metal door rolled open.

CHAPTER 37

DeVille stood behind his desk. There was a big Browning lying on the blotter within quick reach. Also within reach was an overflowing ashtray, a pack of Gauloises, a tall glass filled with scotch, and a half empty bottle of Chivas Regal.

"Come in, *monsieur,* and tell me about yourself."

"Not much to say," Stark responded. "I kicked around a bit, a piece of work here, a piece of work there."

"I judge by your peculiar use of the English language that you're an American."

"Right."

"You seem vaguely familiar."

"You musta seen me around," Stark said.

"Perhaps."

"I will need references before I can trust you," DeVille said. "A previous employer who will vouch for you?" DeVille poured Stark a scotch and handed it to him.

"I knew Nicky Webb in Bangkok."

"Webb? He's no longer in my employ."

"How about Willy Rose?"

The name jolted DeVille, though he managed to conceal his surprise by lighting another cigarette. "Willy Rose?"

"Yeah. I think you know him."

"How is that?" DeVille asked.

"He whacked a guy named Nakamura for you after snatching a rich girl named Hancock." His confident tone belied the fact that he was bluffing, throwing out facts and hoping some of them stuck. "The reason Webb is no longer working for you is Rose killed him. I know Webb was working for you. He told me he was sending money to your Swiss account."

"You do have possibilities, *monsieur,*" DeVille said. The liquor made him feel warmly toward the sole trooper brave enough to stay. "*Monsieur* Rose has been getting sloppy. I have thought about replacing him."

Stark nodded. "What was the story with Kenji Nakamura?"

"Who?"

"The supposed terrorist who kidnapped Diana Hancock. Was he also working for you?"

DeVille was having fun watching this strange man piece things together. The gun on his desk and the liquor in his belly gave him a feeling of confidence. He had an egotistical pride in his work, and had never been able to discuss it with anyone. "Perhaps."

"Lemme guess. He was supposed to rile up the Greeks and the Turks. Then you go in and sell them firepower."

"*Très bien, monsieur.*"

"*Ne rien.*"

"*Vous parlez français?*"

"*Un peu.*"

"Very admirable," DeVille said, switching back to English. "Any other languages?"

"Spanish, German, and a little Thai. I'm pretty fluent in Japanese."

"Ah, Japanese."

"I thought you might be interested in that."

"*Pourquoi?*"

"Rumor was you were shipping out a big load to the Land of the Rising Sun."

"Do you always believe rumors?"

"No. But I've heard about a right-wing youth group that was going to be getting guns."

"You're correct. But that is just the beginning."

"You'll sell more to the Self Defense Forces?"

"*Formidable!* You are very clever. I have established a relationship with the right people. As their SDF grows, so shall my business."

"Are you working with Sasaki?"

"We share common interests," DeVille said coyly.

"General Grant?"

But Stark had gone too far. DeVille reached for the gun. Stark threw the scotch in his face, the liquor burning DeVille's eyes even as his fingers touched the butt of the gun.

Stark chopped down on DeVille's hand and easily took the gun away from him. He let DeVille wipe his face until the tears stopped flowing.

"I've been a fool," DeVille said. "You are the trouble-maker from the docks. The one Rose warned me about. Robert Stark. Who do you work for?"

"Myself."

DeVille looked relieved. "Good. Then we can make an arrangement. You cannot ruin me without hurting your government."

"How?"

"I work directly with top people in the administration." DeVille shifted and Stark tensed. The arms dealer tossed a worn black leather phone book to Stark. Keeping an eye on DeVille, Stark thumbed through the pages. He found phone numbers for the head of the DIA, a deputy secretary of Defense, an assistant to the Secretary of State, two members of the Joint Chiefs of Staff, as well as ranking officials of the CIA.

"You may note that I do not only have office numbers," DeVille boasted. "There are private lines, home numbers. Try them, you can see."

Stark didn't need to. He recognized a private line from the assistant Secretary of State's Foggy Bottom office, and the Maryland home number of one of the CIA officials. "It still doesn't prove anything."

"What I do, *monsieur,* is provoke wars that are in your government's interest, as well as mine. Low intensity conflicts. Keep certain tribes fighting with each other so they don't unite and make trouble. It's easy to provoke Sikh against Hindu, Muslim against Jew, Iranian versus Iraqi. But I work with your government. For example, with the Greeks and Turks, the idea was to encourage the Turks to allow more U.S. bases on Turkish soil."

"What's the purpose with Japan?"

"Because the yen is mightier than the sword." DeVille chuckled at his own pun. "Don't you see what an armed Japan will mean? Supporting a large army will strain the Japanese economy. Produce a more favorable balance of trade."

"And for you, an enormous sale. What happens if someone undercuts you?"

"Certain promises have been made."

"C'mon with me."

"Where are we going?"

"I've got a friend in the Thai government who'd like to talk to you about Nakamura's murder. Meanwhile I'll see what I can do in Washington."

"Robert, you are being naive. I thought you were a man of the world like myself. Join me and you can become a very rich man. Very powerful as well. I promise you I don't ever work contrary to the interests of the United States. After all, your country is the largest arms supplier in the world. I would be foolish to alienate my prime supplier." He was confident in his sales ability and couldn't imagine anyone turning down his offer. "I need your help. We must rehire immediately to make the deadline."

"You are one cocky son of a bitch," Stark said.

"Think before you lose such a golden opportunity."

Stark heard the sound of footsteps and wheeled just as Marcel the Corsican appeared in the doorway with a Bushmaster semiautomatic pistol. The Corsican fired half the thirty-shot clip, chewing up the desk and ricocheting .223 bullets off the walls. Then he ducked back out of view.

"Where's the money?" the Corsican shouted.

Neither Stark nor DeVille answered. The terrified DeVille had hidden behind his desk. Stark was by a metal file cabinet adjacent to the desk. The switch to close the door was on the wall behind the desk, impossible to get to with the Corsican peering around the doorway.

"I've been hit," DeVille hissed, just loud enough for Stark to hear. "My left arm. It's numb."

"Just press down on the wound," Stark said.

Marcel fired the rest of the clip into the room, then ducked out again.

"All the money goes into my Swiss account," DeVille shouted to the attackers. "There's nothing here."

"You lying *cochon,*" Marcel shouted back. "I know you have gold hidden away. We just heard you talking about it."

"I was saying—"

DeVille's words were interrupted by another spray of bullets.

"How much do you have to give them?" Stark asked DeVille.

"A few hundred in pounds, francs, dollars, and yen. Maybe a thousand dollars' worth of gold. It will not be enough. Nothing would be enough."

"You have one minute to give us the money," Marcel shouted. "We have four white phosphorus grenades. I'll throw them in one at a time starting in sixty seconds." Nicknamed Willie Peters, the grenades produce a dense white smoke and scatter burning particles of white phosphorus.

"He'll give you the money," Stark said. "Hand it over, DeVille."

"I won't get up."

Stark had a straight line of fire at DeVille. He aimed his gun at the gun dealer's shoulder.

"You will cover me?"

"Like a mother protecting its baby."

DeVille raised his hands above his head. "Don't shoot," he said in French to the Corsican. "The money is in the safe. I will get it for you."

He moved slowly toward the painting on the wall behind his desk. He pulled the picture forward, then suddenly lunged for the switch to shut the outer door. He threw the switch.

But the Corsican saw the move, pulled the pin on a grenade, and tossed it in.

The heavy metal door slammed shut.

"Merde!" DeVille said. He started to run right toward the grenade.

It exploded. Stark, hidden by the file cabinet, saw the flash and felt the room temperature soar. Anything flammable began to ignite.

Stark crawled out. The heat and smoke were rising. The floor was the safest place to be. Stark looked for DeVille. The arms dealer was lost in the smoke. He had given one scream right after the grenade went off.

Why had DeVille plunged toward the grenade? He certainly didn't seem to be the hero type. And every other instinct screamed to get away from it.

Unless . . .

Stark crawled forward. The spot where the grenade had ignited was still glowing. From a few feet away, it was like staring into a blast furnace. He coughed, and hot acrid smoke burned his lungs.

The smoke was moving over him. An air current. He moved faster, feeling baked. The heat was weakening, almost pleasurable, an overset sauna. He followed the droplets of blood DeVille had left in his path.

A second doorway. He'd expected it. Every rat hole had to have a couple of ways in and out or it became a death trap. This one had been concealed behind a revolving bookcase.

The smoke and heat were chimneying, being whipped out the door and up the stairwell. A metal spiral staircase, shrouded by smoke, went straight up. Stark lay on the floor at the bottom of the stairwell and the hot air breezed over him. As long as all the air wasn't sucked out, he'd be okay.

Then he heard the explosion. Marcel and his accomplices were attacking the door with explosives.

Gerard DeVille had stopped counting stairs after fifty. His feet no longer pounded quickly on the metal rungs. Each step was an effort. He gasped from the smoke. Despite the low wattage bulbs strung every ten meters, he could barely see more than a foot in front of him. Several chunks of flesh had been burned on his legs. He beat out his pants where they smoldered.

He felt a tightness across his chest. An elephant seemed to be pressing on him. Despite the fact he could barely breathe, he craved a cigarette. He could hear the explosions echoing up the long tube.

How many more feet? Each step got higher and higher. Pain shot down his left arm.

He knew what was happening. It was the way his father had died. No. Not here. Sweat poured off his face. He could taste the salt in his mouth, feel the sting in his eyes. The sweat was mixed with smoke. He coughed and fell back a few steps. The loss was frustrating.

The angina got too intense. He leaned against the hand rail. Just for a moment.

Then he got dizzy and the darkness came.

A hole appeared in the metal door and air rushed in. Stark could feel the change in oxygen content in the room almost immediately. It was both wonderful and deadly. Necessary for his body, but a harbinger of an attack.

He still had the Browning. He fired a couple of shots in the direction of where he guessed the door would be.

The explosions stopped.

The smoke had thinned, but Stark still couldn't see the entry door. He pulled the revolving bookcase shut behind him. He moved as quickly and quietly as he could up the stairs. His eyes burned from the smoke, his lungs felt raw.

He'd gone up about six stories when he found DeVille's body. He took the gun dealer's pulse. Nothing.

Down below there was a louder explosion. Stark presumed the Corsican and his allies had made it into DeVille's inner sanctum.

Stark raced up the stairs. He reached a landing and then a solid roof appeared above him. A dead end.

He heard the Corsican cursing below. The voice was clear as it echoed up the stairwell. Then he heard men's feet pounding on the metal treads.

CHAPTER 38

Tears streamed down Stark's face. He fought the urge to grind his fingers against his burning eyeballs. His breaths came in painful gasps. He was at the highest point in the stairwell and the escaped smoke and fumes were at their thickest.

He heard the men below come upon DeVille's body and hoped that they would go back down. After a few moments, the steps continued upward.

"DeVille must've told him where he hid the gold," Marcel said, refusing to give up his dream. His words echoed eerily up the stairwell.

Stark had a few shots left in the Browning. He was too shaky to take the clip out and see how many. There were no heavy objects to drop on his pursuers.

Why would the tunnel dead-end? Uncompleted? Caved in? Deliberately sealed up?

He thought about his time in the Zen monastery, the frustration when a *koan* riddle wouldn't seem to come.

"Keep pushing," his *roshi* would say, and then thwack him with a stick.

Stark drew on all his inner resources and jumped upward, fists extended.

His punch ripped through the dirt and light poured in. The ceiling above him had been quarter-inch plywood, a cap over the mouth of the stairwell to keep it concealed. The tropical fauna had grown over it, making it appear sealed off. That, combined with the smoke, had made it seem like a dead end.

Stark laughed as he clambered up and out into a dense patch of palms and shrubbery. He paused, breathing in and out as deeply as he could, wiping his eyes, and trying to adjust to the sunlight.

There was a pile of debris that had been excavated when the hole was dug. He kicked it over on top of the stairwell hatch.

Stark bullied his way through the foliage, tearing leaves and stomping the soft earth. He came to a small creek and entered. His footprints on the bottom were washed away as he walked. He ran a few dozen yards, then doubled back parallel to his original path, careful to move with a minimal amount of disturbance.

He thought of the Zenrin, "Entering the forest, he moves not the leaves, entering the water, he makes not a ripple."

He made it to a thick clump of banana trees not far from the stairwell and ducked down only seconds before the Corsican and three others emerged from the mouth of the shaft. They were heavily armed, each carrying a couple of machine guns, pistols, and grenades. They'd had quite a shopping spree in the abandoned arsenal.

"This way," Marcel said, spotting Stark's footprints.

"Forget him," one of the others said. The dissenter was a wiry redneck Stark had heard nicknamed Smiley. He had bad teeth and never smiled.

"No. He must know where DeVille's money is," the Corsican insisted.

"Let's load up the trucks with hardware," Smiley said. "We can sell that stuff for a few hundred grand."

"Peanuts," another man sneered.

The men quarreled. The Corsican slapped the dissenter and pointed his pistol at him. "We're losing time. Are you with me or not?"

The other gunmen nodded. Smiley muttered, but agreed. They took off down the path Stark had blazed.

As soon as they were out of sight, he hurried down the stairwell.

The smoke had dissipated and it was much easier going down than ascending. Stark ran to the ammo room, all the time alert for other stragglers.

He found a case of RDX, the powerful explosive developed by the British. The white crystalline solid, also known as cyclonite, was one-third stronger than C-4. Stark rummaged until he found a crate containing blasting caps. Moving as quickly as he could, and still maintain a semblance of caution, Stark put together a half-dozen bombs. He planted them in the ammo room and outside near the five-thousand-gallon fuel tank. He set the timer for ten minutes.

When bending to place the final bomb, he noticed a trickle of blood down his leg. Rolling up the pants, he found a half dozen leeches clinging to the flesh. There was no time to remove them.

He ran to where the vehicles were stored and found a jeep with a full tank and the keys in the ignition. He drove it up the ramp and activated the switch to open the main door.

As it was rolling up, a shot shattered the windshield of the vehicle.

It was Smiley. The redneck ducked out of sight after snapping off a half-dozen shots.

"This place is about to blow," Stark shouted.

"Blow me!" Smiley snarled, and fired a few more shots.

There were about twenty yards between them. Both men had ducked into crags in the cave wall. A Mexican standoff. Stark checked his watch. Four minutes.

Stark dove into the jeep. Smiley's shots punched a few holes into the body. Stark started the jeep and rolled forward. Smiley emptied his clip, puncturing one of the rear tires. Stark drove past him and into the sunlight.

Stark braked. "Get away," he said. "There's just a couple of minutes left."

"Bullshit," Smiley said, and ran down into the underground arsenal.

Stark floored the jeep. The rear tire was gone and he jolted along on the rim. He was about a quarter mile away when the bombs went off. There was a deep roar, like the earth clearing its throat. Then a jolt that lifted the jeep six inches into the air and bounced it a couple of times.

Stark looked back. The ground above the tunnels had caved in, creating a massive sinkhole the size of a football field.

Stark found a pack of cigarettes on the floor. He lit one as he stared back at the hole, clouds of dirt and debris still flying. He puffed on the cigarette a couple of times. When it glowed red hot, he used it to burn off the leeches he'd picked up in the creek.

He threw them to the ground and put the jeep in gear.

A helmeted guard with an M-16 checked Stark's name off a list and issued him a plastic clip-on visitor's badge. The badge entitled him to go to medium level security areas at Bolling Air Force base, about four miles southeast of the Pentagon on the Maryland side of the Potomac. The DIA, established in 1961 to collect and coordinate the intelligence from all military services, was based at Bolling.

A second uniformed guard drove Stark to a sand-colored, two-story building. They were met by a plainclothes security officer, who checked Stark's ID, and escorted Stark to the office of General Todd Grant.

The head of the DIA sat behind a massive nineteenth-century cherrywood desk. The wooden wainscotted office was cluttered with Americana and Civil War memorabilia: paintings by Frederic Remington; muskets and sabers; the horns from a steer; a board with different kinds of barbed wire. An ornately tooled saddle, with silver trim, rested on a stand in the corner. Aside from the multiline phone console and computer on Grant's desk, everything appeared to be at least a hundred years old.

"How did your story work out?" Grant asked.

"I'm still working on it," Stark said.

"I looked you up after we met at that party," Grant said. "I know about your distinguished career." Grant said "distinguished" sarcastically. "You quit the CIA because they iced some Jap unfairly. If you'd been in my outfit, I'd have had you court-martialed."

An F-14 roared off from the airfield. Grant fished a cigar from a humidor and went through the ritual of preparing it. "Too bad about DeVille," Grant said.

"Too bad. Though he did manage to confess before he went to that great ammo dump in the sky," Stark said.

Grant lit his cigar. "Oh?"

"About you and him. Though he did minimize your role," Stark said, hoping the egotistical General would take the bait.

"What I do I do for the country," Grant said.

"How much are you making from your patriotism?"

"None of your business," Grant snapped. "It didn't interfere with U.S. interests. Like the Contragate boys, nothing wrong with mixing patriotism and profit."

"Let me see if I have it right. You'd spark little wars to keep various countries busy. DeVille would sell them U.S. arms which you'd help him get. The latest project was rearming Japan."

"Close enough." Grant grinned and puffed contentedly.

"So Sasaki's working for you?"

"He works for himself. But our interests coincide."

"So this whole deal is just to expand the market?"

"That's it. America needs a strong defense industry."

Stark stood up. "Just out of curiousity, does the President know?"

"Only an elite group knows. The head of the Joint Chiefs, a couple of others. The President's got a rough idea, but not really. He's a civilian at heart, doesn't understand hardball geopolitics. Way down, he's got the balls of a chinchilla."

"I hope you don't mind if I play the tape for him."

"What?"

Stark opened his jacket, revealing a flat Kel recorder the model police use for undercover operations.

Grant moved quickly, reaching into his desk drawer and pulling out a big Colt Army Model percussion revolver with a seven-and-a-half-inch barrel.

"My great grandfather carried this at Appomatox." Grant

set his cigar down in an ashtray, keeping the gun aimed at Stark. "Dates back to 1860. A .36 caliber. You don't see that nowadays. I feel as if I'm holding a piece of history."

"May I see it?"

Grant smirked. "I keep it loaded, of course."

"Of course."

"I'd hate to have to explain how you went berserk and I was forced to shoot you. The paperwork would probably take hours. Now, very carefully, take that gadget out from under your jacket. Keep in mind I was the best pistol shot in the battalion at fifty yards. And we're a lot less than that apart."

Stark reached under his jacket and detached the tape recorder from the mike. He took it out slowly. As he was going to set it down on the desk, he flipped it straight at Grant.

The general flinched and Stark dove toward the desk kneehole. Grant fired, a shot slamming into the wall. Stark crawled forward, reaching to grab his calf. Grant pulled the trigger again.

Maybe Ulysses S. Grant had dropped the gun during a drunken bout. Or maybe deposits had built up during the years of disuse, or the first shot had warped the barrel. Whatever the cause, the firing pin hit the back of the second bullet, and the gun exploded in Grant's face.

The door crashed open and the plainclothes guard raced in. He aimed his .45 at Stark.

"What happened?" the guard demanded.

"He was showing me his antiques and the gun went off," Stark said.

Stark bent to staunch the blood flowing from Grant's neck. A piece of metal had severed his jugular vein.

"Give me a hand," Stark said.

The guard hesitated.

"Damn it, his death will be on your hands," Stark said.

The guard, a Norman Rockwell-esque kid with more freckles than experience, hurried over.

"Put pressure over there," Stark said, directing the guard to another gash on Grant's face.

While the guard pressed, Stark picked up the phone and got the operator. "We've got an injured general. Get an ambulance forthwith."

The guard was so absorbed in trying to stop the bleeding, Stark was able to sneak the tape recorder into his pocket.

Former CIA director Creange and Stark walked down a narrow path in Rock Creek Park. Creange had on a Sony Walkman and was listening to the tape. Periodically, he shook his head.

It was fall in Washington, and the path was lined with red, yellow, and orange leaves. Trees made death so beautiful, Stark mused as they walked. It reminded him of Arashiyama, the area outside of Kyoto where Japanese traditionally go to enjoy the fall colors.

When Creange was done listening to the tape, Stark outlined what had happened.

"But why are you telling me?" Creange asked.

"I presume you can still get access to the President."

"To do what?"

"Bump Sasaki out of grace."

"Any suggestions?"

"Present it to the Japanese officials as a matter of honor. Sasaki was doing an end run around them. Going back channel is frowned upon there even more than here. If the Japanese defense minister wasn't in on it, he'll want Sasaki's head on a platter."

"Can I keep the tape?"

"Sure. I have the original tucked away for safekeeping. In case any of the good guys decide that I know too much."

"You don't trust anyone, do you?"

Stark smiled. "Why should I?"

CHAPTER 39

It's hard for me to concentrate," Stark said, setting down the newspaper. He was on an overstuffed chair in his sparsely furnished one-bedroom New York apartment.

"Why's that?" Diana Hancock asked, stepping back.

"I think your nibbling my earlobe might have something to do with it," Stark said.

"I thought you'd never notice." She tugged at his shoulder.

"Again?"

"We have to make up for lost time," she said.

She was wearing one of his shirts. "I'll make it easy for you. She unbuttoned the two buttons she had done up. "You need help undressing?"

All he was wearing was a pair of sweatpants. She leaned over and tugged at the string with her teeth.

"I'm going to have to give you a dose of saltpeter," he said. He scooped her up and carried her into the bedroom.

"What's so interesting in the paper anyway?" she asked as they embraced in bed.

"Sasaki. He announced his early retirement. His movement flopped, a passing craze. Without his money pumping it up, it sagged like a limp balloon. But there are still a few loose ends."

She pinched his bottom. "I like tight ends. Can we work out again?"

"Is that a double entendre?"

"Yes and no. While you were away all I did is practice aikido. No drugs. No partying. I'm testing for promotion week. Can you be there?"

"Of course."

"Now, that other kind of workout," she said, pressing against him.

A shadow passed across the window outside.

He shoved Diana out of bed and rolled to the floor as the window crashed into a million pieces and Willy Rose swung in on a rope. Shots from his Uzi tore up the bed.

Diana screamed.

Stark grabbed one of his shoes and flung it at Rose, distracting the merc. Rose's shots went high, punching a line of holes in the ceiling. Stark used the bed as a trampoline, bouncing off it and launching a flying side kick.

Stark's foot caught Rose in the chest, knocking him back. Stark landed and charged, speed his only chance at survival. He threw a palm heel strike, hitting Rose under the chin. He wrenched the Uzi from Rose's grip.

But the merc whipped out a tiny .25 automatic. He grabbed Diana and shoved the gun into her temple. "Back off, mate," Rose said. He was dazed from the blows, just wanting a moment to regain equilibrium.

The two men faced off, Diana a hostage between them.

"Nothing on heaven or earth can save you," Stark said.

"What are you jabbering about?" Rose asked.

But Diana had understood. Rose was vulnerable to a *tenchi nage,* heaven and earth technique. One hand high, the other low. Her leg behind him. She couldn't topple him, but she made him stumble. She fell to the floor as Rose tried to regain his balance.

Stark dared not open fire with the ten rounds per second Uzi. Diana was still too close. He dropped the gun and simultaneously threw himself forward in a roll, closing the distance, and coming up with a kick aimed at Rose's groin.

But the merc was quick and caught the blow on his thigh. It made him fall backward, but didn't debilitate him.

Stark fell to the floor and kicked upward. Rose avoided the blow, but had to step back.

Stark dodged. But Diana tried to attack Rose. The bullet tore into her chest.

Stark caught the sight out of the corner of his eye. He was charging Rose even before Diana realized she'd been hit.

The rage in him was overwhelming. Pure white hot hate. There was nothing else. All opposites came together as one, like a light so bright it made the world black, or a heat so hot it felt like cold. Weak and strong, soft and hard, black and white, hate and love.

He grabbed Rose's head and threw his own body sideways. The torque concentrated on the cervical vertebrae, snapping Rose's neck as effectively as a hangman's noose.

Stark's movements seemed slow, dreamlike. He staunched the blood from her chest with a clean towel, then felt her wrist. A faint pulse.

He lifted her body effortlessly and ran to the door.

Diana Hancock lay in bed, a half-dozen tubes letting fluids in and draining fluids out. She was deathly pale, but the doctors downgraded her condition from critical to serious. She had been lucky that they were near to Bellevue, where ER doctors had as much experience with gunshot wounds as a MASH unit.

Stark sat by her bedside. He hadn't left since she'd been released from the ICU.

"I guess I'll live," she said weakly.

"The doctors say it won't be too bad. They had to take your spleen and a piece of lung."

"A quick way to lose weight," she said, then coughed a laugh.

"Take it easy, Tiger."

"You warned me about martial arts beginners being dangerous to themselves."

"What you did was very brave."

"Brave, but stupid."

"But you lived to talk about it."

She was quiet for a long time. "I've been doing a lot of thinking. When I get out of here, I'm going back to Thailand. That was the only time in my life I felt good about myself."

Stark read the message of dismissal in her words, but said nothing. She, however, felt she had to explain. "I love you, Robert, but I can't take the violence."

"I understand."

"Maybe you do. I can't live the way you do. Always looking over your shoulder, never knowing if you might be killed."

"The only way for me to live is as if I might die any moment," he said.

"I know. But it's not just that. The last thing I saw before I passed out was you snapping that horrid man's neck."

"You think I shouldn't have?"

"He deserved to die. But if you could've seen the expression on your face. It was like a Renaissance painting of a saint looking at God. Ecstasy."

The only sound in the room was the gurgle of machines keeping Diana alive.

"What were you thinking?" she asked after another long silence.

"I wasn't. Thinking. It was a moment of pure clarity."

"If that's enlightenment, I don't want it."

"Maybe there's something about death being the ultimate experience in life. Maybe I was just blinded by hate. But you described it perfectly. It was bliss."

She shivered. "I can love a killer, but I can't live with one."

Stark knocked at the door to the old man's Tokyo apartment. When Saito opened it, Stark's face was hidden behind a bag of groceries. "You again?"

"Are you free for dinner?" Stark asked.

"No. The emperor's having me over for tea. Of course I'm free for dinner. Nobody cares about a cranky old man." He said it without self pity.

Stark took off his shoes and entered. Saito carried the bag into the kitchen and went through it.

"I saw in the papers what happened to Sasaki," Saito said. "He'll spend his final years in disgrace. I suppose that was your doing?"

"I helped."

"Good." Saito came to the rice crackers at the bottom of the sack. He opened the cellophane bag and dumped them into a bowl.

He took one and ate it slowly. It was unclear whether he was savoring the taste or suffering with each bite.

"Life is like a bowl of rice crackers," Saito said. "You may hate every mouthful, but before you know it, it's done."

"Is that a Zen saying?"

"No. It's something I read in a fortune cookie. Now, come on and help me."

The two men were cramped in the tiny kitchen alcove. Saito directed Stark as he cut vegetables. The old man criticized his every move.

"You're distracted. When you stand, stand. When you sit, sit. Don't wobble."

"I don't know."

"What don't you know?"

"When I'm meditating or working out at the *dojo*, I feel as if I have it under control. But day to day, it just doesn't seem to work. I wonder about what I do."

"Hmmph. It is easy to be a monk when you're on the mountain. And it's pretentious for a young whippersnapper like you to think he knows anything."

"Am I trapped on the path I've chosen?"

"What do I look like, a fortune teller?"

Saito took the kitchen knife away from Stark. "Like this," the old man said. Each movement was fluid, without waste. Just the outer skin of the carrot peeled off.

Suddenly he lunged at Stark. Stark parried the blow and raised his hand as if to strike a chop to the old man's collarbone. He stopped.

Saito grinned. "When you don't think, you do right. Yet you can control the violence."

"What would have happened if I had struck you?"

"What makes you think you could have?" Saito said confidently.

"But if I had?"

"Then you would have felt terrible. Probably you would have given up your business. Settled down and opened a vegetable stand." Saito handed him back the knife. "Now stop thinking about what might have been. Peel the carrots."

Stark returned to the vegetables. The stroke of the blade went smoothly across the crisp orange skin.

Printed in the United States
By Bookmasters